Colorado Confidential turns up the heat in the search for the Langworthy baby. There's a new agent on board to shake up the case and shake down another lead—if he can handle the very cool, very pregnant Marilyn Langworthy...

"I'm pregnant. I'm not going to make a total fool of myself."

"A fool of yourself? Why would you say that?" Con's expression was unreadable.

"Because it would be foolish of me to believe the things you say. And I can't afford to be foolish anymore. I'll work with you, but that's as far as it goes."

"And if I want it to go further, cher?" Emerald eyes narrowed at her. "I'm out of luck is what you're saying?"

He was the most gorgeous man she'd ever seen, and to pretend she was immune to his brand of sexy Southern charm would be a lie. "A man like you is never at the end of his luck, Con," she said softly. "I don't think I'm going to cause you any sleepless nights."

"You might be surprised nights," Con drawled. "I ness between us I'll do tee anything."

D1011792

Dear Harlequin Intrigue Reader,

Take a very well-deserved break from Thanksgiving preparations and rejuvenate yourself with Harlequin Intrigue's tempting offerings this month!

To start off the festivities, Harper Allen brings you *Covert Cowboy*—the next riveting installment of COLORADO CONFIDENTIAL. Watch the sparks fly when a Native American secret agent teams up with the headstrong mother of his unborn child to catch a slippery criminal. Looking to live on the edge? Then enter the dark and somber HEARTSKEEP estate—with caution!—when Dani Sinclair brings you *The Second Sister*—the next book in her gothic trilogy.

The thrills don't stop there! *His Mysterious Ways* pairs a ruthless mercenary with a secretive seductress as they ward off evil forces. Don't miss this new series in Amanda Stevens's extraordinary QUANTUM MEN books. Join Mallory Kane for an action-packed story about a heroine who must turn to a tough-hearted FBI operative when she's targeted by a stalker in *Bodyguard/Husband*.

A homecoming unveils a deadly conspiracy in *Unmarked Man* by Darlene Scalera—the latest offering in our new theme promotion BACHELORS AT LARGE. And finally this month, 'tis the season for some spine-tingling suspense in *The Christmas Target* by Charlotte Douglas when a sexy cowboy cop must ride to the rescue as a twisted Santa sets his sights on a beautiful businesswoman.

So gather your loved ones all around and warm up by the fire with some steamy romantic suspense!

Enjoy,

Denise O'Sullivan
Senior Editor
Harlequin Intrigue

COVERT COWBOY
HARPER ALLEN

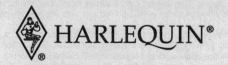

HARLEQUIN®

TORONTO • NEW YORK • LONDON
AMSTERDAM • PARIS • SYDNEY • HAMBURG
STOCKHOLM • ATHENS • TOKYO • MILAN • MADRID
PRAGUE • WARSAW • BUDAPEST • AUCKLAND

Special thanks and acknowledgment are given
to Harper Allen for her contribution
to the COLORADO CONFIDENTIAL series

ISBN 0-373-22735-3

COVERT COWBOY

This edition published by arrangement with Harlequin Books S.A.

® and TM are trademarks of the publisher. Trademarks indicated with
® are registered in the United States Patent and Trademark Office, the
Canadian Trade Marks Office and in other countries.

Visit us at www.eHarlequin.com

Printed in U.S.A.

ABOUT THE AUTHOR

Harper Allen lives in the country in the middle of a hundred acres of maple trees with her husband, Wayne, six cats, four dogs—and a very nervous cockatiel at the bottom of the food chain. For excitement she and Wayne drive to the nearest village and buy jumbo bags of pet food. She believes in love at first sight because it happened to her.

Books by Harper Allen

HARLEQUIN INTRIGUE
468—THE MAN THAT GOT AWAY
547—TWICE TEMPTED
599—WOMAN MOST WANTED
628—GUARDING JANE DOE*
632—SULLIVAN'S LAST STAND*
663—THE BRIDE AND THE MERCENARY*
680—THE NIGHT IN QUESTION
695—McQUEEN'S HEAT
735—COVERT COWBOY

*The Avengers

Don't miss any of our special offers. Write to us at the following address for information on our newest releases.

Harlequin Reader Service
U.S.: 3010 Walden Ave., P.O. Box 1325, Buffalo, NY 14269
Canadian: P.O. Box 609, Fort Erie, Ont. L2A 5X3

The Confidential Code

COLORADO CONFIDENTIAL

I will protect my country and its citizens.

I will stand in the line of fire
between innocents and criminals.

I will back up
my fellow agents without questions.

I will trust my instincts.

And most of all…

**I WILL KEEP MY MISSION AND MY
IDENTITY STRICTLY CONFIDENTIAL**

★★★★

CAST OF CHARACTERS

Marilyn Langworthy—Her nickname's the Ice Queen, but her detached facade hides the guilt she feels over her tiny nephew's disappearance.

Conrad Burke—He's only working with Colorado Confidential because he's hunting an enemy from the past.

Holly Langworthy—Marilyn's younger half sister, she may know more about her baby's kidnapping than she's revealing.

Tony Corso—Nephew of a mobster, he used his position at a Langworthy-owned pharmaceutical firm to steal dangerous viral stock.

Samuel Langworthy—Marilyn's father, he's been estranged from her for too long.

Joshua Langworthy—Marilyn's politically minded brother intends to be Colorado's next governor.

Helio DeMarco—The shadowy mobster has a liking for biological weapons, and a hatred of Con Burke.

Wiley Longbottom—He suggested Con for Colorado Confidential. Now he wonders if he picked the right man for the job.

Colleen Wellesley—The head of Colorado Confidential, she doesn't particularly like Con, and the feeling's mutual.

To Wayne with Love

Chapter One

Nineteen days, five hours, and—

Marilyn Langworthy glanced at the diamond watch on her wrist before focusing again on the computer monitor in front of her.

—thirty-odd minutes. Still no ransom note. Still no leads. Dear God, how can anyone hide a four-month-old baby this long without drawing attention to themselves?

The figures on the monitor wavered. She squeezed her eyes shut against the cold wave of fear washing over her, but the logical part of her brain refused to shut off.

That was why there hadn't been a demand for money. That was why no one had phoned the police to report a crying baby in a house where there hadn't been a baby a few weeks ago, why no curious store clerk had gossiped about someone who looked like a thug or a crazy suddenly coming in on a regular basis to buy diapers and formula. Maybe her nephew's kidnappers had panicked, maybe they'd realized too late that snatching a baby boy was one thing but keeping him concealed while they negotiated a ransom was another.

Maybe Sky was already—

"Ms. Langworthy?"

She opened her eyes. Her expression eased as she saw the older woman standing in the open doorway.

"Don't tell me, Elva," she said, apology tingeing her tone. "Everyone else left hours ago, right?"

Briskly her secretary entered with the same efficient energy she'd displayed hours earlier when her working day had commenced. Elva Hare had started in the typing pool at Mills & Grommett Pharmaceuticals thirty-two years ago and had worked her way up to the position of Samuel Langworthy's personal assistant. *Why she volunteered to become my secretary when I arrived from Boston to become Father's vice president of sales I'll never know,* Marilyn thought. *But I couldn't have handled this job without her.*

"I'm no shrinking violet waiting for you to tell me when it's quitting time, so don't worry about it," Elva replied, laying some papers on the desk. "I wanted to pull these sales figures together for you before your meeting tomorrow."

"God, the meeting." Marilyn sank back in her chair. "I'd forgotten all about it."

"Under the circumstances that's understandable." Beneath an iron-gray perm, Elva's gaze was concerned. "I don't hold with this business-as-usual policy your father's keeping to, especially since as the sole family member involved in his company you're the only one affected. Your brother's canceled all but his most important speaking engagements, and Holly—"

She shook her head. "Now isn't the time to air my opinion of your half sister's life of leisure," she said quietly. "No woman should have to go through what she's had to endure these past three weeks. The police haven't…?"

"They haven't come up with a thing, Elva."

Marilyn heard the hopelessness in her voice as she answered the older woman—heard it, and hated herself for it. She pulled the sheaf of papers toward her, but instead of looking at them she glanced up at her secretary.

"I went to church on Sunday," she said softly. "I can't remember the last time I attended. Oh, Christmas and Easter, of course, and whenever I go back to Boston to pay Mother a visit. But just an ordinary Sunday? It's been a while."

"I don't need to ask what you prayed for." Elva sighed. "I haven't mentioned anything to the rest of the staff, since the family wants to keep a lid on the publicity, but if you hear anything, Ms. Langworthy…"

"If I hear anything I'll let you know right away," Marilyn promised. "Although sometimes I think you're more in the Langworthy loop than I am." She'd meant it as a small joke. It hadn't come out that way, she realized in embarrassment.

Elva didn't pretend not to understand. "Your father's a fine man in many ways," she said evenly. "But he doesn't like admitting he's capable of failure, and rightly or wrongly, he sees the breakdown of his first marriage as a failure. When your mother got custody of you and went back home to Beacon Hill, the only way he could handle it was to close off that part of his life. It helped that he was so crazy about your stepmother," she added dryly. "And to an empire-builder like Samuel a firstborn son like Joshua is a godsend."

"Oh, Josh was always meant to fulfill Father's political hopes, even when he went through his rebellious phase," Marilyn said crisply. "Running for governor is just the start, and if I was ever jealous of my golden-boy brother I got over it long ago."

"But coming back here to Colorado reminded you of how your younger half sister took your place?" Elva probed with characteristic bluntness. Marilyn grimaced.

"I was born on a Thursday. Holly is Sunday's child." She shrugged. "You ever hear the old rhyme?"

"I seem to remember the child born on the Sabbath gets the whole shebang, so to speak." The older woman's normally businesslike tones softened. "What about Thursday's?"

"Thursday's child has far to go." Marilyn's smile was one-sided. "That's me all over, Elva. Sometimes I feel like I just have so darn far to go before I get to where I want to be. Or to *who* I want to be," she added huskily. "I'm not sure I like the person I've become since I moved back here, so I can't complain when the rest of the family make it clear they'd rather I'd stayed in Boston."

She fell silent for a moment. Then she nudged her computer's mouse so that the floral screen-saver disappeared.

"An absolutely perfect example of what I mean." She forced a laugh. "I'm sitting here feeling sorry for my inner child when there's a real baby missing. You're right, Elva—Holly must be going through hell, wondering when the authorities will get a break in this case. Somehow her situation puts my little problems into perspective, doesn't it?"

She sighed. "But meanwhile life at Mills & Grommett goes on, complete with the Wednesday morning meetings I got too used to leaving for Tony to handle when he was here."

"I'll inform security you're working late." Easily Elva slipped back into the persona of efficient secretary. She nodded pleasantly. "Good night, Ms. Langworthy."

"'Night, Elva." Feeling foolishly lonely all of a sudden, Marilyn flipped open the sheaf of papers, but even as she did she realized Elva had paused in the doorway. She looked up.

"Happy birthday, Ms. Langworthy." The older woman's tone was tentative. "At M & G we normally order in a cake for these kinds of occasions. I knew you wouldn't feel like celebrating today, but I didn't want you to think no one had remembered."

A cake. As she heard Elva's footsteps tapping through the outer offices and listened for the thunk of the dead bolt being turned in the reception area door leading to the fortieth floor hallway, a vision of what she'd been spared flitted through Marilyn's mind. She gave a mental shudder. It was bad enough turning thirty-one. Turning thirty-one in a staff lunchroom had root canals and bikini waxing beat hands down in the excruciatingly painful category. And as Elva had surmised, this was one July twenty-second she had no desire to celebrate.

Coming to Denver was the biggest mistake of your life.

The thought dropped into her mind with the suddenness of unwelcome certainty. Unable to continue feigning an interest in the information in front of her, she got up and walked over to the floor-to-ceiling windows that took up one wall of her office. On the same unsettled impulse, she flicked off the overhead fluorescents so that only her desk lamp remained on. Below her the lights of the city spread out like diamonds on velvet.

Maybe coming here hadn't been the biggest mistake, she told herself stonily. Maybe accepting her father's far-from-enthusiastic invitation to take this position at his company had been. Or maybe breaking her own un-written rule of not dating a co-worker took the prize—

yet another reason cake in the staffroom wouldn't have been a fun idea. Since that disastrously eye-opening final evening with Tony Corso and his abrupt resignation the next morning, she'd suspected she hadn't been the first female at M & G he'd shown his true colors to. She had no desire to exchange girlfriend horror stories with Angie, the receptionist, or Leeza, the records clerk.

And none of that mattered a damn, Marilyn thought. Because everything else faded into insignificance beside baby Sky's disappearance.

She'd had the chance to hold him. She'd turned Holly down. Regret, more corrosive than acid, spilled through her. As it had done a hundred times in the days since Sky's kidnapping, the memory of the one and only occasion she'd allowed herself to visit her half sister and her newborn nephew came flooding back.

"Sweetie, it's a Karan blouse and a Jacobs suit," she'd said coolly. "Baby sick-up isn't my idea of the perfect accessory. Here's a little welcome-to-the-world gift for him, by the way. When I told the store clerk what I wanted engraved on it I'm sure he thought we were holdouts from the hippie era or something. Why would you pick Schyler as a name, when you must have known he'd be saddled with such an odd nickname?"

Holly's only reply had been the annoyingly beatific smile Marilyn had privately told herself her half sister must have received along with the rest of the trappings of motherhood. That smile had been infuriating on more than one level, but at the very least it had been a clear indication that the status quo between them had changed, in Holly's mind, anyway.

It had always been so easy to prick Holly's perfect little bubble, she'd thought with a flash of irritation— easy and satisfying and...and *justified*. Except now it seemed her half sister's lifelong lack of self-confidence where their father's first daughter was concerned was gone. Incredibly, that smile seemed to indicate that Holly felt sorry for *her.*

"It's beautiful, Marilee. Thank you."

The use of the foolish pet name that had been the closest a baby Holly had been able to get to pronouncing "Marilyn" had set her teeth on edge. Her half sister had enclosed the solid-silver baby rattle in its nest of tissue paper and ribbon.

"Aren't you going to let him play with it?" Her usual tone when speaking to Holly was a bored drawl. It had been disconcerting to hear a touch of sharpness in her voice, and she'd modulated it with a laugh. "It's never too early to develop good taste, and hallmarked silver beats a chewed-up terry cloth toy any day. Take that disgusting rabbit thing away from him and give him the rattle."

"That disgusting rabbit thing is Bun-Bun, I'll have you know," Holly had replied with a smile. "Sky frets when he can't find him. And besides, Marilee—" Her smile had faltered. "—he's just a baby. The rattle's exquisite, but it's far too heavy for him to lift."

She'd dropped a quick kiss on the top of her son's downy head. "I never imagined I'd feel like this," she'd said softly. "I could just sit here all day and inhale him. Are you sure you don't want to hold him for a minute?"

"I think I'll pass on that thrill, sweetie." She'd barely been able to get the words out. "I'd rather inhale something a little more fragrant, like a dry white wine, and I'm late for my lunch at Zenith with Tony." As she'd kissed the air near Holly's cheek the sight of her discarded gift had prompted her to add, "Next time I come a-callin' on Mama and baby I'll ask him along, shall I?

A little boy should have at least one male figure in his life besides his uncle and grandfather, don't you think?''

As soon as she'd launched the barb some part of her had wished she could recall it…and some part of her, she remembered now with shame, had felt a surge of satisfaction as Holly's complacent smile had given way to a stricken look. Her half sister's back had curved slightly, as if to protect the baby in her arms from the words that had just been uttered.

''You were *jealous.*'' Marilyn stared sightlessly at the glittering panorama that was Denver at night. Her voice rang out too loudly in the shadowed office.

''You wished he was yours. Never mind that either his father didn't want to stick around or Holly decided she and Sky were better off without him. You only used that because you wanted to hurt her, and you wanted to hurt her because you envied her. You were terrified of holding that baby—terrified of showing how you really felt, terrified Holly would somehow guess that you'd give anything in the world to have one of your own.''

Her reflection wavered darkly in the window in front of her, and she stared at the woman she saw standing there as if she were looking at a stranger. Pale blond hair brushed the woman's shoulders. An expensively plain blouse tapered in at the waist and then slightly out again to skim a pencil-slim black skirt. Longish legs ended in narrow, elegant feet shod in narrow, elegant heels. She looked pulled-together, businesslike, attractive.

Marilyn flinched. The illusion shattered. The woman in the glass was a fraud and a bitch. The woman in the glass didn't exist at all, except as a collection of possessions and poses.

The only real thing about her was the dread in her eyes.

"Holly's out of her mind with fear," her brother Joshua had told her curtly when he'd called to notify her of their nephew's abduction a few hours after it had occurred. "She's sitting by the phone clutching that damned stuffed rabbit of his, waiting for the kidnappers to call."

"Sky frets when he can't find him..." More than anything, that had haunted her over the past weeks, Marilyn thought—a tiny baby snatched away from everything and everyone familiar, not even allowed the comfort of a beloved toy. Trivial as it was, that knowledge had brought home to her the ruthlessness of the people who had taken Sky.

The people who had taken him, and who perhaps by now had panicked and—

The pain that had been building in her burst forth in a terrible, keening cry that felt like it was splitting her asunder. A nightmarish jumble of images flashed through her mind and her hands flew up reflexively, as if by pressing the heels of her palms to her eyes she could turn off her imagination. Still the pictures, each one more horrible than the last, seared their way into her soul.

There was only one way to blot them out. Marilyn stopped fighting the blackness and let it overtake her. Her knees buckled. The floor rushed up to meet her.

And the man who had been standing in the shadows the whole time strode forward to catch her as she fell.

HE WAS GOING to have to lie to her, U.S. Marshall Conrad Burke told himself as he carried Marilyn to the couch in the corner of her office. Against the creamy pallor of her cheeks her lashes stirred, and his self-disgust intensified. *Merde.* The lying was going to have to start now.

Me, I was born to hang, sure. Despite the situation he found himself in, a corner of Con's mouth twitched upward as he remembered his great-uncle Eustache's oft-repeated boast. *But you were born to lie, boy, so make sure you do it like a Creole gentleman. Steady eye contact, and with the ladies, a small smile, no?*

Dark lashes fluttered open. Eyes as blue as heaven gazed blankly up at him, and for a moment Con forgot everything Eustache Ducharme had ever taught him. He recovered smoothly.

"Not the way I meant to introduce myself, sugar," he said with a quick, and he hoped, reassuring, smile, his gaze steady on her suddenly widened one, "but it seems I walked in just as you fainted. You feeling all right now, *cher'?*"

He hadn't planned on introducing himself at all and he certainly hadn't walked in only minutes ago, so even if you didn't count the fact that he needed no introduction to Marilyn Langworthy, those were lies number one and two right there, Con thought, guilt rippling unfamiliarly through him. And the lady wasn't buying them, he realized as he saw that heaven-blue gaze focus and begin to harden.

She was going to ask him how he'd gotten past security and into her locked office. He needed to plant other questions in her mind, and fast.

"New Orleans P.D." He slipped two fingers into the inner pocket of his suit jacket and extracted a leather identification case, complete with gold badge. Deftly he flipped it open in front of her. "Detective Connor Ducharme. I'm investigating—"

"Is he *safe?*"

Under his open jacket he was wearing a waistcoat— what those unfortunate enough to be born north of the

Mason-Dixon line and west of the Missouri River called a vest, he supposed. Before he'd known what she intended she'd grabbed its lapels. Slim fingers gave a surprisingly strong tug and she repeated her query, those perfect features of hers etched with strain.

"Is he safe? Have you found him? Dear God—New *Orleans?* Why in heaven's name did they take him there?"

He'd needed her to ask questions. He wished now she'd asked the one he'd been trying to steer her away from.

"*Cher'*, I'm not here about the little one," he said, as gently as he could. "The case I'm working involves a certain Tony Corso, wanted on fraud charges in Louisiana. I wish I had news of your nephew for you, but I don't."

She closed her eyes. When she opened them again he saw the urgently hopeful light in them had disappeared. Her fingers slid from his lapels.

"I—I thought maybe it was all over. The nightmare, I mean. I thought Sky might be on his way home right now."

She took a deep breath. Letting it out, she sat up on the couch. Her head bowed, she swung her legs to the floor. Looking up, she met his look with a suddenly flinty one of her own.

"How did you know my nephew had been kidnapped? Since it's not common knowledge in Denver, I can't believe every last man-jack on the New Orleans force has been alerted."

"Probably not." He shrugged easily, more sure of his ground now. "But when I discovered Corso's trail led here the local law brought me up to speed."

He flicked a glance at her still-white face. Something

prompted him to add, "From what I hear, the rest of your family's sticking pretty close together these days. Why aren't you with them?"

He'd gone too far, he realized immediately. She stiffened, and when her gaze locked on his he could have sworn the temperature in the room dropped several degrees.

"My personal life can't be part of your investigation, Detective, so I'm going to pretend I didn't hear that question."

She smoothed her skirt down her thighs and stood, and despite the perceptible chill emanating from her Con felt sudden heat slam into him. Not everything he'd told her had been a lie, he thought, trying to school his features into impassivity. He *had* asked questions before coming here, and the answers he'd gotten had all been the same. Marilyn Langworthy was a bitch. She was an ice queen. Nothing touched her—not the kidnapping of her tiny nephew, and certainly not the breakup of her relationship with Tony Corso.

Maybe some of what he'd heard was true, but he'd already seen enough of the woman to put the lie to at least two of the labels that had been pinned on her. She cared about the child—cared enough that she was being torn apart by Sky's abduction, judging from what he'd witnessed moments ago. And if she was an ice queen, it was only because the right man hadn't come along to melt her yet.

You gon' be the one who does that, Cap?

The jeering voice inside his head held the same skepticism he'd heard from the late-night denizens of the Canal Street clubs he'd trolled when he'd been young enough that even hardened gamblers had felt a momentary pang of conscience before dealing a tough Creole urchin in on a game of five-card stud. He'd taken them and their consciences to the cleaners, Con recalled without regret. But back then all he'd been risking was money.

The stakes were higher here. And the odds were more overwhelmingly against him than they'd ever been in his life.

F'sure. One of these days I'm gonna come back here and give it my best shot, he answered the jeering voice with a determination that disconcerted even himself. *But whether she knows it or not, tonight the lady just needs someone to be with her. And maybe if that someone gets her good and angry it'll ease her pain for a few hours. Before I leave I can do that for her, at least.*

"Let's get back to the matter you say brings you here, Detective."

Her voice was like everything else about her, he noted—crisp and unemotional on the surface, but shadowed with a hint of vulnerability that the casual observer wouldn't catch. He wasn't a casual observer, Con thought. Not when it came to Marilyn Langworthy. With no enthusiasm he took advantage of that vulnerability.

"Tony Corso," he agreed. "Word is he was your— how did I hear it?—your good right-hand man, *cher',*" he drawled insinuatingly. "That true?"

If she'd stiffened before, now her posture was rigid. Two warning flags of color flew high on her cheekbones, and when she answered him, five generations of Beacon Hill aristocracy on her mother's side came through in every clipped word.

"I'll give you the benefit of the doubt and assume you're just referring to his position at Mills & Grommett, Detective—" She made a show of frowning in forgetfulness. "I'm sorry. Your name again?"

"Ducharme." He deliberately took a step onto thinner ice. "But call me Con, sugar. The other's a mouthful."

Even if he hadn't been trying to goad her he wouldn't have been able to resist letting his gaze linger on the mouth in question, he admitted. Those lips weren't Beacon Hill at all. They didn't go with the prim white blouse and the straight skirt she wore, and they didn't go with the smoothly brushed hairstyle. Those lush lips went with black fishnet stockings, half-undone bustiers, bed-messy tangles of hair obscuring a gleam of blue eye. They were lightly and invisibly glossed—another Beacon Hill legacy, Con guessed. He wondered what that mouth would look like slightly smudged from his kisses.

You're wondering way too much here, Cap, for a man who doesn't intend to do anything about it, the voice inside his head warned. *Maybe you better back off a little and—*

"What is it about me, Detective?" The lips he'd been fantasizing about thinned. "Why do I seem to present a challenge to men of a certain kind, like you and Tony Corso?"

He blinked, feeling obscurely outraged. "Me and Corso, *cher'*, we're not two of a kind. I'll let you take a look at his file sometime and you'll see just what—"

"His references were solid and when he left he certainly didn't abscond with the company's payroll. Whatever you're trying to charge him with, you've obviously made a mistake," she interrupted him. "That's not what I'm talking about. I wasn't Tony's type, I know now. But just the fact that I wasn't particularly interested in him when we met made him determined to get some response from me, whatever it took. Even so, his approach was nowhere near as fast and crude as yours, Detective," she added coldly.

She tipped her head to one side. "The innuendoes, the barely veiled insults. Tell me, do you ever get results with them?"

He'd given in to a reckless impulse by coming here in the first place, Con told himself tightly. He'd compounded that recklessness when he'd revealed himself to her. About the only admirable urge he'd acted upon was his hasty decision to take her mind off her nephew's disappearance by rousing her ire, and that mission, it was all too obvious, had been accomplished.

He'd always known enough to fold his cards and get up from the table when logic and reason told him his run of luck was about to expire. Right now logic and reason were telling him it was time to walk away from Marilyn Langworthy.

Fast and crude? he thought, a tiny spark flaring inside him. *Hell, I could have left you thinking anything else of me, sugar, but not that.*

"You bet I do," he said easily. "And if you were honest, you'd admit that sometimes you wish you could slip out of that ice-water manner of yours and into a little Big Easy fast and crude yourself. If you ever feel a lapse in good taste coming on, look me up, *cher'.*"

"And you'll what?" Her tone was edged. "Be my—how did you put it?—my right-hand man? I don't see my taste lapsing that badly."

Her gaze lasered him. "But I guess I can understand how you work it, Detective. Some women probably just see a big man with dark eyes and black hair when they look at you. Some women might go for that drawl and the riverboat gambler air you put on."

"I was born in St. Tammany Parish, honey. We all talk like this where I come from," Con interjected. "And I put myself through college relieving high rollers of their cash on the riverboats, so that's legit, too. I'm not the one pretending to be something I'm not.''

He smiled into her furious eyes. ''Those shoes. Killer heels, sugar, and barely-there straps. They're your secret sexy vice, aren't they? They're the real Marilyn. And deep down I think the real Marilyn could go for a big man with black hair and gambler's hands if she wasn't so damn scared of letting loose.''

Shrugging, he turned away. ''Too bad for both of us that you're such a coward, *cher'*. If Corso contacts you, try to set aside your fears long enough to let me know, will you?''

He felt suddenly angry with himself. If anyone had been a coward here it had been him, Con thought as he strode toward the door. He hadn't meant to walk into her life this way, had always known there were reasons why Marilyn Langworthy's path and his should never cross at all. And still he hadn't been able to resist this encounter. That was bad enough.

But lying about who he was had been worse.

Didn't have the guts to watch your dreams die right in front of your eyes, did you? the jeering voice said. *Letting her think you're a* cochon *is preferable to what you know she'd feel if she ever found out who you really are.*

''Is it so obvious?''

Her question was so low he almost didn't hear it. He turned and saw she was still standing by the couch, but that was all that was unchanged from a moment ago.

The self-possession she'd exhibited during their barbed exchange was no longer in evidence. Her cool demeanor had fled. And something had replaced the anger in her gaze with total and absolute devastation.

''I keep telling myself it wasn't my fault, Con.'' She

didn't seem to realize she'd used his name. "But it was."

"What are you talking about?"

Frowning, he crossed the distance between them and stood before her. There was something wrong here, he thought—something badly wrong. Lightly he grasped her shoulders.

"What's your fault?"

"I should have been there the day he was kidnapped." Her whisper was raw, her words more directed to herself than to him. "If I had been, maybe I could have prevented it. But I turned around and came home again, because I was too *afraid.*"

Under his palms her shoulders trembled. She turned haunted eyes to him. "It's like you said—I'm a coward. I hadn't been able to stop thinking about Sky since the time I visited him and Holly. I hadn't expected to feel that way about a baby, but I took one look at him and I just fell in love," she added softly. "So I decided I'd set aside my pride and call on Holly that day, put things right between us after all these years. Except I lost my nerve. That must have been just about the time they— just about the time—"

The blue of her eyes sheened over. "I might have *saved* Sky, Con, and it's tearing me apart that I didn't!"

"Don't say that, *cher',*" he began, but with a quick shake of her head she overrode him.

"It's true. By choosing to keep myself sealed off I put a little boy in terrible danger. And God help me, if you were anyone but a complete stranger, I wouldn't even have the courage to admit that much."

Guilt lanced through him. It was way past time to tell her, he thought. If he left it any longer the consequences could be disastrous.

Even as he opened his mouth to speak she forestalled him.

"And maybe I wouldn't have the courage to go through with this, either," she said hoarsely.

Her fingers fumbled with the top button of her blouse. She slipped it free and immediately began working on the second one, her movements clumsy with urgency.

"Holly has family and friends to support her." Her head was bent to her task as if it required her full attention. Without looking at him she continued speaking, her voice little more than a thread. "My father has his wife. Josh may not have found the woman he wants to share his life with yet but he always has someone—someone to hold, someone who can help him keep the nightmares at bay. But I'm the Ice Queen, Con. And ice queens don't have anybody."

He had to stop this, Con thought. Whatever she thought she was doing, it was a sure bet she'd hate herself for it before twenty-four hours had passed. His hands moved from her shoulders to grasp her wrists. The edges of her blouse gaped open to reveal a swell of creamy skin, a delicately erotic edging of lace.

Immediate desire burned through him. He swallowed, and forced his gaze to hers.

"I had no right to say what I did, *cher'*," he said huskily. "I had no real right to come here at all. I should go now."

"*No!*" The single word exploded from her with the desperation of a plea. The blue eyes meeting his were dark with unimaginable pain. "Don't you get it, Detective? I need to make the nightmares go away for a few hours. Sky's disappeared. I might have saved him. For nineteen days that knowledge has been tearing me apart, and I just want to blot it out for tonight."

She undid the last button. His hands slipped away from her wrists, and when she shrugged out of her blouse and let it fall to the floor he made no move to stop her. Cupped by the lacy bra, her breasts rose and fell quickly.

"Take the pain away, Con." Her whisper was raw. "Please take it away, just for tonight."

She needed a stranger. She needed someone who would walk away without a second thought after this was over. She needed someone who wouldn't recall her name a month from now.

And he wasn't that someone, Con thought. He was just the man who'd loved her for as long as he could remember. If he did what she was asking, after tonight she wouldn't only have his heart but she'd own his very soul, and any faint hope he might have had for a future with her would have to be forgotten forever.

Take the pain away, Con. Please take it away...

His arms gathered her tightly to him and his mouth came down on hers.

Chapter Two

With a frown Conrad Burke looked around the massive and rustic great room of the Royal Flush Ranch. It had been three months and two weeks since his encounter with Marilyn Langworthy, he reflected, although *encounter* came nowhere close to describing the conflagration that had consumed the two of them that night in her office. Three months and two weeks of burying himself in his work, of drinking too much, of falling asleep, drunk or sober, with the memory of her haunting his dreams.

He'd promised himself he wouldn't return to Colorado, but when his old friend Wiley Longbottom had come to him yesterday with a request to meet with a certain Colleen Wellesley here at her ranch, located a couple of hours outside Denver, even the fact that Wiley had refused to reveal what the meeting was about and who Wellesley was hadn't given him pause. He'd caught a red-eye flight out of Louis Armstrong Airport, touched down in Denver, and the first damn thing he'd done after renting a vehicle had been to head for the city's lively and upscale LoDo district. He'd parked near the corner of Blake Street and 33rd, within sight of the converted-to-lofts warehouse where he knew Marilyn lived, and had sat behind the wheel of his car all afternoon hoping to catch a glimpse of her. Only when the early November dusk had begun to fall had he left the city, taking I-285 until it hooked up with Highway 9 near Fairplay, just north of the Royal Flush.

Although apparently the house itself had been a bordello in the wild old days, to his mild surprise he'd realized when he'd arrived that the Flush was definitely a working ranch. He was willing to accept that as an excuse for the Wellesley woman's absence so far, Con told himself, walking over to the antique portrait hanging above the gilded mirror running the length of the heavily varnished and well-stocked pine bar.

He gazed without interest at the rest of the decor, an obvious holdover from those same wild days when this room's red velvet furnishings and saloon fittings had probably been the last word in decadent luxury for woman-hungry cowboys. Ranch duties or not, if Wiley hadn't been there, he would have driven back to the airport, Con thought with growing impatience. And this time he wouldn't have indulged in a foolish and futile side-trip to Marilyn Langworthy's neighborhood.

It had ended as he'd known it would. After the third time they'd made love she'd fallen asleep in his arms on the sofa, the cashmere throw they'd been lying on pulled lightly over her hips, her head tucked into the hollow of his neck. He hadn't slept himself, but had spent the few hours before dawn just drinking in the sight of her and breathing in her scent.

During those hours he'd hoped against hope he was wrong. As soon as she'd opened her eyes, hope had died.

Of course she regretted it. What she did with you went against everything she ever thought she was. The only way she could live with herself when she realized she'd

made love with a stranger—made love with a stranger
and liked it, for God's sake—would have been to wall
herself up again behind the ice that's protected her all
her life. Even before she told you to get out you knew
that. Even before she started crying you knew.

So it had ended with her hating herself and hating
him, he thought. And if he had it all to do over again,
for the life of him he didn't see how he could have acted
differently.

She'd needed someone to love her for a few hours.
What she would never realize was that with him she
hadn't had to ask.

"Ray called through to the horse barn and didn't get
an answer." Balancing a thick china plate heaped high
with a Dagwood-size sandwich and a huge dill pickle,
Wiley Longbottom walked into the room. He made a
beeline for the bar and set his precarious burden onto its
scarred surface. "Melody insisted on fixing me a little
snack, as she calls it. Not that I need it," he said, giving
his stomach a rueful pat.

"The Castillos are the ranch's housekeeper and care-
taker," he went on. His next words were spoken around
a mouthful of roast beef. "Ray said he'd try the foreman's quarters, find out if Dex knows where the devil
Colleen's disappeared to."

"So while we're waiting for her to grace us with her
presence why don't you fill me in on a couple of details?" Con suggested, shooting his old friend a sharp
look. "Like what the hell am I doing here in the first
place? You know I don't like the cold, Wiley, so you
must have had one hell of a good reason for dragging
me away from New Awlins and into the snow belt at
this time of year. You've got mustard on your tie," he
added in irritation.

"That might be from lunch. I never was the dandy you are, with your boutonnieres and those extravagant vests." The older man nodded with a grin at the yellow flower in Con's lapel. Under bushy brows his gaze remained hooded. "As for my reasons for dragging you away, yeah, I'd say they're justified, but I think it's best if Colleen's in on this discussion."

"Aren't you playing your cards a little closer than you need to?" Con kept his voice even with an effort. "Dammit, Wiley, this is me. We go back a long way, to before you were appointed director of public safety and when I was just starting out in the Marshall Service. At least give me some background on the mysterious Colleen Wellesley I'm about to meet."

"I haven't given her much on you," the older man informed him with a sidelong glance. "All she knows is that in the past when I've run into a particularly thorny problem I've consulted with my 'conscience' to come up with a solution. She's not aware said conscience is a reformed cardsharp who cooks up the best crawfish étouffée in the French Quarter, bar none."

Con grinned reluctantly. "I appreciate the cover even if it isn't one I'd have chosen myself. And even though you've obviously decided it's time to blow it," he added, more soberly. "She can be trusted, Wiley?"

"With your real identity, and a whole lot more." His friend nodded and took another bite of his sandwich. "Wellesley started out as a cop on the Denver force and made detective in record time. She was a damn good one, too, until a bribery scandal derailed her career ten years ago."

"Nice knowin' you, Longbottom." Con pulled the gold watch that had been a legacy from his great-uncle Eustache out of his pocket. "If I break the speed limit all the way back to Denver I should be able to catch a flight home tonight." His lips tightened. "You know how I feel about dirty cops, Wiley."

"The same way Colleen feels about them," the other man replied testily. "She was the whistle-blower, Burke. Except she wasn't believed, since the son of a bitch she blew the whistle on was a superior officer and the rot went a lot higher than even she'd suspected. She handed in her badge when she realized the corruption was just going to be covered up."

Slowly Con slipped the watch back into his waistcoat pocket. "That took guts, f'sure," he said, his eyes narrowing. "So she bought this place and took up ranching?"

"The Royal Flush was left to her when her father died," Wiley corrected him. "She's got a brother, Michael, but he's just come back from time in the special forces and hasn't been involved with the ranch. Colleen herself delegates most of the day-to-day responsibilities to Dexter Jones, her foreman. Until recently she's concentrated her energies on running an operation in Denver called ICU, which is short for Investigations, Confidential & Undercover."

"You taught me a long time ago always to listen for what the other fellow was leaving out," Con observed. "If she's been operating a private investigation firm until recently, that means she's currently doing something else, am I right?"

"She works for us now," Wiley said flatly. He popped the last bite of dill pickle into his mouth. "The Royal Flush is the headquarters of Colorado Confidential, and Colleen heads the operation. ICU is still operating, but it's also a front for Confidential activity."

Con gave a low whistle. "F'true, Cap? So those cryptic e-mails you've been sending me asking my advice in a case one of the Confidential organizations was working on—they've been about Wellesley's outfit? I knew about the setups in Chicago and Texas, but this is the first I've heard that Confidential had moved into Colorado.''

"Don't forget Montana," the other man reminded him. "Yeah, it's for true, Captain." He grinned as he played back Con's slang to him. "You know, Burke, you're living proof that you can take the boy out of New Orleans but you can't take the New Orleans out of the boy.''

"And you'll only get this boy outta dat sweet Crescent City under protest," Con told him with an answering smile. "All kidding aside, Wiley, what's any of this got to do with—''

He stopped as if he'd been shot. Then he shook his head decisively. "It ain't in the cards, old pal. Check with the Marshalls and see what my boss writes in his reports about me. 'Does not play well with others,' that's what. No way am I interested in joining Wellesley's merry band of undercover cowpokes, not even if our tardy hostess gets down on her knees and begs me to—''

"I'm tardy because I've been in the birthing shed with Dex, saving the lives of a mare and a foal who decided to come out feetfirst.''

The crisp explanation came from the slim, fortyish brunette entering the room. Walking past them to the business side of the bar, she pulled a bottle of scotch from the array in front of the antique mirror and produced a cut-glass tumbler from under the counter. Pouring a hefty shot of the amber liquor, she set the bottle down and favored Con with a piercing look.

"As for the getting on my knees and begging part, I wouldn't hold my breath if I were you. The members of

my merry band—'' her gaze frosted over even further
as she quoted him ''—are all solid team players. By your
own admission it's obvious you wouldn't fit in. Can I
get you men a drink?''

She raised the tumbler to her lips. Con studied her
through narrowed eyes as she took a healthy swallow of
her scotch.

Beneath the ranch-woman exterior of jeans and cham-
bray shirt, Colleen Wellesley was still all cop. It showed
in the spit-and-polish neatness of her attire, the no-
nonsense short cut of her hair—her damp hair, he noted,
realizing that she'd taken time to clean up before she'd
joined them.

But a change of clothes and a few minutes under a
hot shower hadn't been enough to obliterate all evidence
of what she was trying to conceal, he thought. Her lips
were still slightly swollen. Although her gaze had been
sharp when she'd directed it at him, as she set her glass
down on the bar he caught an unguarded flash of warmth
in her eyes.

Colleen Wellesley probably had been helping her
foreman deliver a foal, Con decided. But their maternity
ward duties *had* been completed a little earlier than she
was admitting.

''Bourbon, if you've got it.'' From his waistcoat
pocket he extracted a silver dollar, its surface smooth
from long handling. Idly he passed it under his index
finger and over his middle one, then let it slip under his
ring finger. The worn silver gleamed and disappeared as
he lazily passed it back and forth in his hand. ''He must
be quite a man, *cher'*.''

Her head jerked up and a drop or two of the bourbon
she was pouring splashed onto the bar. ''I'm sorry?''

Con ignored the warning in her tone. ''Your foreman,'' he elaborated. He picked up his bourbon and looked blandly at her over the rim of his glass. ''He must be good at what he does to have saved your mare's life and delivered her foal safely. Breech births can be tricky, or so I hear.''

Dark eyes held his a moment longer. ''Very tricky,'' Colleen said finally. ''And I don't like tricky, Mr. Burke. I presume you're Wiley's fabled 'conscience'?''

''Conrad Burke, Colleen Wellesley.'' Wiley had been watching them during their exchange. ''Why don't the two of you start all over again, and this time let's keep it civil. There's a child's life at stake here, people.''

''I hadn't forgotten that, Longbottom,'' Colleen snapped, but before she could continue Con broke in.

''A child's life?'' he demanded sharply. ''Like when you've asked my advice about cases in the past, Wiley, your e-mails on this one just dealt with details. You never gave me the whole picture. What child?''

''Schyler Langworthy.'' Wellesley barely glanced at him. ''He's the six-month-old son of Holly Langworthy, and in this state the name Langworthy carries a lot of weight. By election day I guess we'll see just how much weight, since Holly's brother's running for governor against the incumbent, Todd Houghton.'' She exhaled tightly. ''Sky was kidnapped almost four months ago. Colorado Confidential took on the case a few weeks later, when the police and the feds ran out of leads.''

She drained her scotch. ''But that's not your problem, Burke. You and I agree you're not team material, so don't worry about it.''

Take the pain away…

He'd known the Langworthy baby was still missing, and his private opinion had been that Sky had been snatched by someone desperate for a child of their own.

There'd never been a ransom demand. So for three months he'd tried to shut out the memory of the agony in Marilyn's voice when she'd spoken of her kidnapped nephew, since unless and until the U.S. Marshalls were called in on the matter his hands were tied.

That was still the case, Con thought heavily. As the oldest federal law enforcement agency in America, the mandate of the Marshalls was primarily centered on federal fugitives, money-laundering prosecutions and the witness protection program. They cooperated with other levels of law enforcement, but only when specifically requested to.

He frowned. Knowing all that, why had Wiley sent for him?

"It's got everything to do with you, Con."

Wiley had shaken his head at Colleen's earlier offer of a drink. Now he hesitated, and pulled the bottle of scotch toward him.

"My ulcers are going to play me hell for this," he muttered as he poured himself a shot and swallowed it neat. He wiped his mouth with the back of his hand. "But then, my ulcers have been giving me hell lately anyway. Ever since Helio DeMarco's name cropped up in this investigation," he added, his suddenly grim gaze fixing on Con.

"Helio DeMarco?"

Con felt as if the blood in his veins had suddenly turned to ice. He heard something strike the floor, and looking down, he saw the silver dollar had slipped through his fingers. With a swift movement he bent to pick it up, grateful for the chance to avert his face.

"You know of him?" Colleen's tone was still barbed. His own was flat as he answered her.

"You could say that. A year ago in New Orleans a

protected witness in a case the Marshalls were building against DeMarco on money-laundering charges was killed by him. Then DeMarco contacted Roland Charpentier, one of our agents, and said he wanted to cut a deal.''

"But instead the Marshalls obviously let him get away, since he's surfaced here in Colorado," the ex-cop said disgustedly. "Was Charpentier on the take?"

"Colleen—" Wiley began warningly, but Con didn't let him finish.

"No, *cher'*, Roland wasn't on the take," he drawled. He met her eyes. "I'd have known if he was. Charpentier's my best friend—in fact, I visited him earlier today, just before I caught my flight to Denver."

Her gaze wavered. "I shouldn't have jumped to conclusions," she muttered. "So how did the Marshalls lose Helio, or Lio, as he now calls himself?"

Instead of answering her question, Con asked one of his own. "Everyone's heard about the Mardi Gras celebrations in New Orleans, but do you know what our other big day is, *cher'?*"

Annoyance reappeared on her features. "The name's Wellesley, Burke. And no, I don't know. I also don't care."

"You should," he informed her. "Because there's a kind of poetic justice involved you might appreciate. Our other big observance is November the first. Today," he added softly. "The Day of the Dead, when we visit the graves of our loved ones and remember how much they meant to us."

He glanced down at the yellow flower in his lapel. "The custom is to lay chrysanthemums by the headstone and have a little chat with the deceased." He shrugged. "Some families even bring a picnic lunch, make a day of it. I didn't have time to do that so I just laid my flowers down and made the same vow I always do.''

"Charpentier's dead, isn't he?" Belated comprehension filled Colleen's eyes. "I'm sorry, Burke, I didn't know. What's the vow you make?"

"That I'm going to take down the bastard who killed him. That I'm going to take down Helio DeMarco."

Con flipped the silver dollar into the air. It flashed upward and then tumbled down again, throwing off glints of light before he one-handedly caught it. Slapping his palm and the coin in it flat against the pine bar, he looked at her.

"Call it," he said tonelessly.

She raised an eyebrow. "Heads."

He lifted his hand. "Tails. I'll work with Colorado Confidential, *cher'*, but on my own terms. No boss, no partners, no rules."

"No deal," Colleen riposted. She turned to Wiley. "For God's sake, Longbottom, *this* is the maverick you're considering to head the New Or—"

"I think you should take him up on his offer." Con heard a hint of steel in the DPS director's normally mild tones. "If Burke says he'll deliver Helio to Colorado Confidential he will. Right now that's all that matters— especially since this whole thing could blow up in our faces if it's not taken care of quickly."

"How's that?" Con frowned at his friend, but Colleen answered him before Wiley could speak.

"We think one of the Langworthys has gone over to the other side," she said coldly. "There was always a possibility Sky's kidnappers had help from a member of the family, and with what we've found out about Helio's involvement, that now seems to be a certainty. A former intern of a certain Senator Franklin Gettys, Nicola

Carson, came close to being killed by a DeMarco hit man when she discovered a link between the senator, the mobster and a mysterious chemical mist that was being tested on sheep at Gettys's ranch, the Half Spur. Fibers found in Sky's crib after his abduction came from the type of sheep on the Half Spur. And Gettys's ex-wife, Helen Kouros, gave us information she copied on a disk from the Half Spur's computer that backs up our belief that some kind of bio-weapons research is being done there.''

She paused. ''But you guessed about the Q-fever virus, didn't you? I'd forgotten—Wiley's 'conscience' recommended we look into the flu that swept Silver Rapids earlier this year.''

''I told him it might be worthwhile to check out any recent influenza-like outbreaks that might have occurred in the area,'' Con said. ''Since I didn't realize this investigation was centered in Colorado I wasn't aware there'd been one in Silver Rapids. But it fits. DeMarco's always been intrigued by nerve gas, biological weaponry, that kind of thing. He's responsible for at least six murders I know of that were passed off as deaths from natural causes, and Roland's was one of them.''

He hoped his voice revealed none of the pain that suddenly swept through him. A vision filled his mind of Roland's lifeless body, slumped over his desk, his hand still gripping the silver pen that had released the deadly vapor which had instantly killed him. That pen had been given to him by Helio DeMarco, it had later been established.

He felt a muscle in his jaw tighten. With difficulty he posed his next questions.

''But where's the connection between DeMarco and

the Langworthys? And which Langworthy is under suspicion, anyway?''

''The Ice Queen.'' Colleen's voice hardened. ''Marilyn Langworthy, Holly's half sister and Sky's aunt. Her nickname's apt. Even pregnancy hasn't thawed her out.''

She was *pregnant.*

Just for a moment Con let himself imagine how he would feel if there was any possibility that the child she was carrying could be his, and fierce joy shafted through him, so powerful and piercing it felt like pain. He wrenched himself back to reality.

She'd had his body. Whether she ever knew it or not, she had his heart and his soul. But the one thing he was incapable of giving Marilyn Langworthy or any woman was a child, he thought bleakly.

So the baby she was carrying had to be—

''We believe that the father of her child is a certain Tony Corso.'' Colleen frowned. ''Since you're an expert on DeMarco, you probably know Corso's his nephew.''

Con reached for the bottle of bourbon and poured himself a second shot, more to have something to do than because he needed another drink. He tossed it back.

Marilyn was pregnant, and by a man who'd walked out of her life. Since earlier this year his own investigation into Corso as a lead to DeMarco had failed to turn up the mobster's nephew, he didn't need Wellesley to fill him in on Corso's absence, he thought grimly as she continued talking, just as he hadn't needed her to fill him in on a number of other details. He wasn't going to tell her that. His flying visit to Denver three months ago, including what had happened between him and Marilyn that night in her office, was none of Colorado Confidential's business and he intended to keep it that way.

There were other aspects to his involvement with this

case that he had no intention of sharing, he admitted. Wiley almost certainly knew some of them, but it seemed he hadn't felt the need to alert Colleen Wellesley to the situation, so that was all right.

That was the only thing that was all right.

Marilyn Langworthy had had an ill-advised affair— an affair she'd later regretted, judging from her assessment of Corso that night in her office—with a man who had connections to a mobster, unbeknownst to her. She gave the impression of being standoffish and unemotional.

If Colleen Wellesley or Longbottom or anyone else associated with Colorado Confidential thought they could hang her out to dry for reasons as flimsy as those, Con thought savagely, it would be his pleasure to set them straight right now. Even as he opened his mouth to speak, Wiley put a hand on his arm.

"If that were all we had on her we'd just keep her under surveillance on the off-chance she could lead us to DeMarco. But there's more. It's pretty damning."

The older man's expression was shuttered. "Marilyn Langworthy arranged a visit to Silver Rapids with Holly just before the flu outbreak, Con. It looks as if the Ice Queen deliberately exposed her half sister to the Q-fever microbe during Holly's pregnancy with Sky."

Chapter Three

"Hold the elevator!"

Marilyn hoped the note of panic in her voice wasn't as obvious to Jim Osborne and Dan Curtis, her neighbors, as it was to herself. Hastening across the gleaming heartwood floor of the loft complex's foyer—waddling, more like, she thought despairingly—she found herself calculating the number of seconds before she reached her apartment and made it to the bathroom.

Living in a trendy converted warehouse had cachet, but there were definite drawbacks. For starters, the elevator had been originally built for freight, and it was slow. Jim and Dan would be getting off at the second floor, so their exit would tack on another ten or twenty seconds. Add thirty more for the mad dash up the industrial-style metal staircase that linked her open-concept lower floor to the upper one where the bathroom and bedrooms were, and there was a chance she wasn't going to make it.

Everything she'd ever read about the physical side effects of pregnancy had emphasized benefits like glowing skin and silkier hair. She'd never expected to be at the mercy of a bladder that felt roughly the size of a pea.

Bad choice of word. As she scooted into the elevator she attempted to maintain a modicum of cool decorum by smiling her thanks at the two men.

"Mama's been shopping for maternity fashions," Dan teased, casting an eye at her parcels and releasing the elevator door. Beside him, Jim raised an eyebrow.

"I saw that look of desperation often enough on my sister's face when she was expecting. Gotta go, sweetie?"

The Marilyn Langworthy of three months ago would have frozen him with a look, she thought. Now she felt grateful for his perception.

"Let's just say I've decided to pack away my favorite CD of Handel's *Water Music* until after next April," she admitted. "There isn't a warp speed button on that panel, is there?"

"Sorry, no." His pleasant features crinkled into a grin. "But we'll go straight to your floor first. Will that help?"

"You're an angel," she breathed fervently.

As the oversize freight doors clanged shut and the elevator began its noisy and excruciatingly slow ascent, surreptitiously she eased her left foot out of its leather flat and felt instant relief. She looked up in time to see both Jim and Dan glance politely away.

Her beloved collection of size seven Manolos were a dim memory, Marilyn thought wryly. Ditto for her wardrobe of designer suits and dresses, all of which she'd seemed to balloon out of within days of learning she was pregnant. Once upon a time she'd concentrated on the label of a garment, but now she'd acquired the habit of riffling through racks of clothes, extracting a likely looking top or skirt, and tugging ruthlessly at the waistline to judge how much stretch it had.

Of course, her shopping expedition today had been only a cover. She'd needed to get away from the office and come to some hard decisions.

She was a thirty-one-year-old expectant single mother. She'd lost her figure, her reputation and after what she'd discovered this morning, quite possibly her job. And she had to go to the bathroom like nobody's business.

Joy soared through her, so pure and exhilarating she felt a prickling moisture behind her eyes. She was going to have a baby. She was going to have a *baby*.

"…bring a plate up to you later, if you'd like."

She'd missed the beginning of Dan's comment, but it was obvious from his expression that he hadn't been expecting tears in reply. She mustered a shaky smile.

"Sorry, hormone overload. It's gotten so bad lately I have to keep a box of tissues by the television in case a heartwarming advertisement comes on. What were you saying?"

"I'm making my special moussaka tonight. I thought if you didn't feel like cooking—" He stopped as Marilyn hastily tried to erase the moue of instant nausea that had shown on her face. "Vine leaves and ground lamb not on the menu these days?"

"I'm finally over the morning sickness, thank goodness," she said as the elevator lurched to a stop at her floor and the doors began to open. "But certain foods still seem to flick the queasiness switch with me. I'll take a rain check on that moussaka for about six months from now, if that's all right with you."

Jim and Dan were good neighbors, she thought as she sped through her open-concept living area and clattered up the metal stairs. That was important, especially in an unconventional building like this. The former warehouse was divided into only three spacious loft apartments, one of which was vacant at the moment, its owners being away in Europe.

"And the best thing about them is that right from the first they were happy for me when I told them I was expecting," she said out loud a few minutes later as she descended the staircase and bent with difficulty to pick up the shopping bags she'd dropped on her frantic way in. "Which is a whole lot more than I got from either the Langworthy or the Van Buren side of my family."

She felt suddenly too weary even to unpack her purchases. Tossing the bags onto the sofa and dropping into an oversize velvet-upholstered club chair, she closed her eyes.

Immediately he was there, the way he always was when she let down her guard.

Sometimes she could almost persuade herself that that whole night three months ago had been a dream—an erotic, sex-charged dream, in which she'd acted with an abandon that was totally unlike her waking self. And Connor Ducharme fit the profile of a dream lover perfectly, right down to his lazy sensuality, his tall, leanly muscled build, his New Orleans drawl. If that night really had been only a dream she would have been able to handle it, Marilyn thought bleakly. But it had happened. She'd slept with a stranger—not once, but three times that night. And she'd loved it.

That was the part she found hardest to live with.

She opened her eyes. From the soaring ceiling twenty-odd feet above her swooped a perfectly balanced wire and metal mobile, its impressive span in keeping with the spaciousness of the loft but its delicate construction a counterpoint to the exposed brick and heavy wooden beams that were an indication of the building's original function as a turn-of-the-century warehouse. A current of air caught the mobile and it swirled lightly, like a swallow changing direction in midflight.

She'd actually phoned the New Orleans police department a week later and asked for him. It had taken seven sleepless nights for her to come to that decision, and when she had she'd felt like the weakest of weak-willed females. She was well aware she'd sent him away, had told him she wanted to pretend the previous few hours had never happened, but illogically, that hadn't mattered. She'd wanted to hear his voice. She'd found herself needing his touch. She'd *craved* him.

So she'd set aside her pride and phoned, and at first she'd had the terrible suspicion that he'd duped her. The desk sergeant had asked her to repeat the name of the detective she was inquiring about, and had put her on hold for what seemed an eternity. At long last he'd come back on the line, only to inform her that Ducharme wasn't in the precinct building at the moment.

But by then she'd lost what little courage she'd had. She'd hung up without leaving her name.

She'd never attempted to contact him again, not even when she'd found out she was pregnant.

Connor Ducharme was a dangerous man. He'd seemed to know instinctively what she'd wanted that night and he'd let her believe he could give it to her. But although he'd made her melt, although his mouth, his hands, his whole body had brought her to mind-shattering ecstasy, what made Detective Ducharme so very, *very* dangerous was that he'd known just how much more she'd needed. He'd pretended to give her that, too.

For a few delirious hours he'd made her believe she was loved.

Marilyn closed her eyes again. Her right hand slid

unconsciously to the swell of her belly, and despite the confusing ache in her heart and the problems she knew she was facing at Mills & Grommett, the beatific smile she'd once so envied on Holly's face crept over her own.

And immediately faded.

"I thought I knew what she was going through, but before now I had no idea," she whispered. "Sky was her whole world, and he's still missing. I'd die if anyone tried to take my baby—"

A loud clanking, the signal that another arduous ascent had begun for the freight elevator, drowned out the rest of her words. Almost grateful for the interruption, with an effort she pushed herself out of the chair and began gathering up her shopping bags for the second time.

A visitor for Jim and Dan, she surmised as the clanking continued. She couldn't remember the last time the elevator had stopped at her floor with a guest, and as far as she knew the Dickenson's apartment above hadn't yet been sublet.

She put her idle speculations aside as her gaze lit upon a fuchsia sleeve dangling from one of the bags. Heart sinking, she pulled the garment out. It was a blouse, made of some silky blend and with ruffles spilling down the low-cut front. The black pants that went with it were what the salesgirl had called a yoga style—stretchy and form-fitting, with a very slight flare at the bottom. The low-rise waistband was meant to sit below the swell of her belly.

What was I thinking? These aren't me at all, for heaven's sake, she thought in exasperation. *For starters, I could hardly have chosen a more attention-getting top. And those pants don't hide a thing. I might as well hang a big Baby on Board sign around my neck.*

She was going to have to return them. Sighing, she began to cram them back into the bag, but then she paused.

This pregnancy, unplanned as it might have been, was the most wonderful thing that had ever happened to her. The baby she was carrying was that most precious of all miracles, an evolving little human being. Why would she *want* to hide it?

"And those pants were a whole lot more comfortable than the ones I've got on." She glanced down in sudden distaste at the navy suit she'd worn to the office that day. Just as suddenly, she began unbuttoning the jacket.

Moments later she was padding barefoot across the carpet to the full-length mirror by the door. She stood in front of it and took a deep breath.

The navy suit's boxiness had made her look bulky rather than pregnant. But the clinging fabrics of the fuchsia top and the yoga pants hugged her curves—all of her curves, she realized. The ruffled V-neck of the blouse skimmed silkily over breasts that were fuller than she'd ever known them to be, and then stretched even more over her stomach. The low-rider style of the black pants made no apology for the roundness of her belly, but the lean cut also accentuated the length of her legs.

She looked pregnant…and in what she was wearing, pregnant looked *sexy*. In the mirror she saw faint heat touch her cheeks, and hastily she turned away.

The elevator clanged to a halt outside her apartment.

"Oh, no," she muttered, aghast. She whirled back to the mirror and her reflection, but even as she fluffed the petal-like ruffles toward the vee of the blouse's neckline the door buzzer sounded.

The ruffles fell back into place. Exasperated, she gave

it up as a bad job, and jabbed the intercom button with her thumb.

"Who is it?"

Marilyn found herself hoping her unanticipated caller was her brother, Josh. Throwing his hat into the political ring seemed to have brought out the stuffed shirt in him and although his recent engagement had loosened him up a little, she was pretty sure the gubernatorial hopeful for the State of Colorado would be none too thrilled with his sister's pregnancy being flaunted front and center where the electorate couldn't help but see it.

Except her mystery guest wasn't Joshua. Even though he didn't identify himself, she'd heard those burnt brown sugar tones often enough in her dreams these past three months to recognize them immediately.

"Let me in, *cher',*" the voice on the other side of the door drawled. "That way you get to tell me to go to hell to my face."

She'd been planning to contact Connor Ducharme tonight, she thought hollowly. It seemed now she wouldn't have to.

TRUST HER Beacon Hill upbringing, Marilyn told herself ten minutes later. Grandmother Van Buren had always haughtily held that a real lady never admitted to an awkward situation, and it seemed her lesson had sunk in. On the sofa across from her, Con balanced the bone-china cup of tea she'd offered him on a carelessly crossed knee, and so far neither one of them had been crass enough to tell the other to go to hell.

But she had no illusions. She'd seen the flicker of reaction in his eyes when she'd opened the door and he'd seen she was pregnant. Beneath the veneer of civility they were like two prizefighters circling cautiously, each waiting for the starting bell to ring.

No matter what his original reason for coming here, the possibility that he could be the father of the child she was so obviously carrying had to be in his mind. She needed to dispel that idea before it took root. She knew next to nothing about the man, but it wasn't inconceivable that he might be attracted to the notion of playing daddy on a part-time basis, and she had no intention of standing by and letting that happen.

No child of mine is going to grow up caught between two worlds, and never fitting fully into either one, Marilyn vowed fiercely. *Grandmother Van Buren's rules of etiquette be damned, it's time to get a few things clear here.*

But she'd left it too late. Before she could speak he beat her to it.

"You once told me you were a coward, *cher'*." Leaning forward, he set his cup and saucer on the large Moroccan leather hassock she used as a coffee table. Under dark brows his green gaze held hers and his mouth quirked up wryly.

"Truth is, it's me you should pin that label on. No matter what you said you wanted at the time I shouldn't have left things the way I did between us, but every time I thought about contacting you I lost my nerve. I took advantage of the situation that night. It wasn't anything I felt too proud about the next day, and I figured you'd have every right to slam the phone down on me if I called."

His self-deprecating honesty took her by surprise. "We both know it wasn't that simple," she said slowly. "I pretty much threw myself at you that evening in my office. I accept half the responsibility for what happened.''

She hesitated, and then went on, her heart in her mouth. ''This—'' she spread her fingers wide over her belly ''—isn't a result of what we did together, in case you were wondering. I know we were insane enough not to take precautions that third and final time, but the dates don't work out. I would have already been pregnant when we—when we—''

She floundered to an halt.

''When we made love, *cher'?*'' Taking her by surprise again, he shook his head. ''Hell, I know I'm not the father, sugar. Tony Corso is, isn't he?''

Her brother had asked her that same question, but in a furious tone of voice. She'd refused to give him an answer, knowing full well that her silence would seem to him to be confirmation of his suspicions, and since she'd had no intention of telling Josh that she'd slept with a stranger his assumptions had suited her just fine.

As Connor Ducharme's same assumption should, she told herself. She didn't *want* him to wonder if he was the father of her baby, so why should she feel even the slightest pinprick of disillusion that he was so easily bowing out from the position?

''Tony's the father,'' she agreed tartly. ''But what made you so sure you weren't in the running even before I told you, Detective? Was it a smidge of relief on learning that if anyone's going to get slapped with a paternity suit, it's not going to be you?''

The green eyes across from her darkened. As if he felt suddenly restless, Con got to his feet and took a few steps into the middle of the room before halting beneath the mobile swaying gently above. His hands in his pockets, he tipped his head back to look at it.

"I never understood men who needed to get their asses hauled into court before they'd pay support, honey," he said softly. "I always saw children as a gift. I'd like a whole houseful of them, with a mama to go along with them."

Still looking up at the mobile he went on, his tone devoid of emotion. "But that's not in the cards for me. I know I'm not in the running, *cher'*, because I can't be in the running. An illness when I was a boy took care of that particular possibility for me."

She stared at him. "But how can that be?" she began unguardedly. Before she could continue he turned to her.

"Just the luck of the draw, I guess," he said, his jaw tight and his gaze unreadable. "From what I've been told, the consequences could have been a lot more serious. Does Corso know he's going to be a father?"

There was an added watchfulness in his gaze as he waited for her answer. This was the reason he'd sought her out, Marilyn realized suddenly. He was still hunting Tony Corso. This was an official visit.

But of course it was, she told herself a heartbeat later. What had she expected—that he'd brokenly confess she'd haunted his sleepless nights, that his search for Corso was just an excuse to see her again, that he'd fallen hopelessly in love with her during those few hours they'd spent together and he hadn't been able to stay away?

She was a damn lead in his investigation. Their unplanned tryst in her office had been an unforeseen perk to him, nothing more.

She didn't owe Con Ducharme anything.

"Tony and I slept together once," she said flatly. "He wasn't the love of my life and I obviously wasn't his, since the next day I found he'd not only walked out on me but on his job at Mills & Grommett. No, he doesn't know I'm pregnant, and if I knew where to find him, I still don't think I'd tell him. But Tony's not planning on being found, Detective.''

''Something's happened.'' His gaze narrowed. ''When I first came to you asking about Corso you made it clear that you didn't believe he was guilty of any criminal conduct. Now I get the feeling you wouldn't put anything past him. When did your opinion change?''

Why couldn't the man have stayed in New Orleans? Marilyn thought hopelessly. What she was about to tell him would have been hard enough over the phone as she'd planned. She wasn't sure if she could go through with it in person.

But she had to.

''Today,'' she said. She looked down at her lap, not wanting to meet his eyes. ''Because today I realized beyond a doubt that when Tony left Mills & Grommett so hastily he helped himself to a severance bonus from the company...except what he took from M & G went way beyond the fraud you told me he'd committed in Louisiana.''

''That fraud I told you about—'' he began, but she didn't let him finish. The next sentence was going to be the worst, she knew. Best to get it out as soon as possible.

''He stole viral stock.'' Even to her own ears her voice sounded strained. ''We're a pharmaceutical firm. That's one of the things our research department works with—viruses, some of them deadly. And somehow Corso got into my computer and authorized the transfer of a batch to a nonexistent company.''

Now she did meet his eyes. ''Either he intends to sell it on the black market, or...'' She'd been wrong, Mar-

ilyn thought sickly. *This* was the sentence too terrible to
finish.

But the dark-haired man in front of her seemed to
have no qualms. ''Or he's got his own plans for the
stuff,'' Con said.

He held her gaze, his features so grim they seemed
carved. Like emeralds on fire, his eyes blazed with some
incendiary emotion in the tan of his face.

That emotion was hatred, Marilyn realized with a sudden chill—a hatred so deep and all-encompassing that it
seemed almost an entity in itself. If Con Ducharme's
hatred didn't consume his enemy, she thought slowly, it
would end up not only consuming him but everything
he held precious.

Fear ran through her. Her hand spread protectively
over the child growing inside her.

''You know what that plan is, don't you?'' Her voice
cracked. ''You know what Tony used me for.''

Just for a second the emotion in those green eyes darkened to compassion. Then it blazed up again, and when
Con answered her his tone was devoid of any feeling at
all.

''It's not his plan, *cher'*, it's his mobster uncle's. And
Helio DeMarco would only want to get his hands on
experimental viral stock for one reason.'' He gave a hu-
morless smile.

''DeMarco intends to use it as a weapon against whoever gets in his way. And that includes anyone who
might be too close to discovering what he's done with
your nephew, Sky Langworthy.''

Chapter Four

"You never wanted Tony at all, did you?" Marilyn looked up at Con in dawning comprehension. "The mobster's the one you're really after."

"Helio DeMarco." He'd drawn something from his pocket, she saw. It gleamed between his fingers as he passed it back and forth, and she realized it was a silver coin. He smiled tightly as he noticed her watching him. "You're right. I've been hunting the bastard for eight months now, ever since he killed a friend of mine. One of these days I'm going to find him, and then—"

The silver dollar flashed upward as he tossed it carelessly into the air. It came down, and he caught it. He spread his palms wide for her inspection, and she inhaled sharply as she realized the coin was nowhere to be seen.

"And then Helio DeMarco's going to disappear, just like that," Con said softly. "That's New Orleans justice, *cher*."

Something in his tone shook her. "Where I come from that's vengeance," she said unevenly. "No police force would countenance one of their own taking revenge like that." Her gaze widened with swift doubt. "Unless that was a lie, too. Are you really a detective with the New Orleans Police, Con?"

For a moment she wondered if he was going to answer her. Then he grinned with real amusement. "Does this sound like a Minnesota accent, sugar?" he drawled. "Sure I'm with the New Awlins authorities, *cher'*. But I'll bet you checked me out already, didn't you?"

"As a matter of fact, I—"

Marilyn stopped, the words dying in her throat. That *grin*. It was absolutely devastating. And why hadn't she noticed before that instead of being completely green, in a certain light those emerald eyes of his seemed sparked with gold? He was definitely too much, of course, with one wayward strand of raven-black hair falling across his brow and thick lashes casting shadows on those hard-cut cheekbones. Even his choice of attire, austere as his dark suit and white shirt seemed at first glance, was a world away from both Boston and Denver. His vest was a black on black brocade. His shirt wasn't cotton, but creamy linen.

He was a throwback. Even as the thought occurred to her she knew she'd hit upon the key to the man. Con Ducharme was pistols at dawn, bourbon on the verandah, a risky dalliance with another man's wife in a jasmine-scented and moonlit garden. He was a quick temper flaring over a card game. He was heated hours entwined in satin sheets.

He was wearing a gun.

Hard reality returned in a rush as she glimpsed the sliver of worn leather briefly revealed under his jacket. He'd as much as confessed to her that he intended to kill a man. That lazy charm camouflaged a resolve as cold as bare steel.

"As a matter of fact, I did check up on you," she said slowly. "But tell me, aren't you a little out of your jurisdiction? You said it yourself—it's New Orleans justice you're dispensing, and Denver's a long way from the Big Easy.''

''I had some time coming to me. I took it. This is a private hunt, not an official one.'' He looked away. ''You're right, from the first I was only after Corso because I hoped he'd lead me to DeMarco, and when I found out he'd left his position at your company I got a real bad feeling. When I learned that Mills & Grommett dealt with viral material and that the family who owned the company had just had a child kidnapped, the bad feeling got worse.''

He met her confused gaze, his own shadowed. ''But I needed a solid link between his nephew's disappearance and Sky's abduction before I could know for sure he was involved, and there didn't seem to be one until this week when the Denver police forwarded the reports I'd requested on the kidnapping. I'd told them it sounded similar to an unsolved case I'd worked on years ago,'' he added.

And why did you feel you needed to give me that information? Marilyn wondered, watching as he looked briefly away again and then back at her, his gaze once more steady and clear. He was lying, she thought with sudden certainty. Not about everything, maybe not about anything important, but it hadn't happened the way he was telling her.

Still, he was a police detective talking about a case, whether it was officially sanctioned or not. Maybe he was holding back details he couldn't—

''Denver CSI found traces of eggshells in Sky's crib.'' His words ran through her like an electric shock, driving all else from her mind. He took in her reaction. ''Apparently that means the same thing to you as it did to me.''

"I've visited M & G's research facilities often enough to know that one method of cultivating viral stock is to inject it into eggs." Too agitated to remain seated any longer, she got to her feet and faced him. "I assume you've already informed the local police that you suspect Helio DeMarco's involved in Sky's kidnapping, but with what I found out today about the missing viral stock, it's obvious they should widen their investigation to include Corso."

She swallowed. "I—I'm willing to provide a statement to the Denver P.D. as soon as you can arrange it with them. Just give me a few minutes to compose a notice of resignation from my position at Mills & Grommett. It could save the company some embarrassment when this all comes out, and it might lessen the impact on Josh's campaign."

She placed a hand on the back of the sofa for support against the dizziness that swept over her. "Governor Houghton's people are going to make political hay with this as it is. My brother's run his platform on the premise that biological weapons research and testing should continue to be restricted, and Houghton is all for opening up the field and bringing a new lab facility to Colorado. Josh won't have a leg to stand on when the public learns his own sister allowed potentially lethal stock to be stolen right out from under her nose."

"The public isn't going to know that." Dark brows knitted together in a scowl, and without warning he strode to her side. She felt him take her arm in a firm grasp. "Dammit, *cher'*, when did you last eat?"

His unforeseen change of subject startled her. "Lunch?" she ventured. She passed a shaky hand across her forehead. "I know I had an apple this afternoon."

"*Merde,* it's no wonder you look like you're about to

take another header on me," Con muttered ungallantly. "What the hell were you thinking, going without food for so long when you're supposed to be eating for two?"

"I was about to order in a pizza or something when you showed up on my doorstep." Marilyn's dizziness subsided. She tried to pull her arm away but he didn't relinquish it. "And for your information, women aren't encouraged to eat for two anymore when they're pregnant."

"When they start out as scrawny as you were three months ago they should. Show me what you've got in the fridge and I'll make you a meal."

Releasing her arm, he shrugged out of his suit jacket and slung it over the back of the sofa. He looked down at the leather shoulder holster he was wearing as if he'd forgotten it was there, made a low sound of annoyance, and slipped out of it, too, laying it beside his jacket.

Her first annoyed impulse was to take him up on his scrawny remark. She was going to have to let it go, Marilyn admonished herself edgily. They'd gotten way off track here, and—

She jerked her head up. "What do you mean, the public isn't going to know?"

"Just what I said. The public isn't going to know, the police aren't going to know, Mills & Grommett isn't going to know. What you told me tonight about Corso stealing viral stock is our ace in the hole and I don't intend to lay it on the table just yet." He looked surprised. "You didn't think I was going to let you take the heat for this, did you, *cher'*?"

"But I deserve to." She pressed her lips together. "We can't just keep this information to ourselves, Con."

"I'll make sure the right people are informed." He grimaced. "But in this case, the local authorities aren't the right people. I'm pretty sure DeMarco's bought off some of the boys in blue, and although I'd be willing to trust the rest of the department with my life there's no way of knowing right now who's dirty and who's not. If one of his paid informants gets word to him that we're on his nephew's trail, both Corso and DeMarco will sink out of sight as completely as an old she-gator and her pup in a swamp."

He smiled tightly. "And as a born-and-bred Louisiana boy like me knows, it's the gator you don't see that's most dangerous. No, we're going to let them keep thinking they're safe. Meanwhile, we'll be gator-hunting. And baby-hunting, too," he added in a softer tone. "I don't know what DeMarco wants with your half sister's baby, but I know he's definitely behind the kidnapping."

I have a chance to save Sky. Marilyn felt as if a crack of light had just pierced the clouds that had shadowed her world for the past four months. Tremulous hope leaped in her.

"Oh, Con, I'd give anything to bring him home safely! You don't know what a nightmare it's been since the day Josh phoned me and told me he'd been taken."

"I've got a pretty good idea of what you've been going through." He hesitated, and then his hands came up to lightly clasp her shoulders. "And I know that night in your office never would have happened if you'd been able to turn to your family for support."

She shook her head in sharp negation. "That night in my office never would have happened if you hadn't been a stranger. Right now wouldn't be happening—I couldn't go to anyone in my family about how I provided the opportunity for Tony to get his hands on that virus."

She frowned, wondering how she could make him understand. It was important that he understand, she realized in faint surprise. She didn't know why, but it was.

"My father divorced my mother and remarried when I was just a little girl," she said slowly. "He insisted on retaining custody of Josh, and didn't contest it when Mother decided to move back to Boston with me. I was only five years old and I adored my father, so instead of blaming him I blamed his new wife. I decided she'd been the one who'd persuaded him he didn't need me anymore."

"That's Celia Langworthy?" Con's gaze was shadowed. "I remember reading her name in one of the police reports."

"Celia Grace Langworthy." Marilyn tried to keep the censure from her voice. "I don't think I'll ever fully forgive her. Who knows, my parents might have gotten back together again if she hadn't come along."

She shrugged. "I'm not a little girl anymore and I've even come to see that she makes my father happier than my mother ever did, but I still can't feel close to the woman. She's an ex-southern belle type—fussy and fluttery. And I guess I've always felt it would be disloyal to Mother to forget that Celia replaced her. So I became an outsider in my own family, never feeling I could be myself with them, always knowing there was a barrier between us. Now I almost prefer it that way."

"I'd better stay a stranger, then." A corner of his mouth lifted in wry appraisal. "If we're going to be working together and living in the same building for the next little while, I'd like the barriers to stay down."

"Living in the same building?"

"I've taken the loft upstairs on a short lease," Con said offhandedly. "I like what you've done with your place better, especially that mobile. Who's the artist?"

She was beginning to know the way the man operated, Marilyn thought. He was a master at distraction, not only when he was performing some baffling piece of sleight-of-hand, but in any conversational confrontation, too. Except this time she wasn't going to allow herself to be distracted.

"A local. The LoDo area's an artistic haven," she said firmly. "Which as a new resident you might find interesting, Ducharme. Why did you sublet the Dickenson's loft?"

"I needed a base of operations for while I was in Denver. I wanted that base to be near you." He fixed her with the same steady gaze as before, but this time she instinctively felt he was telling her the truth. "DeMarco isn't a cute movie gangster, sugar. He's the real deal, and as cold-blooded as they come. From the moment you became pregnant with his nephew's baby you were in danger, because that made you the link between him and the Langworthys—and if he finds out that Corso's theft from Mills & Grommett's been discovered, he'll want to sever that link."

His grip on her shoulders tightened. "DeMarco took one person away from me. I won't give him the chance to do it a second time, *cher'*."

She'd seen him in the romanticized role of pistols at dawn, Marilyn thought, shaken by the icy implacability in his tone. Maybe some part of Con Ducharme fit that vision. But he'd be equally adept in a back alleyway knife fight.

She didn't know if that was a good thing or not. She felt a tiny tremor run through her, and repressed it immediately.

"That night in your office I thought you were the most beautiful woman I'd ever seen." As if he sensed her doubts, gently he tipped her head back so her eyes met his. His drawl wrapped around her like velvet. "Too thin, for God's sake, but beautiful. I shouldn't have let things go so far between us, *cher',* but I'd be lying if I said I regretted it. Don't fight me on this, okay? Maybe I should have told you before I arranged the sublet, but I needed to move fast."

"I don't intend to fight you. That woman you met three months ago might not have agreed to your high-handed plan, Con," she acknowledged somberly. "I'm not that woman anymore. For one thing, I've got another little person inside me who needs your protection even more than I do, and for another—"

She attempted a laugh and pulled away, feeling suddenly that the moment had become too intimate. "For another, I'm far from slim or beautiful right now. I'm about as big as a house, and I'm only in my second trimester."

She had the feeling that not much disconcerted Connor Ducharme. It seemed what she'd just said had.

"Have you looked in the mirror lately, *cher'?*"

"About thirty seconds before you rang my doorbell," Marilyn informed him. "I was wondering what had possessed me to buy something that fit me like a second skin. I know what I look like, Con. It's all going to be worth it, but I'm hardly—"

"You were beautiful before. Now you're so damn sexy it hurts."

"It hurts?" It was her turn to be disconcerted. "What do you mean, it hurts?"

"It hurts," he said bluntly. "It aches. I don't know how else you want me to say it. It's the kind of pain a better man than me might grit his teeth about and take a cold shower to get over. I'm not that kind of man."

"Oh, for heaven's sake." She stared at him. "I'm almost four months *pregnant.* How could you possibly find that sexy?" She lifted a disbelieving eyebrow. "No cold showers. Right. Tell me, just how would a man like you handle those painful urges a sex-bomb mama-to-be like me probably sets off each time I lumber into view?"

"You really don't get it, do you?"

She stifled a sound of exasperation. "No, Con, I don't—"

His mouth was on hers before she could complete her sentence.

Everything else Con Ducharme did had a kind of controlled grace about it. His walk was more of a prowl. When he'd stripped off his suit jacket there'd been an economical spareness to the action. Even when he'd spoken of his plans for Helio DeMarco he'd shown no more agitation than a tiger would display in attacking a jackal…but there was *nothing* controlled about his kiss, Marilyn realized instantly, shocked heat running through her. With a second shock she acknowledged that there was nothing controlled about her reaction to it.

Before she realized what she was doing her lips had opened under his and her hands had slid up his chest to clutch tight fistfuls of his shirt. She felt immediately and totally drenched, as if she'd stepped into a waterfall fully clothed.

His right hand was spread wide against the back of her head, his fingers entangled in her hair. With his other arm he pulled her closer to him, and she felt his bicep tightening against the outside curve of her breast, felt herself tauten in automatic response. The tip of his tongue flicked against the roof of her mouth, licked along the vulnerable inside of her lip, pushed past hers without any hesitation at all, as though he'd been waiting all his life for this one moment and had no intention of letting anything hold him back a second longer.

She was being invaded by him, Marilyn thought dazedly. The man was as good as laying claim to her. And whereas only minutes ago she would have found the notion completely outrageous, right now there was something dangerously erotic about the possibility of being claimed by Con Ducharme and in turn claiming him for herself.

When they'd made love three months ago his embrace had numbed the pain that had been tearing her apart. How was it that this time the same pair of arms, the same mouth, the same *man* was touching off a chain reaction of sparks in all her nerve endings?

Before she could come up with an answer Con took his kiss deeper, and the sparks that had been sizzling inside her flared into a thousand tiny explosions, short-circuiting whatever rational thought she was still capable of and replacing it with pure sensation.

He tasted like chocolate—dark, bittersweet, melting chocolate. Her tongue flicked against his inner lip and then licked again, savoring the essence of him almost guiltily, as if she were indulging in some expressly forbidden treat.

Except chocolate wasn't forbidden. Wine was forbidden, liquor was a no-no, but even the most cautious of mamas-to-be could have chocolate—

For the second time in the space of a few heartbeats shock electrified her, and for the second time she felt as if she'd been suddenly doused with water. But this time it was ice-water, and it brought her violently back to her senses. She stiffened and began to pull away from him, but even as she did she realized there was no need.

Already Con had lifted his mouth from hers. Wry

comprehension overlaid the desire in his eyes as his gaze searched her face.

"I think I get it, sugar," he said hoarsely. "How 'bout you tell me anyway, just so I'm sure we're on the same page here?"

"The same page?" It took everything she had to force the words past the constriction in her throat. "All you have to do is take one look at me and you should know what page I'm on, Con. I'm on the pregnancy page. The mother-to-be page. What I'm not on is the hot and heavy, roll in the hay, make a total *fool* of myself page. I don't know what got into me to—"

"A fool of yourself?" His expression was unreadable. "Why would you say that?"

The iron band around her chest tightened further. Abruptly Marilyn turned away, only to halt just as abruptly as she caught a glimpse of herself in the mirror.

Her hair, normally sleekly brushed and obediently in place, tumbled waywardly around her head. Her lips were slightly swollen. The fuchsia top was barely containing her.

Unbidden, an echo of her grandmother's words when she'd learned her only granddaughter was pregnant came back to her.

…some ill-advised attempt to emulate the daughter my former son-in-law had with his doxie? Is that why you've humiliated our side of the family in such a way— because you thought you could win back your father's love by presenting him with a grandchild to replace Sky, or Schyler, or whatever your flighty half sister named her baby? If so, my dear, you've acted like trailer-trash to no avail. Samuel Langworthy discarded you years ago. What father could do that if his daughter meant anything to him at all?

She met Con's eyes in the mirror. "Because it *would* be foolish of me to believe the things you say. And I can't afford to be foolish anymore, now that I'm going to be a mother. I'll work with you to find Tony, Con, but that's as far as our relationship goes."

"And if I want it to go further, *cher'?*" Emerald eyes narrowed at her. "I'm out of luck is what you're saying?"

An attack of common sense didn't mean she was blind, Marilyn admitted reluctantly. He was probably the most gorgeous-looking man she'd ever seen, and to pretend she was totally immune to his brand of sexy southern charm would be a lie.

"A man like you is never at the end of his luck, Ducharme," she said softly. "I'm just saying you're not getting lucky with the Ice Queen. I don't think that's going to cause you any sleepless nights, whatever you said earlier."

"You might be surprised at what keeps me awake nights." He shook his head. "The Ice Queen, sugar? You're anything but. Your trouble is you let the world label you, and then you figured you had to live up to the label. But now and again you slip up and let the real Marilyn out."

He jerked his head upward at the mobile overhead. "Metal and wire. And still it soars. You made it, didn't you?"

She frowned, nonplussed. "How did you—" Her brow cleared. "That night at my office. I'd been sketching out some ideas for another design. I suppose you saw them."

"Half-hidden under some other papers," Con acknowledged. "Don't worry, sweetheart, I won't tell anyone you're secretly an artist, not a corporate drone. Just like I won't tell anyone you wear fuchsia when you're not expecting company.''

With one strong finger he reached out and touched a ruffle. ''You look like a pink peony, *cher',*'' he drawled. ''You're out of place in a Denver November, and I'd lay odds Boston's climate's too dreary for you, too. If you want to keep it business between us I'll do my best, but I can't guarantee anything. And I still intend to make you dinner. We can brainstorm a plan for tracking down Corso while we're eating.''

She probably should make some excuse and send him on his way, Marilyn told herself. But she wasn't going to, and not just because they needed to talk about Tony. All of a sudden the thought of seeing Con to the door and then facing a solitary meal all by herself seemed unbearably empty.

She was attracted to the man. There, she'd admitted it. She was attracted to him. His compliments, as extravagant as they were, made her feel a little less bulky. The fact that he didn't see her as Mills & Grommett's V.P. of sales, didn't see her as Holly Langworthy's ice-queen half sister, didn't see her as a Van Buren of the stiffly proper Beacon Hill Van Burens was strangely liberating. So she was attracted to him. And it would be easy to let that attraction veer unwisely into something stronger.

She wasn't going to be that unwise, but she was going to have dinner with the man, she thought stubbornly. And if she chose to tell herself it was merely because she wanted company tonight, her little deception was no one's business but hers.

''Dinner it is, then, Detective,'' she conceded. ''There should be a couple of steaks in—''

She stopped, feeling her heart crashing against her

ribs. Immediately Con's arms were around her again, and this time she had no desire to pull away.

"What is it?"

"It's a deception," she said thinly. "A cover. That's why Sky's kidnapping makes no sense—because it doesn't have to. Because it's smoke and mirrors."

Con's grip on her tightened. "A deception? Sorry, *cher'*, I don't underst—"

"Of all people you're the one who *should* understand." She stared desperately into his face. "You're the cardsharp. You're the sleight-of-hand artist. Isn't that how it works—while the audience is concentrating on what's just disappeared in your left hand, your right is palming the ace of spades?"

"Merde." Con's tone was flat. "The child means nothing to him. The child's just the distraction, as far as DeMarco's concerned."

"Which means that as soon as Helio no longer needs to distract us—" The words stuck in her throat. He completed her sentence for her.

"As soon as DeMarco no longer needs a distraction, he'll dispose of Sky," he said, his voice harsh. "This never was a regular kidnapping. That's why there never was a ransom demand. Like you said, it's all smoke and mirrors. While everyone's occupied with finding Sky, DeMarco's setting up the crime he really wants to commit, starting with getting his nephew to steal the viral stock he needed from Mills & Grommett."

A muscle moved at the side of his jaw. "The election's in three weeks. What better way to ensure that the candidate he's backing gets elected by a landslide than to link Governor Houghton's opponent to the most terrible biological disaster this country's ever known?"

"Helio's going to release the virus just before the election," Marilyn whispered.

Con nodded curtly. "DeMarco's going to release the virus. And then he's going to get rid of Sky."

Chapter Five

"We need to establish a contact schedule, Burke. Going for a week and a half with no word from you just isn't good enough." Colleen Wellesley shot the third person in the room an impatient look. "Tell him, Wiley. He's your man."

"I'm my own man, *cher'*." Con turned to the bar, his narrowed gaze meeting the brunette's frustrated one in the antique mirror. "And you agreed to let me play a lone hand when we set up this operation, remember?"

"A deal I only agreed to on the condition that you'd hand Colorado Confidential Helio DeMarco on a plate," Colleen snapped. "Not on the condition that you'd play rottweiler at the suggestion we bring in and question the one person who probably knows where to find him."

Con swung around to face the ex-cop directly. "The Langworthy woman's an innocent bystander in all this. If it weren't for what she told me last week we wouldn't have learned that DeMarco's nephew stole viral stock from M & G. More importantly, we'd still be in the dark about his real agenda."

"That virus was stolen by the man who fathered the baby she's carrying. The transaction took place on Marilyn's own computer. Innocent bystander?'' Colleen gave a sharp laugh. ''Accomplice is more like it.''

She paused. Her lips thinned incredulously. ''For God's sake, don't tell me you've gone and fallen for the Ice Queen, Burke. Is that what this is all about—she batted those cold blue eyes at you and spun you a tale about how Corso used her and dumped her, and that manly southern chivalry of yours fell for it, hook, line and sinker?''

''Out of bounds, Colleen.'' From the far end of the bar Longbottom spoke, the very mildness of his tone a warning. He favored Con with an equally mild glance. ''But we wouldn't have to take off the gloves in this conversation if you'd be a little more forthcoming, Con. Is there something between you and Marilyn Langworthy that we should know about?''

''Not a damn thing, Cap,'' Con replied curtly. ''Not a single, goddamn thing. You two through grilling me now?'' His smile was tight, and it encompassed both Colleen and the man who'd been his friend for more years than he could remember. ''Because if you are, I'll head back to Denver. There's a poker game I don't want to miss out on tonight.''

''A *poker* game?'' Anger warred with disbelief on Colleen's features. The anger won. ''If you're an example of how they run things in the New Orleans marshalls's office, Burke, no wonder the place is called the Big Easy. But we run a tighter ship here in Colorado, and if you think I'm going to sanction you taking a break from this case just to play cards—''

''Corso sees himself as a high roller,'' Con drawled. ''The woman you insist is his accomplice told me as much when we were discussing where he might have disappeared to. She also gave me the names of the clubs he gambles at on a regular basis.''

''I see.'' Colleen bit the words off. ''And just what do you intend to do if and when you run into Tony Corso at one of these clubs? Pull up a chair beside him and join in the game?''

''That's right.'' He held her angry gaze. ''And then I'm going to raise the stakes, *cher'*. I'll let you know how it turns out.''

The woman rubbed him the wrong way, Con thought as he let himself out of the ranch house and headed for his vehicle. Or maybe it was more accurate to say this whole setup rubbed him the wrong way—the insistence on toeing the line, the team structure, these meetings, as infrequent as they were.

Except that wasn't it either. The real reason why he'd acted like such a prick just now with the woman who ran Colorado Confidential was that he was even more angry with his lack of results on this case than she was. Like Wellesley had noted, it had been a week and a half since that night with Marilyn in her apartment and he was no closer now to finding Corso or DeMarco than he'd been then.

''Colleen wants you off the case.''

About to open his car door, Con turned. A few feet away stood Wiley, his slight puffing an obvious indication that the older man had hastened to catch him before he left. The director crossed the gravel drive and joined him.

''I told her you stay on. Maybe I made a mistake.''

''Maybe you did.''

He was pissed off with Longbottom, too, Con thought darkly. How the hell had Wiley figured he'd be a good fit in one of the Confidential organizations? Trying to shoehorn him into Wellesley's group was an obvious indication his old friend was losing his touch. There'd been a time when nothing had gotten past the portly man now standing in front of him.

"You're no stranger to Marilyn Langworthy, are you?" Wiley had come out without a coat. He stamped his loafer-shod feet against the November chill and tried to pull the edges of his suit jacket over his comfortable girth. "And you're what—a second cousin once removed to Sky? I never could figure out those genealogical charts," he added, frowning, "but I guess the actual relationship's not important. The main thing is you and the Langworthy woman are almost family, except I get the feeling you'd rather the connection was something different."

Con stared at his friend. "You haven't lost it at all, have you, Cap?" he rasped. "You're still the sharpest knife in the drawer, and then some. Sharp enough to cut me, at least." He attempted to keep the annoyance from his voice. "How long have you known?"

"A few days." All of a sudden Wiley's casual manner dropped from him like a glove. He met Con's glare, his own normally mild brown gaze sparked with fury. "You know what really gets my goat, Burke? Not the fact that you kept this up your sleeve, although that's bad enough on a sensitive investigation like this one. But what's harder to swallow is that you underestimated me. That shows incredible arrogance on your part. Like I said, maybe I made a mistake about you."

A few moments ago he'd shrugged the exact same accusation off, Con acknowledged. This time it stung, and not only because it was a slur on his own capabilities.

If he'd learned one thing over the years, he told himself in chagrin, it was that friends were harder to come by than a straight flush in a game of Cincinnati draw. He'd been lucky enough to have had two of them—men he would unhesitatingly go to the wall for, men he'd known would go to the wall for him, too, no questions asked. One of those friends had been Roland. The other was the tough and loyal man confronting him right now with some hard home truths. And although Charpentier had been taken from him by DeMarco, if Wiley washed his hands of him it would be no one's fault but his own.

"First cousin once removed to Sky. A tenuous relation by marriage only to Marilyn. Her stepmother's my aunt." He cleared his throat. "Hell, Wiley, have I been that big a jerk?"

"You know you have." Although Longbottom's tone was crisp, it lacked its previous antagonism. "The Delacroix sisters, right? The eldest being your mother, Felicity, then Celia and finally your aunt Jasmine."

"*Maman* likes people to assume the age order is reversed, but yeah, they're sisters." Con looked away. "Celia's the only one who moved away from Louisiana. She ended up in Colorado with her first husband, Dr. Edward Grace, who came close to destroying her before she found the courage to divorce him."

"As a boy you used to stay summers with Teddy Grace and your aunt, didn't you?" Wiley's question wasn't posed as such, and with a disconcerted start Con realized the director had done his research. Longbottom went on. "And if I'm correct, you had one last visit with Celia after her marriage to Samuel Langworthy—coincidentally, at a time when Marilyn was also in Colorado, visiting her father. Goddammit, Con, the woman *knows* you! How could you have jeopardized this case by keeping something like that from me?"

"It probably wasn't even necessary to use a fake ID and name. She doesn't remember me," Con said tonelessly. "I doubt Marilyn remembers much about that visit to her father. She was five years old and her world had been ripped apart. I was only a couple of years older than her, but even so, I knew I'd never seen anyone so fragile. Or so beautiful," he added in an undertone.

He felt something cold pressing against his palm. Looking down at his hand, he saw he'd unconsciously retrieved the silver dollar he carried in his waistcoat pocket. "Even if you kick me off the case, Wiley, I'm sticking close to Marilyn and I'll track down DeMarco before he decides she's another liability he needs to get rid of. Yeah, I wish the relationship was something other than it is between us, but if she learns I'm the nephew of the woman she feels was responsible for taking her father away from her all those years ago, she'll think I've played her for a fool."

"Haven't you?" The older man looked troubled.

Con shook his head. "Marilyn Langworthy's the reason I never married, Cap. I'd sooner break these ten gambler's fingers of mine than hurt one hair of her head."

He hesitated. Longbottom was a friend, yes, but not even Charpentier had guessed at the secret he'd carried around most of his life. He'd only ever told one other person what he was about to tell Wiley, and that other person had been Marilyn herself. He took a deep breath and went on, his tone harsh.

"She doesn't remember me, but like I said, I remember her. And I remember her telling her brother, Josh, that when she grew up she was going to have a family of her own that no one would be able to tear apart. I can't give her children. If I'd met Marilyn in the normal way we might have gotten past the Aunt Celia thing, but we never could have created the family she needs so much. I wasn't going to be the man who took that dream away from her.''

Wiley exhaled. ''But now the picture's changed. She's carrying the child she's wanted all her life.''

Con nodded. ''That's right, the picture's changed.'' He held his friend's gaze expressionlessly. ''So am I off the case or not?''

''What I told Colleen stands.'' Wiley reached past him and opened the door of Con's car. ''Looks like there's some nasty weather brewing, Burke. You'd best be heading back before the driving gets hairy.''

He stood there, a short man, balding, and carrying a little too much weight for his stocky frame. Wiley Long-bottom was true blue, Con thought. He was a friend.

''This reporting-in schedule.'' Con slid in behind the wheel and inserted his key in the ignition. With a grimace he jacked the car's heater all the way up and set the fan's blower on high. ''Every few days suit you?''

He looked up in time to see Wiley grin. ''That'd be fine. And Burke?''

Con grinned back, relieved that they were on their old footing again. ''What?''

''I hope you run into Tony Corso at that gambling club he frequents. If you do, good luck at the card table.''

''Hell, I always was lucky at cards.'' Con's grin faded. He shrugged, and moved the gearshift into reverse. ''It's my love life that's been shot to pieces lately. But I'm workin' on that, Cap. I'm workin' on that.''

''COULD I LOOK more out of place?'' Marilyn muttered as she lowered herself into the chair the maitre d' was holding out for her. She sat down before he had a chance to push it closer to the table, heaved herself slightly off the seat again, and sat down for the second time. She looked up to see Con waiting politely before he took his own seat.

"The eagle has landed," she snapped. "Or the blimp, I should say. Tell me again why I'm here, Con."

"Because I wanted the pleasure of your company," he said without missing a beat. "What you drinking, *cher'?* Perrier? Soda and lime? Bourbon and branch for me," he told the waiter hovering by his elbow.

"Soda and lime, I suppose." Marilyn heard the peevish note in her voice, but couldn't suppress it.

Whereas once upon a time her svelte pre-pregnancy self would have glided into this room like a swan, surveyed the competition and basked in the comforting knowledge that she had every other woman there beat hands down in the elegance department, right now her confidence was nonexistent.

She'd expanded to the point where she couldn't fit into any of her dressy dresses, so when Con had dropped this last-minute dinner date on her earlier today she'd had to go out and scour the stores for something to wear. She'd despairingly come up with what she had on now— a deep purple, shot-silk tunic-like affair with, heaven forbid, a Nehru collar. It billowed over elastic-waisted pants in the same shot-silk fabric. It was designer. It had cost too much. Every other female in the room seemed to be wearing backless and skintight and black—exactly the kind of dress pre-pregnancy Marilyn would have worn to an exclusive club.

"*Merde,* the rings."

Before she knew what he intended, Con reached into his pocket. The next moment he'd lightly grasped her hand and was slipping something over her finger. It was a plain gold band, she saw, a match for the one he was suddenly wearing himself.

"Is this a joke?" She started to tug the ring off, but he laid his hand over hers.

"It's not a joke, it's a disguise." He lowered his tone. "You asked why you had to come here with me tonight, *cher'*. Aside from the fact that I really did want to take you out for dinner, I need to look like a married man, especially later when I wander on out back to the gaming room and ask to sit in on a couple of hands of poker."

"I don't—" Seeing his warning look, Marilyn fell silent as their waiter returned with the drinks order. As the man left she went on impatiently. "I don't get it. I thought we were on the lookout for Tony. If he shows up he won't be fooled into thinking you and I are a married couple, and if he doesn't come here tonight, why bother trying to convince strangers?"

"Because without you I look like a pro, honey." Con shrugged. "With a very pregnant wife at my side I just might be taken for an amateur ripe for the fleecing, and the local sharks are gonna think they smell fresh meat. I won't have any trouble joining a game."

"Except that as soon as you walk away with the whole pot your cover's blown," she said skeptically. "Which means you won't be invited back again anytime soon."

"Yeah, you right, like they say back home." A slow smile lifted one corner of his mouth. "Losing on purpose takes almost as much skill as winning. If and when our high-rolling friend does turn up, I'll have established such a reputation as a free-spending rube he won't be able to resist getting in on the action."

He frowned. "At that point I start playing it by ear. All I want is an opportunity to get close to the bastard."

"And all I want is to stay as far away from him as I can."

Marilyn pressed her lips together, wishing she hadn't been so frank. She picked up her menu, scanned the selections, and laid it back on the table again. "Pan-fried trout," she said decisively. "And don't let me even look at the dessert cart when they wheel it by afterward."

"Why not?" He looked genuinely astonished. "They probably don't hold a candle to New Orleans desserts, but what does? Indulge yourself, *cher'*."

"I'd rather fit into a size four again one day," she answered promptly. "If I keep indulging myself, as you put it, outfits like this will become a staple in my wardrobe." She gestured with distaste at the shot-silk tunic.

"That's new?" His tone was carefully noncommittal, but looking up quickly, Marilyn was sure she detected a glint of humor in the green eyes watching her. "Did you buy it today?"

"No, I waylaid the Pakistani ambassador to the United Nations and made him hand over his outfit." Her eyes shot daggers at him. "Of course I bought it today. And I hate it, but at least it's big."

"Damn straight it's big." Now the humor was impossible to miss. "I can barely see what you look like underneath all that, *cher'*."

"That's the whole point." She frowned. "Let's talk about something other than me and my beach-ball figure. What's so great about New Orleans desserts?"

Across the table from her he leaned back in his chair. "The same thing that's so great about the city herself, sugar. They're sinful and decadent and sexy as hell. Berries Artesia. That's served in a syrup made with Pinot

Noir wine and vanilla bean. Or Creole bread pudding with whiskey sauce—you eat that and then you have to say ten Hail Mary's because it's just so wickedly good.''

He grinned. ''I'll bet even you couldn't resist my specialty, though. Chocolate crepes with fresh strawberries. The trick to them being you feed the strawberries to your sweetheart by hand, one by one.''

''And then you go to church and say penance?'' she asked weakly. The man was talking about food, she told herself. There was no need to get all hot and bothered over a discussion on recipes, for goodness' sake.

One dark eyebrow lifted. ''Oh, no, darlin' heart,'' he drawled. ''Then the two of you go to bed and sin all night long.''

Now hot and bothered was appropriate, Marilyn thought, feeling a delicious tingling sensation right down in the very tips of her toes, and a dizzier, darker warmth spreading upward from her thighs to the pit of her stomach. Now he wasn't talking about food—or if he was, it was so tangled up with a completely different delight that she wasn't sure where one left off and the other began. She looked swiftly down at the pink linen tablecloth to hide the heated color she could feel in her cheeks as their waiter approached.

She had a problem, she told herself as Con gave first her order and then his before proceeding to ask a question about one of the restaurant's wines. Her problem was she didn't know how to handle a man like Con Ducharme, for the simple reason that she'd never known anyone remotely like him before. She glanced through her lashes at him. Take right now, for instance—he and the French-accented waiter were discussing the lineage of a certain Burgundy as if the fate of the world hung upon it, but unlike other escorts she remembered from her dating past there was no pretension or snobbery about Con's interest. He just liked good wine, the same way he liked good food—the steaks he'd grilled the night he'd made dinner at her apartment had been perfect—and the same way he liked women. He was a sensualist, she thought. And she didn't have the first idea of how to go about being sensual.

She had a sudden vision of the type of woman who would be able to match Con sexy smile for sexy smile, languid indulgence for languid indulgence. That woman would be dark-haired and sloe-eyed, and when she laughed she would lean forward across the table and lay polished fingertips on his hand to establish a physical contact between them.

That woman wouldn't be pregnant. So she wouldn't have to keep reminding herself that Con Ducharme, as devastatingly good-looking and sexy as he was, had to be kept at arm's length. She wouldn't have to worry that if he ever found out the baby she was carrying was—

"And when Josh gets in, you can be sure he'll take a hard look at that very issue, Dwight. We can count on your newspaper's support, then?"

"Only if you promise to give me a chance next week to win back what you just took off me, Samuel. Good God, man, I really thought I had you until that last hand."

A wave of laughter rippled through the group of older men who were making their way from the direction of the gaming rooms at the far side of the restaurant area toward the exit. A strong scent of bay rum cologne and the lingering odor of expensive cigars trailed in their wake as they passed by.

"Something the matter, *cher'?*" Con's eyes were on

her, his features shadowed with sharp concern. Marilyn managed a stiff smile.

"Not really." She nodded her head at the broadest-shouldered man in the group as he clapped a companion heartily on the back and exited the restaurant.

"Except that was my father, Samuel Langworthy. He saw me, Con. He saw me…and he walked right by as if he didn't care to know me."

Chapter Six

"Not the most exciting evening for you, sugar," Con apologized as he stepped aside to let Marilyn exit the elevator first. Absently he held out his hand for her door key. She bent to unlock her apartment herself.

"It got a little boring when you were on that winning streak for a while," she replied. "But then you started losing. It was well worth it just to see the frustration in your face."

"Let me." Gently he nudged her aside. "Not just being a southern boy here, hon. DeMarco has an uncanny sixth sense where his survival is concerned, and he may already guess someone's on his tail. From now on I want you to be extra cautious when you come back here after being gone for any time. If something seems out of place or if it just doesn't feel right when you walk in, leave immediately and use your cell phone to call me. Like I said before, you're a link between him and the Langworthys that he might want to eliminate."

"Because I'm carrying Tony's baby," Marilyn said, looking away. "I guess you're right."

She waited while he went ahead of her into the loft apartment. The open concept of the ground floor made his security check a matter of seconds, and with a reassuring smile at her he took the metal stairs two at a time to the second level and the bedrooms, disappearing briefly from view as he strode down the hall.

He was right, the evening hadn't been exciting. Tony hadn't appeared at the club, and during the four hours that Con had played cards she'd spent her time making desultory conversation with other lost souls whose escorts had temporarily abandoned them for the gaming tables.

But all the while her nonencounter with her father had lingered unhappily just beneath the surface of her thoughts, despite Con's suggestion during dinner that Samuel's seeming slight had been inadvertent.

"He probably didn't see you, *cher'*. He wouldn't be expecting to run into you here."

"We made eye contact. But he was with his political cronies—the ones he's rallying to Josh's cause, although I'm sure Josh is quite capable of mustering his own support without resorting to the backroom deals men of my father's era think are necessary. And I'm an embarrassment to him."

She'd placed a hand on the swell of her belly. "When Holly was pregnant with Sky the campaigning hadn't gotten underway. But with the election coming up this month the media spotlight is as hot as it's ever going to be, and Father's afraid that if it focuses on Josh's unmarried and pregnant sister it could be detrimental to his chances."

She'd added slowly, "Josh himself hasn't said anything along those lines. I sometimes think he and I might have been friends if we'd had the opportunity to get to know each other. Do you have any brothers or sisters, Con? You've never mentioned."

He'd seemed to hesitate before replying, but when

he'd spoken his manner had been easy. "My mother's a belle, just like you say your stepmother Celia is. You probably know what that's like."

"I'm not close to my father's wife, as I'm sure you've gathered." She'd tried to keep her tone detached. "I know next to nothing about her background."

He'd looked thoughtful. "Well, Felicity's one of those legendary charmers men shoot each other over, with about as much maternal instinct as a butterfly and twice as flighty. My father adores her, but then, about the only parenting he ever gave me was to teach me how to play poker with a straight face. They spend most of their time jetting from one party capital to the other all over the world, since Skip was born one of the idle rich. I love them, but I knew early on I was the adult in the family and that they weren't going to provide me with any siblings."

He shrugged. "I went to boarding school and vacationed with relatives during holidays until I was about ten. Then I put my foot down and told Skip and Felicity I didn't want to be farmed out to every far-flung aunt and cousin anymore. They had a married couple who took care of the New Orleans house, so that worked out."

"For your parents, maybe. I wouldn't call it an acceptable environment for a child." The words had rushed from her mouth before she could call them back. "I'm sorry, Con, I shouldn't criticize your family."

"No harm, no foul, sweetheart." His grin was swiftly amused. "You should hear my Aunt Jasmine on the subject. She's a history professor at Tulane, as unlike *Maman* as two sisters can be. Never married, but in a long-term relationship with Jean-Claude, a jazz saxophonist in the Quarter. He's the last of the cool cats and about as New Awlins as Mardi Gras, since he's directly descended from one of the original Creole families that came to the city as free people from Haiti back in the 1790s, as he never fails to tell me.''

"Did Jasmine take you in?''

If he'd meant to distract her from her own less-than-satisfactory relationship with her family, he'd succeeded. Jazz musicians, cardsharps, intriguing females—Con's background seemed as sprawlingly exotic and boisterous as the city he so obviously loved. Completely enthralled, she'd leaned slightly toward him over the table in a most un-Beacon Hill like way.

"Yanked me by the scruff of the neck right out of an all-night game of Omaha stud, *cher',*'' he said in rueful reminiscence. "I was fifteen. Jasmine told me if I didn't start applying myself I'd end up on the wrong end of a gun, or worse yet, living the same pleasure-seeking life as my parents. No one had ever rapped me over the knuckles like that before. I took it to heart.''

"And ended up a police detective,'' she'd finished for him. "Your Aunt Jasmine must be proud of you.''

He'd shrugged off her observation and turned the talk to Tony Corso after that, Marilyn remembered now as Con, his upstairs inspection completed, came down the stairs again. He paused halfway, reaching out to lightly set the mobile in motion. Dark brows lifted.

"I hadn't realized.'' An appreciative grin crept across his tanned features. "It's scrap metal soldered together.''

"Old silver spoons, some bells from the harness of the pony I had before Mother and I moved back to Boston, a whole lot of junk,'' she said, feeling uncomfortable and not knowing why. "It's just a hobby. Mother used to say it wasn't ladylike, scrounging through secondhand stores for things other people had thrown away.''

"What are these?" He was looking at a cluster of darker metal just out of reach.

"Broken typewriter keys. I found a boxful in one of the storage rooms at work. They must be decades old." She gestured at the hated shot-silk tunic. "I was going to make us some tea, but before I do anything else I'm determined to take this off. I'd drop it into a charity used-clothing bin tomorrow, except I don't want to inflict it on anyone else."

As she spoke, she mounted the first few steps, expecting him to stand aside to let her pass. Instead, he blocked her way.

"Truth. Beauty." His tone was bemused. "Are there any others?"

"Love." Reluctantly she pointed out the third set of welded typewriter letters, swaying gently on the far side of the mobile. "You've got good eyesight."

"These things were all discarded," he said, still looking at the ink-blackened keys. "Only you realized they were valuable. I'd say you're the one who sees farther than anyone else, *cher'*."

Belatedly he stepped aside. "Put on your peony top, we'll drink tea together and I'll sit across from you pretending I'm not staring at those sexy ruffles. Go on, sugar."

Almost absently he gave her a swat on her derriere as she moved past him. Turning in shock, she saw he was already halfway to the open kitchen area.

The words of protest she'd intended died on her lips, but as she stood uncertainly before her bedroom mirror a few minutes later, her eyebrows were still drawn together in an expression that was half-frown, half-confusion. Marilyn Langworthy, Mills & Grommett's Ice Queen, just didn't get swatted on the behind like that by a man, she told herself edgily. Marilyn Langworthy wasn't the type to be teased, didn't enjoy being touched, insisted on observing the proprieties. Her nickname had come about because everyone *knew* that was what she was like—just like everyone knew she would never wear anything as foolishly feminine as a plunging fuchsia blouse, just like everyone knew she would never do anything so outrageous as sleep with a man she didn't know.

And just like everyone knew getting pregnant had been the last thing she'd wanted. Her thoughts ground to a halt. In the mirror her gaze widened as comprehension flooded through her.

She'd been living her life as if others knew who she was better than she did...but none of those people had ever really known her at all. It had taken a stranger to look past the protective casing of ice and see the real woman trapped within.

Except Con Ducharme wasn't a stranger anymore, she realized hollowly. Con Ducharme was the man she was falling in love with.

"Dear God, you can't be," she whispered to her suddenly white-faced reflection in the mirror. "It's too much of a risk. All you know about him is he's a gambler and a flirt and a bedroom-eyed, sweet-talking—"

She stopped. Unconsciously her hands crept to the rounded swell of her stomach.

"A sweet-talking liar," she said slowly. "The man's been lying to me since the day we met, I'm sure of it. Maybe I can see the signs because I've been lying too, but whatever the reason, whatever he's hiding, I can't trust him. Not with my heart, and certainly not with the baby I'm carrying."

His hunt for Helio DeMarco wasn't part of the lie, Marilyn thought as she descended to the living room a few minutes later, the yoga pants topped not by the fuchsia blouse but by a black tunic in a silky jersey knit. She was as certain of that as she was of the other, so continuing to work with him to find Tony and his mobster uncle was still on the agenda. Even as she acknowledged her decision she felt an illogical sense of reprieve, as if she'd managed to find a reason to stave off a moment she was dreading.

And that was stupid, she told herself stonily. Sooner or later she and Con Ducharme would part ways. Just because it wasn't happening tonight didn't mean there was a chance it could somehow be averted.

"It's not chicory coffee but it's hot."

He'd prepared the tea while she'd been upstairs. It wasn't the first time he'd done so during the week and a half since the night he'd cooked dinner for her, but now it seemed unsettlingly symbolic of how at ease she'd become with having the man in her home. A strand of blue-black hair fell across his brow as he came toward her, two mugs in his hands.

"And to a thin-blooded Creole far from home hot's the important thing. You were shivering a little too, *cher',* when we walked from the car."

"Despite my Boston upbringing, I never could take the cold."

Her voice betrayed none of the turmoil she felt, Marilyn noted thankfully. She curled up in the velvety club chair as he set her mug on the leather hassock, his beside it. Sitting down on the sofa with the economical grace she'd come to associate with everything he did, briefly he pinched the bridge of his nose, a quick crease appearing on his brow. He caught her watching him and let his hand drop.

"Four hours of holding a gris-gris down on my cards," he said wryly. "Like I told you before, that's more work than winning."

She frowned. "What's a gree-gree?"

One side of his mouth lifted. "Dat's juju, sugar. Voodoo magic." A shadow passed over his features. "And if I did have access to a witchy woman and her spells I don't know that I wouldn't buy one off her, just to conjure up Tony Corso," he muttered. "It's taking way too long to flush him out and time's running short."

Fear shafted through her, overriding everything else. "What are you saying? Do you think Helio might already have made the decision that he doesn't need Sky anymore? Dear God, Con—if he has I don't know how Holly's going to survive. I don't know how *I'm* going to surv—"

"That's not what I meant, *cher'.*" He shook his head sharply, cutting off the rising flow of her words. "I meant that although we're pretty sure releasing a virus is his intention, we're not sure exactly when he's going to do it. We're not even sure where he's going to release it," he added, "although odds are he won't choose Silver Rapids again. Apparently the small hospital there has developed a contingency plan since the last time."

What was that noise? Marilyn wondered faintly. It was like the waves of a mighty sea roaring around her, blotting out every other sound around her. Dimly she realized Con was still talking, but his voice seemed to be coming from far, far away.

"Since the last time?"

Now the faraway voice was her own. Carefully she

formulated more words, her tongue feeling too thick to deliver them.

"What last time? Are you saying that there's been a viral attack on Silver Rapids in the past?"

"Forget I said that, *cher'*." Through the haze that seemed to be surrounding her she was aware that he was suddenly in front of the club chair. He reached for her hands and pulled her almost roughly to her feet. "That was told to me by the authorities on a need-to-know basis, and it's nothing you need to know."

"It was in January, wasn't it?" Her lips felt numb. "Late January. People got sick—two elderly patients actually died. The newspapers said it was a particularly virulent strain of influenza."

"Silver Rapids flu." The emerald gaze confronting her darkened with an unidentifiable emotion. His hands came up to cover hers. "Like I said, honey, put it out of your mind. Right now we should be concentrating on—"

"I was responsible for *infecting* her, wasn't I?" She pushed his hands away, her own trembling violently. The roaring sound in her ears grew louder and she raised her voice.

"Dammit, Con, *tell* me! A few months after I moved to Denver Corso persuaded me to invite Holly along with us to the Silver Rapids winter festival. Apparently he and she had met socially several times prior to that and he said she'd told him she wanted to get to know me better. Except the day of the festival he said he couldn't make it after all. To show him I wasn't hurt I insisted on going anyway—and even though Holly wanted to beg off too, I practically bullied her into accompanying me."

"You were trying to repair the relationship between

you and your stepsister. You acted from the best of motives—'' he began, but she cut him off, her tone thin.

''My motives were about as despicable as they could be. She was six and a half months pregnant by then, and she hadn't told anyone who the father of her baby was. Tony's eagerness to have her with us made me wonder if they'd been closer in the past than he was admitting. I spent the whole time we were in Silver Rapids trying to trap her into confessing that he and she had been lovers, because I was jealous.''

''You were that much in love with him?'' Con drew an audible breath. She shook her head in quick frustration.

''I never was in love with him, I realize that now. I was just lonely and flattered by his interest. But at the time the thought that he'd been with Holly first made me feel like I was his second choice.''

Her gaze had been fixed on his. Now it wavered. ''I just took it as one more instance of Holly getting everything she wanted—everything *I* wanted. I saw her pregnancy the same way, and what with my attitude and her defensiveness, that day in Silver Rapids convinced both of us we were never going to be friends. Shortly after that she fell ill, and for a while there was a possibility she was going to lose the baby.''

She forced her eyes to meet his again. Sometime in the past few seconds the roaring sound had faded away, she realized. ''It wasn't the flu, was it?'' she asked him. ''It was a virus—a virus that was deliberately released in Silver Rapids as some kind of test. That's why Holly had to be there. Someone needed to see how it would affect a mother-to-be and her unborn baby. Tony set the whole thing up and I carried it out.''

"No, *cher'*—" His denial was automatic. Tears blurred her vision.

"Don't lie to me," she whispered. "Not about this. If you have to you can lie to me about everything else, but not about this. Was I responsible for what happened to Holly? Was it an experimental virus that nearly killed Sky before he was born?"

He was silent for so long she began to think he wasn't going to reply. Finally he did, reluctance weighing his every word. "You're right, the Silver Rapids flu wasn't just a flu. It was a combination of a genetically engineered virus and Q-fever microbes and there's a chance it was developed from stock meant for Mills & Grommett. But you're not responsible for exposing Holly to it, Marilyn. You didn't know it was going to be released in Silver Rapids that day."

He held her gaze. "From what I know of Corso, probably even he wasn't aware of the full extent of what was going to happen. I think the original plan was to release a killed bug into the population—something that wouldn't pose any real danger, but would stimulate certain trackable symptoms. Instead, a live one was substituted and people died, but you couldn't have guessed any of that when you took Holly there that day, *cher'*."

"Just like I couldn't have known I might have prevented Sky's kidnapping when I let my pride get the better of me and drove back here, instead of continuing on to see Holly the day he was snatched." Her smile was crooked. "Goodness, Con, I'm a regular saint, aren't I? They should name a holiday after me. Of course, it would have to be held sometime in the winter—it would be more appropriate if the effigies of me were carved in ice, don't you think?"

"Stop thinking that way, dammit." He clasped her

shoulders, his grip tight. "You're no ice queen, *cher'*, whatever the rest of the Langworthys think. If you were you wouldn't be beating yourself up about all this. You wouldn't be doing everything you can to bring Sky home safely. Your family doesn't know the first thing about who you are—they never have."

"I was absolutely horrible to the woman my brother loves. Now they're engaged, and I wouldn't blame her if she never spoke to me. When news of the theft from Mills & Grommett gets out my father's company will be destroyed. I'd say I've done more than enough to justify the nickname the family gave me, Con."

It would be so easy to cry, she thought. The tears were right there in her eyes, and with the first blink they would squeeze onto her bottom lashes, tremble for a moment, and begin to slide down her cheeks. Since Con, liar or not, seemed inexplicably to be on her side, he would hold her and comfort her and try to take her pain away as he'd done three months ago.

But she wasn't going to let herself cry in front of him. She didn't deserve to be comforted. Somewhere out there was a child she hadn't allowed herself to hold, and if Sky was never returned to his family again the blame for that would rest squarely on her.

"I need to be alone." She stepped away, forcing herself to ignore the sudden coldness that wrapped around her. He frowned, and she went on more forcefully. "I need to be alone, Con. Running into my father the way I did shook me badly enough. Now to find I put Holly into a situation that could have had tragic consequences for both her and her unborn child…" She took a shaky breath.

"Please go," she whispered unevenly. "I—I've got a lot of thinking to do."

"You're sure you're going to be all right?" Her tight nod did nothing to erase the worry from his features, but after a moment's hesitation he turned toward the door. "If you need me, call, *cher'*," he said quietly. "I'll be down here before you can hang up the phone."

He would be, too, Marilyn told herself as she closed the door behind him, realizing from the sound of his ascending footsteps that he'd taken the stairs—an option she'd had to forego weeks ago in favor of the balky and slow—but given her condition, more convenient—elevator.

The man was an enigma, and not only because of her conviction that he was withholding something from her. From the first he'd seemed to ally himself unconditionally with her, a gesture of faith her own father hadn't displayed, and yet his attitude toward Helio DeMarco was chillingly single-minded.

Trying to figure out Con Ducharme was a luxury she couldn't afford right now. Despite her incipient tears, falling apart wasn't something she could afford, either. With the fate of a child hanging in the balance there were questions she needed to find answers to, and the most important of those dealt with Tony Corso's involvement in Sky's kidnapping.

Her gaze clouded, Marilyn reached for the door's chain-lock. As she did the unfamiliar gleam of gold on her finger caught her attention, jerking her abruptly from her thoughts. The pretend wedding band glinted mockingly at her, as if to underscore the shaky reality of her situation.

It was the last straw in a nerve-racking evening. Seconds later, her lips firmed to a line, she was in the hall and pressing the elevator's call-button. The man in the apartment above might have chosen to live a lie, she told herself edgily. That didn't mean she had to do the same, especially in the privacy of her own home. As the too-angry protest ran through her mind she tugged at the ring, illogically unwilling to wear it for a moment longer, but to her frustration the thing wouldn't budge.

"Silky hair and glowing skin?" she said furiously under her breath, twisting the band to no avail as the elevator arrived and the doors started to open. "Why don't they tell you about the swollen feet and sausage fingers?" Head bent to her task, as she spoke she took a step forward...

"Why don't they tell—"

...into thin air.

Chapter Seven

"Connn!"

The terrified scream tore from Marilyn's throat even as her right foot stepped into space and she pitched into nothingness. Her arms windmilling wildly in an already-too-late attempt to reverse her forward momentum, she felt her left heel lift from the hallway floor, felt her weight shift to the ball of her foot, then to her toes, felt herself completely lose contact with solid ground.

Ever after she found it almost impossible to believe what she did next. Ever after she knew she owed her life to a woman she barely remembered, and certainly with no fond memories.

You—the blond one! One of Madame Olga's quirks had been to refuse to learn the names of any but her star ballet pupils. *You move like elephant! Up lightly and turn in air—like so!*

For one whole Boston winter's worth of Saturday mornings the elderly former prima ballerina had forced fourteen-year-old Marilyn to work on the intricacies of the *tour en l'air,* her sarcasm an integral part of the lesson. When the day had finally come that Marilyn's performance earned a grudging, *Satisfactory, girl. Not good, but not absolute horror.* Marilyn had gone home, informed her mother and grandmother that she was giving up ballet, and had burned her satin shoes in the back garden of the Beacon Hill estate.

Seventeen years later, in the black hole of an empty elevator shaft, Madame Olga's tortuous drilling paid off and somehow Marilyn, calling on physical resources she would have said she no longer had, executed a lightning-fast *tour en l'air*—literally a turn in midair that brought her facing the elevator opening instead of the blank wall of the shaft—as she fell. Her outstretched fingers scrabbled at the ledge of floor she'd just been standing on as it blurred past, found purchase, frantically grabbed.

Another involuntary scream left her lips as her wrists and shoulder joints seemed to pop completely out of place. Her body's free fall jolted to a halt. Her grip slipped and terror sliced through her as she tightened her precarious grasp.

Sweat, cold and clammy, poured over her.

She could keep it up for a minute, maybe two, she thought, her brain already fogged from the excruciating pain searing like white-hot knives through her arms and hands. Then one hand would fail her—probably her left, since she was right-handed. A split second after that she would complete her fatal plunge.

She'd come out of her apartment wearing the flat velvet slippers she'd put on when she'd changed earlier. One of them had been lost right away. Now she felt the other slide slowly from her dangling foot and fall off.

A soft thump from far below signalled its final resting place on what she assumed was the elevator car's roof. She squeezed her eyes shut to dispel the sickening image of her own body hitting that same far-below roof.

Even if she'd been months further on in her pregnancy, no unborn baby could survive such a fall by its mother, she thought desperately. Her child would die with her. Her child would never come into the world, never howl in outrage at the unsettling transition from comfortable womb to brightly lit delivery room, never feel the loving touch of the one pair of arms that had been aching to hold his or her tiny body since the day the pregnancy test had come back positive.

There was nothing complicated about this, Marilyn told herself grimly. It was simple. She had to live. She had to live to save the life of the baby growing inside her.

And her only chance of survival lay in Con hearing her in time. She opened her mouth to call out his name again, but even as she did she heard his hoarse shout.

"Marilyn! *Marilyn*—hang on, *cher'!*"

He had to have seen the yawning opening of the empty shaft as soon as he'd burst through the fire exit door that led to the stairs, because even as the fingers of her left hand began to slide inexorably from the ledge of floor she could hear him pounding down the hall toward her. Her grip gave way. Her body, no longer balanced, swung sickeningly sideways like a half-unpegged piece of clothing on a line and began twisting around in a semicircle, the movement prying loose the fingers of her right hand.

I've become one of my own mobiles, she thought. The fog of agony rolled in thicker. *I thought if I turned myself into something he could value, Daddy would realize he'd been wrong to throw me away all those years ago. But tonight he threw me away all over again. And this time it hurt a thousand times more.*

Truth…

Con's racing footsteps were only yards away, but he wasn't going to make it in time, she knew.

Beauty...

Her left hand cupped protectively around the swell of her stomach, in a final caress of the baby inside.

Love...

Con had never been a stranger—not really. Her fingers began to slide free. Even in the shadows of her office that first night, on some level hadn't she felt she'd always known him? Hadn't that lazy drawl, those emerald eyes, seemed achingly familiar, reassuringly comforting? Hadn't she known then that he was the man she was destined to love, the man she'd been waiting for all her life?

Lies had been told, on her part, as well as his. But there had been one unspoken truth between them that cancelled out everything else.

She was in love with him. She would die knowing she'd had that.

The fingers of her right hand, frozen now in a sweat-slick claw, slid from the ledge. Her eyes flew open in terror. Con appeared in the opening. She plunged downward.

"No!"

Even as his shout resounded through the shaft his arm shot out and his hand clamped around her wrist like a band of steel.

"Con!" Five minutes ago—no, a lifetime ago—she hadn't allowed herself to cry in front of him. Now she could taste the tears, feel them wet on her cheeks. "Con, get me out of here!"

But already he was one-handedly pulling her up, his features etched with strain, his body dangerously and unevenly braced against the steel frame of the elevator opening. The sound of running feet came down the hall, and from behind him she saw Jim and Dan appear, their faces white with shock.

Shock was replaced immediately with determination.

"Use both hands to grab her, buddy," Jim said tightly, his arms locking around Con's waist. "Dan, latch on to my belt and see if you can reach the doorknob of Marilyn's apartment behind you to anchor us."

Swiftly Con sought her other wrist, and her outstretched fingers found his. As soon as his hold was secure, he began hoisting her up and toward him.

"Almost there, *cher',*" he rasped. "Stay still and let me get you past the edge here. We don't want that little one inside you to get hurt."

One final heave and then her knees were barking against wood and steel. Frantically she drew them up, and as her bare toes felt the blessed solidity of floor beneath them Con pulled her safely into the hall and away from the gaping emptiness behind her.

The next moment his arms were around her in a crushing embrace. He eased it immediately and drew slightly back to look into her face, his eyes darker than she'd ever seen them. Deeply carved lines bracketed his mouth. At the edge of her vision Marilyn was dimly aware of Jim and Dan's shaky grins of relief, but all she could do was meet Con's gaze.

"I nearly lost you, *cher'.*" His voice was raw. "When I saw that open shaft I—"

His eyes closed tightly and his hand came around to the back of her head to press her face into his chest. Her own eyes squeezed shut, Marilyn felt the beat of his heart beneath her cheek.

"The cables must have snapped." A few feet away, Dan's terse comment held a touch of anger. "This thing was inspected and certified only a month ago. Building management assured us it was safe.''

''If the cables had snapped sometime this evening, we would have known.'' There was an odd note in Jim's voice. ''Forty feet of steel falling onto an elevator car right beside our apartment would have made quite a racket, Dan. And what's that?''

Around her she felt Con's grip tighten. Jim went on, and now she could identify the odd note in his voice as apprehension.

''It looks like something's jammed against a gear a few feet up. It's hard to see without a flashlight…but isn't that a length of lead pipe, for God's sake?''

Dan's disbelieving reply became appalled confirmation, but Marilyn barely heard their conversation. She lifted her head to meet Con's shattered gaze.

''It wasn't an accident,'' she whispered.

''It wasn't an accident, *cher*,'' he agreed, his jaw rigid. ''This was deliberate sabotage, and DeMarco had to be behind it. He tried to have you killed.''

''It wasn't DeMarco who arranged this.'' Her voice shook. ''He's not the only powerful man who sees me as an obstacle he needs to eliminate.''

Her nails were broken and cracked. They dug into his shirtsleeves.

''I think my father tried to have me killed, Con.''

SHE WAS SAFE, Con told himself almost twenty-four hours later as he readied a tray of tea and toast to take up to Marilyn. He'd left the apartment only once, to have a quick shower and change of clothes in his own. Even then he'd arranged for Jim and Dan to stand watch over her while she obeyed doctor's orders and exhaustedly slept the day through.

Last night after the elevator incident Marilyn's own OB-GYN had come from the hospital where she'd just finished delivering a baby—apparently the Langworthy name had enough pull to rate a house call—and had checked Marilyn over thoroughly, pronouncing her none the worse for her ordeal except for her broken nails and abraded fingertips, and suggesting an ultrasound be scheduled for the coming week to be absolutely sure the pregnancy was proceeding as it should.

So the woman he loved and the baby she was carrying was safe, and that was the main thing. If she hadn't been…

If she hadn't been, your own life wouldn't have meant jack, he told himself harshly. *The only reason you would have had to go on living would have been to hunt DeMarco to the ends of the earth and watch him die— slowly and in as much pain as you could arrange. Hell, that's still an attractive option.*

But although Marilyn was safe, she was far from secure. How could she be, when she was convinced her own father had been behind what had happened to her? How could she be when there was a possibility she was right?

"You didn't see how he looked at me when he saw me at the club," she'd said after Jim and Dan had left and she and Con were in her apartment awaiting the arrival of Dr. Roblyn. "Like I was the last person in the world he wanted to see. Like I was his…his *enemy,*" she'd added in agonized confusion. "I know how outrageous it sounds, Con, but look at the facts. That elevator was disabled after you and I came back here tonight, and before you went upstairs. That's a pretty precise window of opportunity. Someone followed us home from the club, and the only person I know who saw me there was Father.''

"Let's start with motive before we move on to means and opportunity,'' he'd argued. "You said Samuel sees you as an obstacle he needs to eliminate. How do you figure that?''

"I could derail Josh's chances. Having an unmarried and pregnant sister reflects badly on him in the eyes of a certain portion of the electorate, which is why I haven't been asked to campaign for him. But having an unmarried and pregnant sister who's been cooperative enough to die in a tragic accident gets my brother the sympathy vote.'' She'd shrugged tightly. "Just like having an unmarried and pregnant half sister whose baby was abducted seems to have garnered Josh some support in—''

She'd stopped. He'd been close enough to her to see the dawning horror in her eyes and he'd known he needed to extinguish it immediately.

"By all accounts your father doted on Sky,'' he'd said roughly, taking her hands in his. "For God's sake, *cher'*, you can't seriously be suggesting he had anything to do with the kidnapping. Do you really think Samuel Langworthy is cold-blooded enough to sacrifice his grandson for his ambition?''

"Why not?'' Her voice had been a thread. "He gave up his daughter rather than be dragged through the messy and public custody battle Mother threatened him with—a custody battle that would have distanced him from the politically powerful friends he was already cultivating back then for the son he had such lofty hopes for. And in this case, once Josh gets into office, what's to prevent Sky from miraculously being returned to Holly? I can even see how it could play out as a further gilding of the golden boy's image, if Father's tame kidnappers are told to arrange the handover so newly elected Governor Joshua Langworthy brings back his nephew himself.''

She'd looked away. "That didn't come out the way I meant it. We've had our differences in the past, but Josh wouldn't knowingly be a party to anything like that.''

"And yet you believe Samuel could.'' He'd fought against the doubt her words had aroused in him. "Come on, sugar, think logistics for a minute. We're dealing with someone who not only knows elevators but who's agile enough to have shinned up a cable to disable it. Then he overrode the safety feature on the doors on your floor so they opened when they shouldn't have. Like you said, the window of opportunity for all this was damned brief, which wouldn't be a problem for a man like DeMarco who can pick up the phone and arrange the most specialized hit in moments. Your father might have political connections, but he's no mobster.''

"No, he's not a mobster,'' she'd agreed, her gaze haunted. "But he owns several prime office complexes in the heart of the city, and properties like that have maintenance supervisors on the payroll. My father knows the kind of people who would have a working knowledge of elevators, Con.''

She'd drawn her hands from his and pressed them to her belly. "Motive, method and opportunity. He had all three. Maybe you're letting your hatred for Helio DeMarco blind you to the possibility that the theft of the virus and Sky's kidnapping could be completely unrelated.''

The doctor had arrived then, and their conversation had ended there—mainly, Con admitted now to himself, because he hadn't been able to muster a convincing enough rebuttal to Marilyn's suspicions. In fact, her last comment had prompted him to rethink his own position.

Was she right? Had he allowed his personal feelings for DeMarco to color his attitude to this case?

The question had been an unsettling one, and it had occupied his mind throughout the remaining hours before dawn this morning. Not that he hadn't welcomed having something to keep his thoughts on track, he acknowledged as he set a bowl of soup on the tray and headed for the upper level of the loft. As it was, all night long he'd still been all too aware that she was curled up in bed only a few yards away. At least once an hour he'd found himself in the doorway of her room on the pretext of checking on her, fighting the urge to stroke back the pale hair from her brow and press a kiss to those softly exhaling lips.

He'd resisted that urge. He'd wrestled with his conscience. And finally he'd called the number Colleen Wellesley had given him on his first visit to the Royal Flush headquarters of Colorado Confidential.

He'd expected two reactions from the ex-cop—annoyance at being roused at three in the morning and irritated dismissal of the questions he'd posed to her. Colleen had answered the phone on the second ring, sounding wide-awake, and instead of brushing aside his queries she'd fallen momentarily silent. When she'd eventually spoken her normally brisk tone had sounded shaken.

"I can answer that first one right now, Burke. When we took on this case we canvassed the backgrounds of anyone who had a connection to the Langworthys, and a certain Hoyt Jackson came up on the radar as being an ex-con who'd done time for armed robbery. He's a janitor at Mills & Grommett now and by all accounts he put his criminal past behind him years ago, but I seem to remember…''

Her voice had trailed off. He'd heard the sound of papers being rapidly paged on her end of the line.

"Yeah, I thought so." Her voice had hardened. "At one time Jackson was an elevator repairman. Those people have to be bonded, which is why he couldn't get back in the field after he'd done his time."

"So Samuel had the means of arranging what happened to his daughter tonight. Opportunity, ditto," Con had said tersely, "since if Jackson's his hired thug as well as a janitor in his company, all it would have taken was a phone call when Langworthy left the club. What about motive? And what about Marilyn's theory that her father could be involved in the kidnapping?"

"I'll have to get back to you on those questions," Colleen had said slowly. "But I can tell you that right from the start this smelled like an inside job to me. I've always suspected either someone in or close to the family had a part in Sky's abduction but as you know, my money was on the Ice Queen."

"Except the Ice Queen, as you call her, came damned close to being killed herself a few hours ago," he'd countered sharply.

"Still championing her cause?" Colleen had sighed. "Dammit, Burke, I can't cross her off the list just yet. Have you considered she and her father might have been in this together and had a falling-out? I know the accepted version is that the two of them aren't close, but that might just be a facade."

He and Colleen Wellesley were fated never to have a completely civil conversation, Con told himself as he knocked on Marilyn's bedroom door. And if it weren't for his promise to Wiley yesterday, as far as he was concerned Colorado Confidential could go—

"Come in." From the bedroom came her muffled invitation, and he pushed open the door.

"Your doctor said you should keep your strength up…" he began. He stopped in midsentence, halting on the threshold.

"She's probably right. I've got the feeling I'm going to need all the strength I can muster." Far from being tucked under the covers as he'd expected, Marilyn was fully dressed and standing by the dresser, a hairbrush in one hand and a determinedly set look on her pale features. "I can't just lie here any longer. I'm going out of my mind with boredom."

"Toast and clear soup. I thought I was cooking invalid food," he said mildly, advancing into the room and setting the tray down on a bedside table. "If not bed rest, what were you planning on doing?"

"I took yesterday afternoon off to go shopping for that outfit I wore last night." Turning from the dresser she walked over to the bed and sat on the edge of it, wincing as she did. "I should put in some time at the office. I always get more done on a Saturday when there's no one else around, anyway."

Her tone was detached, her expression evasive. Not only were they in marked contrast to the Marilyn he'd thought he was beginning to know—the woman who seemed to have been growing more comfortable with him, the woman who'd blushed across the table last evening and whose tongue had flicked against his in that all-too-brief but meltingly delicious kiss the night he'd come back into her life—but in this setting her cool manner was even more out of place.

Her bedroom decor wouldn't have suited the wide-open areas and exposed brick walls that recalled the warehouse origins of the main part of the loft, but this room projected a much more intimate feeling than the rest of the apartment. Faded cabbage roses slipcovered the chairs, and softly worn velvets and lace gave an air of deliberately shabby romanticism to the fainting couch against the far wall, the two small glass-topped tables cluttered with books and bowls of potpourri on either side of the bed, the curtains pooling on the floor by the French doors leading out onto the miniscule balcony she'd told him had once been one of the warehouse's loading platforms.

Her bed was white-painted and ornately rococo wire and brass, obviously from a bygone era. The tiny crystal chandelier cascading from a plaster rosette in the center of the ceiling was another antique, Con surmised, judging from the one or two missing prisms and the glowing patina of the silverwork. Over everything hung the faint scent of some old-fashioned flower—heliotrope, or maybe lilac.

But the woman sitting in the middle of all this charmingly elegant nostalgia and femininity was wearing no-nonsense brown flats and a brown-and-tan houndstooth jacket over a pair of dark gold wool slacks. Her hair was brushed smoothly back into a tight clasp at the nape of her neck.

You've pulled your Beacon Hill armor around you again, cher', Con thought, looking at her. *And I understand you well enough to know you only do that when someone's hurt you…or when you're scared you're going to be hurt.*

An image from long ago flashed into his mind—long ago, but never forgotten. Hell, when it came to the woman sitting on the bed in front of him, every flicker of an eyelash, every word she'd ever spoken, had been carefully retained in his memory. This particular image was of a five-year-old Marilyn in Christmas green velvet, white stockings, gleaming black Mary-Janes. Her hair had reached to her waist then, and it had been held off her forehead by a thin velvet band. She had been coolly eyeing the enormous turkey that took pride of place on the table before her, and her mouth had turned down at the corners.

"I'd rather have a cheese sandwich, please, Father. Tell Luz she can bring it into the library with a glass of milk when it's ready." She'd risen from the dinner table, her small shoulders stiffly set, her whole demeanor icily disapproving. "If it was just you and me and Josh it would be different," she'd enunciated coldly before giving the barest of nods to Samuel Langworthy's new wife, Celia. "Surely you can't expect me to sit down to Christmas dinner with *her*. And why isn't he with his own family, instead of trying to be part of ours?"

That final barb had been directed at him, Con recalled. Even at the time it hadn't hurt, maybe because even at seven years old he'd known the small blond princess staring scornfully at him had been trying her hardest to hurt someone—anyone—in order to conceal her own pain.

Marilyn Langworthy no longer wore a velvet band to keep her hair back, but the expression on her face was the same as it had been all those years ago—tightly stubborn and closed off. He had the sudden impulse to sit down on the bed beside her, pull her onto his lap, and just hold her.

Except in the mood she was in right now that would probably earn him a black eye, he thought wryly, and so it should. She was a grown woman well on her way to having a child of her own, and although he could think of situations where cosseting and babying her might be appropriate—an inappropriate heat spread through him at the idea and he quickly tamped it down—this wasn't one of those situations. He narrowed his gaze at her.

"I don't believe you, *cher'*. Wherever you're going, it sure isn't the office—especially since your hands are in no shape to use a computer. You want to tell me what's going on?"

Whatever she'd been expecting from him, it hadn't been plain speaking. For a split second he was sure he glimpsed a flash of contrition behind those blue eyes.

It disappeared. The shuttered look fell over her features again. She reached for a slice of toast.

"I didn't want to tell you because I know you'll try to talk me out of it." She didn't look at him as she spoke. "But my mind's made up and nothing you can say is going to stop me."

She bit off a small corner of toast. It seemed as he watched that she could barely chew it, and when she swallowed it was with an obvious effort. She set the scarcely nibbled triangle back on the plate with a suddenly trembling hand.

"I'm going to call on my father, Con. I—I need to know for sure if he had anything to do with what happened last night."

Chapter Eight

"Mother would hate what Celia's done to the place," Marilyn said in an undertone to Con as they entered the wide drawing room of Samuel Langworthy's Capitol Hill mansion. She cast an appraising eye over the pale floral upholstery of the furnishings, the white-painted brick of the bijou fireplace where, despite the brightness of the crisp November day outside, a small pinecone fire was cheerily flickering.

"Your father's on an overseas conference call, Ms. Langworthy. He'll be down as soon as he's off the phone." The black-uniformed woman standing in the doorway glanced toward Con, who was emphasizing his detachment from the conversation by examining an ornament he'd picked up from a nearby table, and then politely switched her attention back to Marilyn. "Can I get you anything, Ms. Langworthy?"

"Nothing, thanks, Antonia." Trying to quell the sudden butterflies in her stomach, Marilyn pulled off her gloves and drew them carelessly through her fingers. "And my father's wife?" she said with assumed lightness. "Is—is Celia in?"

With a rush of relief she saw the older woman shake her head. "Mrs. Langworthy's at the Aspen cabin with

Miss Holly this weekend. She thought a change of scenery might—''

''Sorry.''

Con had set the ornament back down sharply enough that it had made an audible click against the polished tabletop. His one-word apology was delivered in a curt mutter. Deliberately turning her back to Con, Marilyn pretended to make a closer survey of the room.

He'd been angry with her, she recalled, still shaken by the memory—really angry. Without consciously thinking of it before, she'd somehow been of the unworried belief that no matter how much she might push him, with her Con's reactions would always be tempered. In fact, she admitted, over the past two weeks he'd met her mood swings with unruffled indulgence, as if even at her most snappish he found her endearing.

It was another example of his disregard for her ice-queen reputation, she thought. Con Ducharme treated her like an adorable female. And although coming from any other man such an attitude might have been annoying, he managed to pull it off by making it clear that doing so didn't mean he underestimated her in any way.

But back at the apartment when she'd informed him of her intention to have it out with her father, he'd come close to exploding. Disconcerted by his vehemence, she'd countered with an automatic anger of her own.

''Father's hardly likely to attempt anything in his home with the servants around,'' she'd riposted when he'd tersely told her he couldn't agree with her plan. ''And frankly, Con, if I decided I wanted to strip naked and go for an elephant ride at the Denver Zoo, I really don't see how it would be anything to do with you. I'm helping you find Tony Corso, and through him, Helio DeMarco. A working relationship like ours doesn't give you the right to tell me where I can go and who I can see.''

That comment had been patently unfair, Marilyn admitted now with a twinge of guilt. His objection had been because he'd been worried for her safety, and under more normal circumstances she might have acceded to his request that she delay confronting her father for the time being. Why *had* it been so important to her that she assert her independence?

Because you're not completely independent anymore when it comes to Con Ducharme, she told herself with raw honesty, fixing her gaze on a cluster of Persian violets massed in a Limoges cachepot on the table beside her. Small silver-framed photos were grouped around the plant, and idly she traced the delicate chasing around the edge of one of them with her fingertip. *You admitted as much to yourself last night—you've gone and fallen in love with the man. From now on he can hurt you without even trying.*

From now on? He already had, she thought unhappily. On some disturbing level she sensed that despite his easy charm and effortlessly sexy manner he hadn't revealed himself to her at all, and that part of what he was hiding had absolutely nothing to do with the investigation.

His anger over this visit had been honest, at least. In a way, that made it easier to deal with…and in a way, it made it harder. She didn't like this grim-faced, silent Con. He was too much like the man who had coldly admitted to an all-consuming hatred of Helio DeMarco. He was too much like a gambler who would stake everything he had, everything he held dear, on winning the game.

She was suddenly grateful for the heat thrown off by the crackling pinecones, suddenly glad that her surroundings weren't the formal antiques and dark colors she remembered from her childhood in this house.

"Let's get out of here, *cher'*."

Con had crossed the pretty Aubusson carpet so quietly that Marilyn gave a slight start as she felt his hand on her arm. She turned to face him and felt the tightness in her chest ease a little. The driven gambler had disappeared. The Con who stood before her was the man who'd ruefully forced himself to throw a poker game last night, who'd managed to make a list of desserts sound sinful, who had held her in his arms as if he would never let her go.

"I came on too strong back at the loft. Hell, I know that's not the way to handle you." His grin flashed briefly at her, but when he went on his tone was sober. "Whether your suspicions about your father are correct or not, just the thought of meeting him has you as nervous as a cat, sugar, and don't try to tell me you were trembling a minute ago because you were cold."

His gaze was dark. Uncomfortably Marilyn looked down at his grip on her jacket sleeve. What would he say if she told him what had been going through her mind only moments ago? Naturally she wouldn't. Bringing uncomfortable truths out into the open wasn't the Beacon Hill way or the Van Buren way. She moved her arm enough so that his hand slipped from it, and her lips began to formulate some meaningless reply.

And then she stopped. She raised her eyes to his. Unconsciously she placed her palm on the curve of her belly, her chin lifting slightly.

"I'm so tired of observing the proprieties, Con," she said clearly. "I don't intend to raise the child growing inside me to play foolish parlor games, so I guess it's time I gave it a rest myself. I wasn't trembling because

I was cold or because I'm worried about meeting with Father. I was trembling because I'm afraid, and the person I'm afraid for is you.''

''Me?'' The green-gold eyes looking down at her widened in astonishment. ''*Merde,* honey, I can take care of myself. I always could.''

''Really?'' She gave him a searching look. ''In a bar fight or a card game, yes. But I'm not talking about that kind of danger, Con. I'm talking about losing your soul. I'm talking about destroying yourself in a single-minded crusade to bring down a man you've vowed vengeance on. You become a different person when you talk about DeMarco…and I'm beginning to wonder if that other personality isn't starting to spill over into the real you.''

''Because of the way I reacted earlier?'' His frown was quick. ''I've already admitted I could have handled it better, but I still stand by my reason for not wanting you to come here. You—''

''That's just it,'' she interrupted. ''You *haven't* told me the real reason you're so on edge about this. Oh, part of it's what you said—we both know this interview with my father is going to be devastating and you'd like to spare me that if you could. But there's more to it, isn't there? Funnily enough, I'm not the one who's as nervous as a cat about being in this house. You are. I want to know why.''

''I've already told you.'' Con's tone was flat. ''If you don't believe me there's not much I can do to convince you.''

''You could try laying your cards on the table, Ducharme,'' Marilyn suggested, anger sparking inside her. ''Or is that too hard a concept for a New Orleans gambler to—''

''After spending the past half hour on the phone calling a spade anything but a spade with a group of Japanese investors, I'm about ready for some good old American plain-speaking, so give it to me straight, Marilyn.''

The craggy-faced man striding into the room rolled his shoulders as if to brace himself. ''What's the crisis? Did the office burn down? I know only business would bring you here.''

''The office is still standing, Father.''

She wasn't sure how long she would be, Marilyn thought, her knees turning immediately to rubber as she met the hooded gray gaze being directed her way. It flicked toward Con, standing beside her, and hastily she pulled herself together.

''This is Con Ducharme, a friend of mine.''

In the few sentences they'd exchanged on the drive here to the Capitol Hill mansion, Con and she had decided that was how she would introduce him. It was explanation enough for his presence with her the evening before, if her father needed one, and Con hadn't wanted his connection with the New Orleans P.D. mentioned to Samuel. *So much for plain-speaking right from the start,* she thought shakily.

''But you're right, this isn't exactly a social visit. I'm—''

''No, it wouldn't be.'' With a grunt, Samuel Langworthy settled himself on one of the pair of floral sofas, jerking his head toward the other as he lifted the lid of a round wooden jar on the table beside it.

''Cap'n?'' Con raised an eyebrow. ''I've got nothing against the occasional good cigar, even if it is a smuggled-in Havana from the looks of it. But you don't want to smoke that now.''

Her father looked disconcerted, she noted. It was an

expression she couldn't remember seeing on his face before.

"An old habit, and one Celia's been after me for years to break. My apologies, Marilyn." He spoke stiffly. "I wasn't thinking."

Something about the comment struck her, but for a second she couldn't pinpoint what it was. Then realization came. Carefully she lowered herself to the sofa, perching on the edge of it rather than sitting back.

"That's the first time you've come anywhere close to alluding to the fact that I'm expecting, Father." She glanced down at herself. "It's not as if it's easy to overlook. I mean, when I get pregnant, I really get pregnant, don't I?"

She forced a laugh, and even to her own ears it sounded brittle. "That's why I'm here, actually. I want to ask you—with Josh's campaign coming to a head, just how inconvenient has it been having not one but both daughters sullying the family image?"

Gray eyes frosting over in his perfectly barbered face, Samuel Langworthy began to rise. "This isn't a topic we need to discuss, especially in front of—"

"You're *wrong*."

The words rushed from her with an intensity she couldn't control. Struggling to her own feet, Marilyn took a step toward the man who had sired her. She couldn't allow herself to think of him as her father anymore, she told herself tightly. He'd given up that role years ago, and if what she feared was correct, last night he'd completely discarded it. Con's earlier edginess had given way to a wary and watchful monitoring of the situation, she noted distractedly.

"It's the only topic you and I need to discuss," she said flatly. "It's the only one left, because we've long since passed the point where we can discuss the kinds of things other fathers and daughters talk about. I'm not in grade school, so we can't talk about my science projects or my book reports or the teacher who gave me a B when I thought I deserved an A. High school and college are behind me, so exams and the way I missed making the swim team by a tenth of a second aren't relevant anymore. My first job, my first car, my first kiss, the first time a boy broke my heart and I pretended I didn't care—they're all *gone.*''

He hadn't blinked once during her outburst. There was no expression at all on that tanned, still craggily handsome face. She was boring him, Marilyn thought incredulously. She had poured out a lifetime's worth of hurt in a few short sentences, and the man who had caused it was *bored.* Anger and pain cut through her, scything down the last of her doubts.

"You weren't in a conference call when I arrived, were you?'' she asked thinly. "When Antonia told you I was here, you needed time—time to decide how you were going to play this, time to toss back a little of that Dutch courage I'm pretty sure I can smell on your breath. Was it a bad shock, Samuel? Did even your iron nerve fail for a minute or two when you realized it hadn't worked?''

"What are you talking about?'' She was sure she detected a hint of bluster in his growl. He swung a frowning gaze to Con, standing a few feet away. "Ducharme, right? Dammit, man, do you know what this is all about?''

"I think so, Cap.'' Con's drawl was more pronounced than usual. "It's about betrayal. It's about abandonment. Mainly I think it's about trust. You need it spelled out further?''

"I forgot. You're a businessman, first and foremost, so maybe I should have put it in business terms." Marilyn took a breath, willing her voice to steadiness. "I spent most of today taking inventory—not of Mills & Grommett stock, but of my life. Somehow it seemed appropriate to assess what I'd almost lost. I realized that a lot of what I'd held valuable meant nothing to me...and to hang on to it I'd let the really important things slip away over the years. One of those important things is truth, Father. If you won't admit you're capable of sacrificing me to win the election for Josh, how about coming clean on your part in Sky's kidnapping? You're involved in that somehow, aren't you?"

No matter what she'd said to Con, even as the accusation left her lips Marilyn knew she'd been hoping against hope that her suspicions were wrong. She stared at her father, and saw a sick pallor muddy the healthy tan of his cheeks, saw the shutters slam down over those gray eyes just an instant too late to hide the guilt flashing through them.

The pretty, sunlit room appeared suddenly dark and shadowed. In the fireplace a flame discovered a touch of pine resin, and the resultant hiss sounded malevolent instead of cosy.

"Sky's my grandson. I'd give anything—*anything,* do you hear?—to get him back." Samuel's declaration seemed wrenched from him. "If I thought the deal I made—"

He stopped in midsentence. Slowly his hand came up to his face, and for a moment he held it there as if to shield his eyes from her gaze. Once upon a time those big hands had placed her on a pony, Marilyn thought. Once they'd lifted her high in the air and then swooped her down again.

Once she'd been this man's daughter—a daughter he'd loved and cherished and spoiled.

She felt Con's arm go around her shoulders. His touch didn't take away the aching in her heart, but it gave her strength to ask her next questions. "What was the deal? Was it something to do with the election?"

Samuel Langworthy dropped his hand, shaking his head as he did. "No, it couldn't be," he muttered hoarsely. "There can't be a connection between the two—there just *can't* be."

He drew in a deep breath. Then he lifted his gaze to Marilyn's, and she saw that once again his brief smile was completely emotionless, distantly courteous.

"Celia will be sorry to hear she missed you. Ever since you moved back to Denver she's been hoping you'd take her up on one of her dinner invitations."

Her mouth dropped open. An incredulous little bark of laughter came from her before she could prevent it. "That's *it?*" she asked. "End of discussion? For God's sake, Father—this isn't a meeting of Mills & Grommett's board of directors. You don't get to adjourn this with a quick show of hands. We just heard you as good as confess to being in on Sky's—"

"You didn't hear me say anything of the sort, Marilyn," Samuel interrupted crisply. "Ask Ducharme here."

"He's right, *cher*'," Con said slowly. "He didn't give us anything we could take to the authorities. But he gave us more than he realized."

He narrowed his gaze at the older man, his grip tightening around Marilyn's shoulders. "He's the devil, Cap. Whatever he promised you in return for your cooperation, it wasn't worth it, believe me. Deals with the devil never are."

This time the emotion that appeared and disappeared on her father's features was fear, Marilyn was almost sure, but when he spoke his voice was harshly steady.

"You sound like you speak from experience. *Ducharme*…with that name and that accent, you must be a long way from home, am I right?"

"You right, Cap." Con's tone sharpened. "New Awlins, to be exact. What's your point?"

"No point. I believe I may have relatives there on my wife's side, that's all." Samuel shrugged. "I have an appointment downtown in half an hour, Marilyn, so we'll have to cut this short. Perhaps we can have a more convivial visit over Thanksgiving dinner? Celia was going to phone you this week with an invitation, although after the times you've turned her down I'm sure she won't be surprised if you decline."

She'd come here expecting…what? That the man in front of her would break down and confess all? That he'd ask her forgiveness for every old hurt and wound he'd inflicted over the years? That he would say the three words she'd been waiting to hear from him for as long as she could remember?

Whatever she'd been expecting from Samuel Langworthy, he hadn't given it to her, Marilyn thought tiredly. He was right, it was time for her to leave.

"I'll probably spend Thanksgiving with Mother in Boston," she said. "But let Celia know I appreciate the invitation. And tell her—"

She hesitated. In some ways she was still her father's daughter, she acknowledged. It was almost as hard for her to make up for a decades-old omission as it obviously was for him. She saw that one of the small, silver-framed photographs beside the cachepot was of herself on a pony, a smiling man's hands around her five-year-old's waist.

"Tell her I like what she's done with this room," she said softly. "We'll let ourselves out, Father."

"Very well." Samuel turned away and lifted the lid of the humidor. The seemingly dismissive action didn't match the raw emotion that lurked below the surface of his final words.

"Take my advice and make sure your building's management has a certified inspector approve the elevator before they deem it safe to use again." He cleared his throat, as if to steady his tone. "I know from experience that these fellows try to cut corners on a weekend rather than pay for a qualified tradesman to come out."

Absurdly grateful for Con's supporting hand on her elbow as they made their way to the front door, Marilyn didn't trust herself to speak until they'd proceeded past the bayberry bushes lining the brick walkway and had reached the circular drive where he'd parked his rental SUV. Then she turned to him, and even though she realized he was aware of what she was about to say, she put it into words anyway.

"I didn't tell him about the elevator, Con," she said hollowly. "I didn't have to." She fought back the nausea she could feel rising in her.

"I didn't have to because he already knew."

Chapter Nine

"Tony was hired on Father's recommendation."

Marilyn closed the dishwasher door with a thump. Since their visit to the Langworthy mansion a few hours earlier she and Con had gone over this subject a dozen times, but she couldn't see they were any further ahead than they'd been when Samuel had inadvertently dropped his bombshell on them.

"That must mean that even then Helio had some kind of hold on him, but we still come back to asking ourselves what that hold was. Or is," she added. "And I don't understand how you can think it's possible Father wasn't involved in the attack on me. You heard him. He *knew* what had happened."

She leaned back against the dishwasher in frustration and almost immediately pushed herself away from it again. She saw him lift a quizzical eyebrow at her actions and felt embarrassed warmth touch her cheeks.

"The agitator's off-balance," she said, feeling foolish.

"And?" His eyebrow rose higher.

"And if I was peacefully dozing away in a cosy womb I wouldn't want to suddenly wake up and find myself on the Teacup Ride at Six Flags," she snapped. "It's bad enough that the two of us were doing acrobatics in that elevator shaft last night.''

''The doctor told you there was no harm done, *cher'*.'' He took her arm and steered her toward the living room area. ''But maybe now's a good time to bring up something I've been thinking about today. You said you're going to Boston for Thanksgiving. Why don't you make plans to leave a little sooner—like tomorrow, say?''

They'd reached the couch. She didn't sit down, but instead turned to face him.

''I thought you might suggest something of the sort,'' she said. ''I just can't do it, Con. Not while there's a chance I can help you bring Sky home safely. And what can happen with you keeping a twenty-four hour watch over me from now on?''

She lowered herself to the couch and tucked one silk-slippered foot under a thigh, the stretchy jersey of the yoga pants she was wearing—this pair in deep violet, to contrast with the soft rose of a long-sleeved, ribbon-tied chiffon blouse—a comfortable change from the wool pants she'd worn to her father's house.

''I still don't think it's necessary for you to sleep here tonight, for heaven's sake. Those dead bolts on my door are top of the line, and the main entrance in the lobby is equipped with a card-entry system.''

''It's nonnegotiable, *cher'*.''

He was wearing the same dark charcoal suit he'd worn to the meeting with her father earlier, although he'd discarded the jacket while he'd been helping her prepare dinner. His vest—how many did the man have? Marilyn thought distractedly as Con sat in the chair across from her—was carelessly unbuttoned, the snowy white cuffs of his shirtsleeves casually rolled up against the tan of his forearms. He leaned forward, those same well-muscled forearms braced on his thighs, his hands hanging loosely down between his knees.

"You and me, we're gon' be stuck to each other like lime syrup on a snowball, shug," he drawled. "If you won't go stay with your *mère* in Boston—"

"Back up," she interrupted. "I haven't a clue what you just said, Ducharme. Snowballs and lime syrup? And what's a shug?"

"Short for sugar, sugar." His grin flashed white. "And snowballs? Aw, honey, they're pure heaven on earth on a hot New Awlins summer day when you're nine years old and hangin' around waitin' for the streetcar with your friends. Shaved ice—that's important, *cher'*, shaved, not crushed—and whatever flavor of syrup you want poured over it. Me, I was always a lime man myself."

"Oh." She nodded. "We've got those, too, except here they're called slushies."

He looked pained. "Naw, shug, nothin' near. Just like what they call a po-boy outside of Awlins is only a sloppy sandwich. You got to come to my neck of the woods for the real thing."

A few hours before she'd been certain she would never smile again. Now Marilyn felt her lips curving reluctantly upward. "You're homesick, aren't you?" she accused softly. "Fess up, Detective—you hate being away from your beloved Big Easy."

"Like old Adam must have hated being driven out of Eden after he took a bite of that apple," he agreed, a corner of his own mouth quirking up. "Like you must miss Boston."

"Oh, no," she said swiftly. She groped for an explanation. "I mean, Boston's home to the Van Burens. And there've been Langworthys in or around Denver ever since before Jefferson Langworthy, who helped turn Colorado from a territory into a state," she went on more slowly, frowning down at her hands. "But I never felt either city was home." She looked up at him. "I hadn't quite realized that before."

"You're wrong about Samuel, you know." Con's gaze on her was intent. "He loves you. My guess is he was told about the elevator incident after the fact—and I think it was presented to him as a warning about what might happen if he didn't continue to toe the line."

For an instant hope flared in her. Quickly she extinguished it. "That's ridiculous," she said flatly. "For one thing, by his own admission my father made a deal with someone—probably Helio. He had guilt written all over him, Con."

"Yeah, I saw the guilt." The silver coin was between his fingers, she saw. It flashed back and forth as he spoke. "But more than that, I saw fear, *cher'*. What if he had what he thought was a harmless arrangement with DeMarco, and by the time he realized what he'd gotten into it was too late?"

"A harmless arrangement like what?" Her question was edged. "And again, what possible hold could Helio have over my father? I may not be close to him and I know he can play pretty rough in the business world and the political arena, but I'd swear he's never done anything that would lay him open to blackmail. The only time he ever let his heart rule his head was when he fell in love with Celia—and even then he waited a respectable time after his divorce from Mother before he married her."

She shook her head, and this time her smile was wistful. "He and Mother never would have gotten back together, no matter what she's always told me. Somehow it took me until today to realize that. I don't think she was ever happy with him, but she turned completely against him when he decided to end the marriage.''

''Divorce can get pretty brutal,'' Con said thoughtfully. ''You suppose the custody arrangement might not have been exactly how she told you, either?''

''You mean Father didn't want me used as a pawn in a messy court battle?'' The idea was unsettling. Without realizing she was doing it, her hand slid over the pregnant swell of her stomach, her fingers spreading protectively. ''But if that's why he let me go, Con, then…''

Her words trailed off. Her eyes opened painfully wide. He reached across the space between them.

''Then he must have loved you so much he couldn't bear to see you torn in two, *cher'*. By the time you were old enough to handle the truth, the gulf between the two of you was too wide to bridge. He's not the most demonstrative man, I'll give you that.''

''But at the club last night he looked straight through me. Almost since the very day I came back to Denver he's deliberately kept a distance between us.''

Abruptly Con let go of her hand. He stood.

''That's it.'' There was suppressed excitement in his tone. ''Two questions, *cher'*. First, was Corso already working at M & G when you arrived?''

''He'd been hired a few weeks previously.'' Marilyn frowned. ''What's that got to do with anything?''

''Maybe nothing. Maybe everything.'' Con's expression was grim. ''Secondly, how did you get the position of vice president of sales?'' He saw her confusion. ''Was anyone fired to free up the job for you? Did someone retire?''

She shook her head, her puzzlement growing. ''No. In fact, I'm not sure Father would have come to me if he hadn't been left in the lurch. Janet Bukowski, the woman who'd held the position forever, simply failed to show up for work one Monday. When Elva, my father's secretary at the time, tried to contact her she learned Janet had moved out of her apartment over the weekend without telling any of her friends. Foul play might have been suspected, Elva told me, except for the fact that an acquaintance of Janet's ran into her by chance in Aspen a few days later. She refused to talk about why she'd left Denver so suddenly, but she said she was never coming back. I had the qualifications for the job and the firm I worked for in Boston wasn't in the greatest financial shape, so when Father offered me the position I took it.''

"The Bukowski woman was a loose end.'' Con sounded as if he were talking to himself. "I'll lay you good odds she's not in Aspen anymore, sugar. When the authorities look into it, I think they'll find out she met with a fatal accident not long after she ran. She was blackmailed into leaving,'' he said tightly, meeting Marilyn's shocked gaze. "Blackmailed or threatened.''

"But why?'' Appalled horror ran through her. Suddenly the notion of having the big man in front of her as a twenty-four-hour-a-day bodyguard no longer seemed a needless precaution. "What was the point?''

"The way I see it, your father was approached by DeMarco to hire his nephew, Tony.'' A muscle jumped at the side of Con's jaw. "Who knows what he offered Samuel to sweeten the deal—maybe a contribution to the election fund, maybe a promise of political support from one of the unions DeMarco controls. Whatever it was, to your father it would have seemed like a pretty good trade-off for merely adding another salesman to his roster. But what DeMarco was really after was to get Corso into the V.P. of sales slot.''

''Because that would make it easy for Tony to steal the viral stock Helio needed.'' Marilyn closed her eyes sickly. ''But before Helio could tell Father that was the second part of the deal I'd been hired.''

''And they couldn't get rid of you like they did the Bukowski woman—not if they still hoped for Samuel's cooperation.'' Con swore with quiet vehemence. ''So they went to plan B, which was for Corso to use your password and steal the viral stock that way. Dammit, *cher'*, you were close when you said Sky's kidnapping was a distraction for the real crime. Your father must have put two and two together at some point—probably after the Silver Rapids incident. He confronted DeMarco with his suspicions, but before he could act on them his grandson was abducted.''

''And with Sky's life at stake, Father would have no choice but to let Helio call the shots.'' Marilyn bit her lip. ''If we're right, he's been keeping me at arm's length for my own protection, Con. He doesn't want to give Helio another weapon to use against him.''

''Hostages to fortune,'' Con supplied bleakly. ''But despite Samuel's careful avoidance of you—he was even afraid to acknowledge you at the club—DeMarco guessed how he really felt. You were supposed to die in that elevator shaft last night, but though you survived, the result was the same. Your father was informed of what almost happened to you and reminded that Sky's continued safety depended on him. If there was the slightest chance he was thinking of going to the police with what he knew and suspected, last night brought him firmly back into line.''

''Helio doesn't miss a step, does he?'' Marilyn heard

the bitterness in her own voice. "He's like a chess player, always five moves ahead of his opponent."

"No, he's like a poker player," Con contradicted her. "Which means he's always ten moves ahead, *cher'*. But you were the wild card he wasn't expecting to come up against in this game—you, and the fact that you're carrying his nephew's child."

Actually, that's not quite true, Con. You see, Tony isn't the father of my child at all. He couldn't be. Because the one and only time we got anywhere near any kind of physical intimacy I backed off—and when I did, I found out what kind of man he really was.

The words ran through her head. She opened her mouth to say them out loud but they wouldn't come.

Although the meeting with her father today had been shattering, the brief exchange she'd had with Con in the Langworthy mansion drawing room before Samuel had walked in on them had left her feeling just as hopeless. She hadn't gone looking for a man like Con Ducharme, and before she'd met him she would have said a sexy, green-eyed gambler wasn't her type at all. But last night had changed everything—or at least it had changed her.

She'd faced her own personal truth. She'd admitted to herself that she'd fallen in love with him. And if that wasn't the stupidest thing she'd ever done in her life, Marilyn acknowledged, it came pretty close…and not just because she was sure he'd lied to her. After all, she'd been far less than honest with him. What made wanting Con Ducharme so insane was that she knew he didn't want her.

Or not enough, anyway. He wanted Helio DeMarco more.

"Father should have trusted me with the truth," she said distantly. "Maybe he was afraid to, maybe he was ashamed, but he shouldn't have kept secrets from me. I'm a mother-to-be. The decisions I make affect the baby I'm carrying, and his lies could have been disastrous for my child.''

''And if he felt it wasn't his secret to tell, *cher'?*'' Con's gaze was unreadable. ''Your half sister's involved here, too. It's her son who's missing.''

He wasn't talking about Holly any more than she'd been speaking of her father, Marilyn thought. They were both talking about Con himself, and this was the first time he'd come close to even an oblique admission that he was keeping anything back in his dealings with her. She held his gaze.

''Yes, Holly's son is missing. Helio's probably behind Sky's abduction, Tony Corso was somehow involved, and my father knows more than he's willing to admit. Holly's keeping a secret, too—the secret of Sky's father's identity. And you arrived on the scene three and a half months ago with some trumped-up story about wanting to locate Tony for a fraud he committed in Louisiana, although when you returned to Denver that story had changed.'' She shook her head. ''The difference between Holly and my father and you is that the safety of my child doesn't depend on Samuel or my half sister. You're the one I have to trust. I don't think I can.''

She got to her feet, her heart thumping in her chest. ''It strikes me that the Colorado authorities wouldn't cooperate as fully as you say they have with a renegade detective working on his own time. You're not with the New Orleans Police at all, are you, Con?''

He raked an indecisive hand through midnight-black hair and exhaled audibly, the glance he slanted at her no more than a sliver of green through dense lashes. He let his hand drop.

"Merde." His tone was soft with regret. His shoulders lifted slightly. "Great-Uncle Eustache must be turning over in his grave right about now, but if being a Creole gentleman means I have to keep lying to you I guess I'm going to have to pass. You right, heart. I've been palming cards left, right and center with you, hoping you wouldn't find out. I'm New Awlins, through and through, but I'm not New Awlins P.D., though the boys in blue back me up when I'm working undercover."

"Working undercover?"

Marilyn's throat felt as if it had completely closed up. Her lips were frozen. There was a hot, burning sensation behind her eyes.

She'd known he was lying to her. Knowing was a world away from having him confirm it to her face.

"For the U.S. Marshalls." He took a step toward her. "But this isn't their case. I'm on loan to an outfit called—"

"Come any closer and I'll rake that handsome face of yours, Ducharme. Right from the start you played me for a fool, and I fell for it! You even made *love* to me while you were lying. Is that what you mean by undercover work, Con?"

She caught her bottom lip between her teeth. "I'm still being a fool, aren't I? That's probably not even your name." Something flickered behind his gaze and her wrath turned suddenly to dull sickness. "Tell me you lied about that, too, and I swear this is the last time you'll ever set eyes on me."

Thick lashes swept briefly down over those emerald-gold eyes. His mouth tightened to a line. "The name's real. The history's real. The only thing I wasn't straight with you on was the Colorado Confidential connection, Marilyn. And if it gets out that I've come clean with you on that, I'll be yanked off this case faster than I could shuffle a deck of cards.''

This time when he came closer she made no move to stop him, but her posture remained tensely rigid. ''Colorado Confidential?'' Her tone dripped sarcasm. ''Wait, don't tell me—a secret crime-fighting organization operating out of a remote base deep in the Sangre de Cristo Mountains, right? You all get decoder rings and you're chosen for your special powers. For God's sake, Con, can't you come up with something better than that?''

''That was pretty much my first reaction, *cher'*.''

He rubbed his jaw, and in the gesture there was such defeat that for a moment she felt herself softening. She gathered her outrage around her again.

''And your second reaction?''

He lifted his head. His gaze met hers with no subterfuge at all. ''My second reaction was that I'd been handed the best damn chance I was ever going to get to bring Helio DeMarco down. It was Christmas and Mardi Gras and my birthday all rolled into one, sugar.''

He'd just given her the plain, unvarnished truth, Marilyn told herself hollowly. His hatred rang true, his determination rang true and the black, implacable satisfaction in his voice could only have come from the darkest corner of his soul. This was the real Con Ducharme.

She was afraid of this man.

''Don't look at me like that, honey.'' Now there was no space at all between them. Slowly he brought his hand to her chin and tipped it upward, his thumb sliding to the corner of her mouth. ''I'm the gator-killer, not the gator. Someone's got to take that bastard out, and I won't apologize for the fact that the job fell on me.''

''You don't have to apologize,'' she said unevenly.

"But you're talking about *killing* a man, Con. That should be something you face with regret, not with—"

She stopped. His thumb stroked upward.

"Not with what, heart?"

"Not with—with joy," she whispered.

Unhurriedly he slid his other hand from her shoulder and past the beating pulse at the side of her throat. Both hands now framed her face, both thumbs stroked the corners of her parted mouth. His expression unreadable, he bent his head until his lips were just touching hers.

"Don't tell me how to do my job, *cher*'," he murmured hoarsely. His breath stirred a stray strand of hair on her cheek. "Don't ever do that, okay? I told you he killed a friend of mine. Did I tell you how?"

"No, you—"

Those two words were all she got out before his mouth came down on hers.

Chapter Ten

His kiss was open-mouthed and almost burningly hot, but even as a flinch ran through her his palms drew her face closer. His tongue licked hers with slow, languid strokes, as if he was coaxing her to give in to the dark heat she could feel soaking through her thighs, her breasts, the suddenly damp roots of her hair. Abruptly he withdrew—just enough, Marilyn realized with a sudden little shock, so that his teeth could close lightly on her bottom lip.

Her eyes flew open. His were still veiled behind spiky black lashes. Only a gleam of barely focused green showed.

"Roland Charpentier and me, *cher'*, we were the terrors of New Awlins' bad old lower Ninth Ward when we were kids," he breathed, his teeth still holding her lip and his drawl soft against her mouth. "Crazy, crazy…oh, man, were we crazy."

He sounded drunk. She knew he wasn't, Marilyn told herself faintly. But his voice was hypnotically low, dangerously slurred.

Without warning, the heat she'd been feeling cascaded over her in a shower. Her knees buckled weakly. Not missing a beat, Con ran a hand down the thin chiffon of her top, skimming her nipples as he did. His hand continued downward, as if she were a spooked mare who needed gentling, and snugged tightly under the curve of her derriere, hoisting her up.

"We both joined the Marshalls' service. We worked the occasional case together, even though I normally didn't have a partner. And one day Helio DeMarco surfaced in our Big Easy swamp of felons and criminals. Give it to me again, honey."

He was a bad man, Marilyn thought dizzily as he released her lip and flicked his tongue against it and past it. He was bad and outrageous and sinfully sexy, and even if he'd waited for her consent she wouldn't have had the strength to resist him. Through the clinging jersey of the low-riding drawstring pants she was wearing she felt his hand spread wide to scoop her bottom. His kiss went even deeper than before, and this time when he lifted his head his gaze was wide and glazed.

"You got this Creole boy wrapped around your little finger, you know that, *cher'?*" he said huskily. "Took one look at you and fell to my knees, f'sure. Never got up. The Marshalls run the witness protection program. Rollie and me tucked away a mob accountant who'd spilled his guts to a grand jury, but a year later DeMarco's people found the accountant and used him for mudbug bait. I was on another case by then so Roland went after DeMarco by himself. Made things hot for him, too—so hot that the bastard sent word he was willing to turn himself in, maybe shave some time off the hundred-and-fifty-year sentence he was probably going to get. You like kissing me?"

She couldn't keep up with him. One moment he was relating a story she knew couldn't have anything but a doomed ending, and in the next breath his tone was edgily erotic. She shook her head helplessly, and then changed the movement to a nod.

"I do." Her voice sounded rusty and unused. "But I don't think I should. Not like this, Con. Not while you're telling me this."

"I like kissing you, too." If he'd heard the second half of her reply he gave no sign. "That's partly because I've got such a thing about your mouth, honey. You know, you don't have to wait for me to take the first step every—"

Her hands had been against his chest. Even as she slid them quickly up his shirtfront to twine her arms around his neck she wasn't sure she had the nerve to go further. She rose on her tiptoes and pulled his head down to hers. She felt an unmistakable hardness pressing against her, heard him exhale sharply, saw those sooty lashes fall against the faint ridge of color on his cheekbones.

She wanted to take the darkness away, Marilyn thought dazedly, her tongue circling his and her arms tightening around his neck. Was that what this was all about—did he want to blot it out, too? It seemed he was veering back and forth between desire and obsession, the past and the here and now, and the words she'd thrown at him earlier today came back to her.

"I'm beginning to wonder if that other personality isn't starting to spill over into the real you…"

"Roland wanted him too badly." Con moved his mouth from hers. "That's the only reason I can think of for him agreeing to DeMarco's terms on the take-in— no backup, no one else informed, just the two of them alone in Charpentier's office. DeMarco had a typed statement already prepared, apparently. The way we reconstructed what happened, he let Roland read it over and then he took it back and signed it with his own inkpen.''

Amazingly, he gave her a rueful smile. ''Sorry, *cher'*, that's pure New Awlins. Pen, ballpoint pen, whatever you all call it in these parts. This thing.''

In his free hand was a silver pen. She hadn't seen him extract it from his vest pocket but seemingly that was where he kept it, Marilyn realized as he slipped it away again.

''Then he handed Roland that expensive silver pen so the statement could be countersigned. Even then De-Marco liked the possibilities of biological weapons and nerve gas.'' Con shrugged. ''The thing was rigged to release a vapor the second time it was used—a vapor that would bring death within ninety seconds of it being inhaled. All DeMarco had to do was hold his breath and watch Roland take his last one. Then he walked out and sank back into the swamp again.''

''Who found Roland's body?'' She knew, Marilyn thought. She just needed to hear him tell her what she was up against.

''I did.'' Con brushed his lips against hers, his tone faraway. ''I did, heart. You understand now why it'll be pure pleasure for me to carry out this assignment for Colorado Confidential?''

He wasn't asking her a question. Even if he had been he didn't give her a chance to answer. His mouth trailed along the side of her jaw to her earlobe, and then moved down the vulnerable line of her neck. As if a feather was stroking upward from the flare of her hips, slow heat prickled along the skin on her back and convulsively she arched her body toward his.

She'd asked him to lay his cards on the table, and at long last he had. He couldn't help it that she didn't like what he'd showed her any more than he could change the way he played the game out, so if she wanted to win this there was only one thing to do.

She was the wild card. She had to deal herself in.

Deliberately she discarded the last of her resistance, and as if he sensed her infinitesimal shift Con slanted a dark emerald gaze at her.

"You want this, *cher'?*" he murmured lazily.

Instant heat suffused her. She swayed, he steadied her, she managed to nod her head. "I want it, Con. I—I want you now."

A slow smile lifted the corner of his mouth, and to her consternation he shook his head. The next moment he'd straightened, putting her slightly away from him. Where his hands gripped her shoulders was the only part of her that didn't feel suddenly chilled, Marilyn thought in confusion as his eyes widened guilelessly at her.

"See, that's the difference between New Awlins and the rest of the world," he said softly. "I want you too, sugar. I want you so bad I can already taste you…and that's part of what makes it so damn good, so let's take it slow. Now tell me again—do you think you might want this the sweet and lazy Big Easy way? 'Cause if you do, this Creole's your man."

This was the Con Ducharme she'd fallen for, Marilyn told herself breathlessly—the sexy, laid-back gambler with the wry grin and the teasing drawl. Right now he might never have heard of a man called Helio DeMarco, might never have stood over the body of a dead friend swearing to take an eye for an eye, a life for a life, no matter what the price to his soul.

She wanted this Con Ducharme to stay.

"Would the Big Easy way include those strawberries you picked up at the grocery store with me this afternoon being dipped in melted chocolate?'' she asked, hoping the nervous quaver in her voice was only audible to herself. ''And then would it include being hand-fed those strawberries by you?''

She knew her face had flooded with color. She wasn't very good at this, Marilyn thought in embarrassment. She just didn't have a light and playful touch when it came to this kind of thing.

This kind of thing? she thought a heartbeat later. God, was she so Beacon Hill that even in her own mind she avoided coming right out and using the word? *Sex,* she told herself firmly as she forced herself to meet Con's eyes. The word was sex. The man was pure sex. She and he were going to have—

''Dessert first?'' There was a spark of wicked humor in his gaze. ''Aw, shug, you bin holdin' out on me, f'true. You sure you don't have a little New Awlins blood in you somewhere? 'Cause strawberries and chocolate, *cher',* that just don't sound too Boston to me.''

Marilyn giggled. An instant later she clapped her hand to her mouth in shock. Con gave her a quizzical glance.

''You look like a little girl who just said a bad word she wasn't supposed to know, heart,'' he noted laconically. ''What's the matter, bay-bay?''

Behind her fingers a second gurgle rose up at his drawled tongue-in-cheek endearment, and she took her hand away. ''I don't giggle,'' she said helplessly. ''I don't know how to play games, I don't flirt, I don't act this way. What's *happening* to me?''

His quick laugh held startled amusement. ''Hell, you're just havin' fun, sweetheart. That never happen to you before?''

He pulled her to him, and before she knew what he intended his hands slid down to cup her jersey-clad rear.

"You were just as gorgeous, but you didn't have a rump this sweet when I first met you. Keep this after the baby comes, Mar'lyn, honey, would you? You might not fit into those designer suits you wore before, but this is going to look like poetry in motion in a tight black skirt and those sexy heels you go for. Got a double boiler?"

She gurgled again, and this time she didn't try to hold back the sound. "If that's not one of those New Orleans phrases you keep throwing at me you'd better let me know right away, because you wouldn't believe how I'm translating it."

Maybe she was getting the hang of this flirting business, she thought as he grinned. His palms tightened momentarily on her behind, and then he released her.

"Boiler as in for melting chocolate, not booty as in melting a poor defenseless male," he said reprovingly. "Walk ahead of me into the kitchen, honey, just to drive me crazy a little."

Grandmother Van Buren would definitely not approve, Marilyn told herself twenty minutes later as she lit the final wick on an outsize pillar candle and placed it on the living-room floor's polished cherrywood planks just beyond the fluffy flotaki rug that anchored the seating area. Its triple flames joined the rest of the haphazard grouping of candles she'd gathered from all corners of the apartment and arranged in a wavering line around the rug, and kneeling back on her haunches, she surveyed the scene. On the Moroccan leather hassock sat a glass bowl of melted chocolate. Beside it was a second bowl, this one brimming with ruby-toned, out-of-season strawberries. She only had to glance over her shoulder toward the open kitchen area to see Con, a dish towel slung with panache over his shoulder, checking the burners of the stove before joining her.

The large overhead light flicked off, leaving the golden glow of the dozen or so candles the sole illumination. Suddenly her easy mood deserted her, and it was with an effort that she smiled at him as he pulled her to her feet.

"Looks like fairyland, *cher'*," he said softly. "And see up above? The heat from those pretty little things is making your mobile turn."

He could make her laugh. He could make her knees go weak with desire. But at his inconsequential observation Marilyn felt her heart turn over. He couldn't have said anything that would have taken away her nervousness so completely, she thought, sinking into the down-filled cushions of the sofa and watching as he loosened his tie enough to undo the collar button on his shirt. And he was right—the tiny pools of light threw the open expanse of the loft's main floor into velvety shadows, creating an oasis of golden warmth that seemed mysterious and magical.

Truth, beauty and love.... She'd known when she'd impulsively added those words to the mobile now slowly swirling overhead that they completed her creation. But without those three sentiments, life itself was arid and empty.

He completed her. She'd waited far too long to tell him he—

"Open."

Startled out of her thoughts, automatically Marilyn opened her mouth just as Con held a dipped strawberry to it, but she was a moment too late to catch the drop of melted chocolate that trickled warmly onto her bottom lip. She bit down, and immediately her taste buds were flooded.

The chocolate was bittersweet, its creamy richness a

decadent contrast to the juice that exploded from the plump strawberry. She closed her eyes in ecstasy, and when she opened them she saw Con was watching her.

"Was it good for you, *cher'?*" His tone held a touch of hoarseness. Even in the flickering glow of the circle of candles the hard flush mounting his cheekbones was unmistakably evident. "'Cause it was good for me. You think you might be able to make that little groaning sound again?"

He sat down on the couch beside her, deftly swinging her legs up onto his lap and laying her back against the softly pillowed armrest as he did. He reached forward, selecting another gleamingly red-hulled strawberry and plunging it into the bowl of dark melted chocolate before sitting back again.

"Isn't it your turn?" she asked unsteadily, still shaken by the rush of heat his not-quite-teasing words had sent through her.

"Yeah, it's my turn. This is how I take my turn, honey."

Even as he spoke he was touching the chocolate tip of the strawberry to her lips, and instinctively her tongue darted out to lick it. Her teeth closed on the luscious berry, and sweet juice spilled through her mouth. Through her half-closed lashes she saw Con's gaze darken as her sigh of pleasure came out in a throaty purr.

"You missed some," he rasped.

Leaning toward her, he nudged the other half of the strawberry past her parted lips at the same time as his tongue licked the smear of melted chocolate from her mouth. Liquid heat instantly suffused her, and from the sudden rigid hardness in his muscles she knew the same heat was running through Con.

"You're a messy eater, *cher','*" he whispered against

her lips. Slowly he licked her again, his gaze never leaving hers. ''Am I gonna have to do this every time?''

Marilyn didn't trust herself to speak. She nodded, and even that small motion set the room spinning dizzily around her. Nothing she'd ever experienced had prepared her for this, she thought faintly. Who would have guessed that the simple act of eating could be so *erotic?*

But Con Ducharme could probably turn washing a car into a sensuous pastime. Those green-gold eyes, those thick dark lashes, the leanly muscled build under his suit—he was sinful delight personified. Add to all that his drawl and those skilful gambler's hands that seemed to know just what to do with a woman, and it seemed almost illegal that he should be let loose to wreak havoc on a staid and inexperienced Beacon Hill female like herself.

She'd been nicknamed the Ice Queen, Marilyn thought, letting her lashes drift over her eyes as Con pressed a kiss to the corner of her mouth, but if anyone who'd ever called her that could see her now they'd realize she wasn't anything—

A drop of chocolate touched her lip. She opened her mouth for the next strawberry, but as soon as her tongue flicked out her eyes flew open in shock.

''I skipped a step, heart.'' Con's drawl was lazier than she'd heard it before. ''So sue me.''

He'd been inching her toward the far edge of desire from the moment he'd first kissed her tonight, she thought dazedly. Once or twice she'd come dangerously close to slipping, but this time he was coaxing her to step right over the line.

Her gaze holding his, slowly Marilyn took Con's chocolate-dipped middle finger into her mouth. Even more slowly, she let her tongue run along the length of it, licking it with languid deliberation. She saw his teeth catch hard on his lower lip, saw his eyes glaze over with heat, heard him exhale tightly.

Lightly she grasped his wrist with both her hands and pulled him closer. She gave a tentative little suck and felt a shudder run violently through him.

"Don't do that, *cher'*." His words came out in a strangled gasp. "Not if you want me to be any good to you when we get right down to it."

She hadn't understood, Marilyn thought wonderingly. She'd seen it as Con teasing her into losing all control, but what she hadn't realized was that she had that same power over him. She could make bad-boy Con Ducharme melt. She could drive him crazy with desire. She—very pregnant ex-ice queen Marilyn Langworthy—could make this big and sexy riverboat gambler plead with her to slow down and beg her to keep going.

And she wanted to do all that, starting right now.

She licked the tip of his finger one last time, and let him withdraw it. Without taking her eyes from him, she reached over to the bowl of strawberries on the hassock beside her. Grasping one and still not breaking their locked gazes, she swirled it in the warm chocolate, coating it extravagantly.

"This is how I take my turn, Con," she murmured, bringing the berry to just above the swell of her breasts revealed by the vee of the chiffon blouse's neckline.

Dark and gleaming, the melted chocolate dripped from the rosy tip of the berry to spill across the creamy paleness of her skin. Slowly it pooled into the hollow between her breasts.

"Tell you a secret, sugar." Con's breathing was shallow and fast. He watched as the last drop of chocolate fell to her breasts, watched as she brought the strawberry to her lips and took a bite. "I've been known to finesse a card game into coming out in my favor once or twice. But what you're doing here is stacking the deck, and that's not fair. I don't stand a chance, *cher'*."

As if she'd pushed him past all endurance, his hands went swiftly to the beribboned neckline of her blouse. Almost impatiently he spread it wide, exposing the lacy trim of her front-fastened bra. The next moment his head had bent to her breasts, and his tongue was lapping at the sweetness pooled between them even as he one-handedly unlatched the small clasp holding her bra together.

It sprang open. His palms moved immediately to the twin globes now revealed, his thumbs circling tantalizingly around the raised peaks of her nipples. Looking down through her lashes at herself and at him, Marilyn felt an instant's panic.

She was pregnant. What was she thinking, behaving this way? And could he really find her so attractive without a flat stomach, a tautly slim figure?

A strand of midnight-black hair brushed against her skin. One of his hands slid from her breast to the rounded curve of her belly. His palm caressed her there with the same attention he was giving the rest of her.

He was a man who was comfortable with his maleness. He liked embroidered vests, so he wore them without worrying whether they were old-fashioned or not. He didn't apologize for the fact that the shoulder-holstered gun he wore when they were out and about was obviously a weapon he'd used in the past, and neither did he feel the need to explain why he'd chosen a tough profession like law enforcement. Where another man might feel it necessary to remain gruffly inarticulate as a sign of masculinity, Con used words like "fairyland'' and described her as a peony with no reticence at all.

He liked being a man, Marilyn realized slowly. And he loved it that she was a woman. He'd made it obvious that everything about her that made her different from him aroused him, including the fact that her rump snugly filled his spread palms when he held it, that her breasts needed a fuller cup size than she'd ever worn before, and that she was capable of nurturing a growing little life inside her.

She felt his mouth gently take in one of her nipples, felt his tongue teasing it to a tight pink bud. Everything else slipped away and a blissfully languid heat began lapping over her.

''I want to see you get bigger, month by month, *cher'*.''

Con's whisper was barely audible against her skin. He kissed her nipple, kissed the soft underside of her breast, pushed the flimsy chiffon up and began leading a trail of kisses toward the fullest curve of her belly. Lightly he pressed one above her navel, and then began trailing down to the drawstring waist of her pants. Without conscious volition, Marilyn moved her hips restlessly toward his mouth. In the flickering light from the candles she saw him lift his head and flash her a quick grin.

''That's right, sugar.'' There was a husky undercurrent in his tone. ''That's how you tease me till I can't wait anymore. I told you you cheated.''

''And you said you'd been known to palm a card once or twice yourself,'' she managed unevenly. ''I think you're doing it now, Con. Here I am with practically everything on display for you and you haven't even shown me one teensy square inch of your hide. For heaven's sake, you're still wearing your tie. *That's* cheating.''

"We'll make a deal." He pulled at the drawstring of the silky violet pants. "You let me slip you out of these—" The cord released and he shot her an innocent look. "And then I'll slip out of everything I'm wearing. Fair enough?"

"Fair enough," she agreed shakily. "But I'll be watching you closely while you strip down, just to make sure you're keeping to the rules."

"Yeah, honey, I kind of thought you might," he drawled, already tugging the stretchy jersey over her hips and down her thighs. "I'm gonna have to—aw, hell, heart. You're a thong girl, and a low-rider thong girl at that. You win, I lose, no contest."

Somehow during the last few minutes she'd sunk into the squashy feather-filled couch pillows. Now Marilyn raised herself up on her propped elbows, carelessly blew a tumbled strand of blond hair out of her eyes, and gave Con a more guileless look than the innocent one he'd favored her with moments ago.

"They're comfortable," she protested, glancing at the bra's matching scrap of lace snugged under the curve of her belly. "And you didn't lose because I'm a thong girl, you lost because you're a rump man…and a weak-willed rump man at that." She waited a beat, and then added wickedly, "Sugar."

The candlelight emphasizing the hard planes of his face and picking out the reluctantly amused gleam in his gaze, Con slid the violet pants past her knees, her ankles, her arched feet. He stood and shrugged out of his vest before slipping the loose knot of his tie free and letting it drop to the rug.

"You know how to play poker, Mar'lyn?"

She watched as he unbuttoned his shirt. Against the white linen his skin was a dark gold, and a faint arrow of fine black hair shadowed his washboard-flat abdominals. She shook her head, her mouth suddenly too dry to speak.

''Good.'' He let the shirt drop to the floor beside the vest, his hands going to the buckle of his belt. ''Remind me never to teach you, heart.''

Marilyn barely heard his words. She'd seen his body before, she acknowledged, but the night he'd come to her in her office she'd been so trapped in guilt and grief only the physical act itself had gotten through, and that only as a way to alleviate the terrible pain wracking her.

He was big and rangy and even more heavily muscled than she'd realized, seeing him in the well-cut but necessarily concealing suits he favored. High up on one shoulder was what looked like an old scar, and as her gaze lingered on it Con gave an unconcerned shrug.

''Courtesy of a poor loser.'' He unzipped his fly before sitting again on the couch to remove his shoes.

She wanted him, Marilyn admitted shakily—wanted him in her, wanted him to take her, wanted to give him everything he wanted from her. But she was over three months pregnant, and although the books she'd bought by the dozens all were comfortably reassuring on the subject, she still couldn't repress the tiny flicker of doubt she had about making love in her state.

The missionary position was out of the question, she thought worriedly. What did that leave? She wished suddenly that her past experiences had been more varied and venturesome, but the few relationships she'd had that had progressed to the physical stage had been almost drearily conservative.

''It's going to be all right, honey.''

As if he'd been reading her mind, Con's soft comment broke into her thoughts. She blinked, and saw he was watching her intently. Without taking his gaze from hers, he got to his feet, and pushed the dark briefs he was wearing down his thighs before stepping out of both them and his pants. Showing no self-consciousness at all, he reached for her hand.

"No teacup ride for your little passenger, *cher'*,'' he said hoarsely. "We'll take it nice and slow and we'll do the whole thing lying on our sides so we can watch each other, okay?"

Just like that, her doubts fled. Marilyn let him pull her to her feet, and as he snugged her up against him and thumbed the flimsy waistband of her thong down her thighs she let her fingers trail daringly down the vee of hair to the shadowed tangle between his legs.

Her hand closed around him. She caught her breath and heard him do the same.

He was warmly and solidly big in her nervous grasp. As they sank to the deep-piled fluffiness of the rug her gaze sought his.

"You don't have to teach me how to play poker, but you're going to have to guide me through this, Con."

To cover her discomfiture she began fumbling with her blouse. He pushed her hands aside and pinned both her wrists in an easy, one-handed hold.

"Rule number one, then. The blouse stays, *cher'*. It's practically falling off you, and I'm finding it sexy as hell to keep catching glimpses through that see-through stuff."

Why did it seem somehow more wanton to be lying here half-clothed with him, rather than totally nude? she asked herself as soft tufts of the rug lapped sensuously against her legs and her derriere. Not only did it feel wanton, she knew she looked wanton, too. The expression on Con's face was proof of that.

"Messed hair, juice-stained mouth, satin-doll skin." His throaty murmur was accompanied by a slow licking of her lower lip. His tongue went farther into her mouth, and then out again. "Back home we got voodoo women who couldn't mix up a love-potion stronger than what you're puttin' on me, shug. Gimme some of that."

Even as he growled the teasing plea his mouth covered hers, and as his kiss went deep Marilyn felt a lean leg move underneath her. Instinctively she hitched her top leg closer to her body and over his, and it was only when she felt him entering her that she realized the opportunity she'd given him.

Being Con he'd taken that opportunity, she thought, her eyes widening as the gentle pressure between her legs increased. And being her, she wasn't sure if she was absolutely ready.

"Li'l tight, sugar, but we gon' love it in a second," he slurred against her mouth, still kissing her as he muttered the words. "You got the promise of a Creole gentleman on…okay, now, baby, that's where we wanted to be, f'true. Tell me you like that, honey. Tell me how I make you feel."

He was completely inside her. She could feel every hard inch of him. Heat blossomed through her, and she felt the same heat dewing the swollen curve of her top lip.

Con licked it away. The action was startlingly, shudderingly erotic. Marilyn opened her eyes fully and saw a corner of that bad-boy mouth quirk briefly up.

"Hell, *cher',* I'm from New Awlins, and down there we like our sex like we like our rice—just a little bit dirty, heart," he muttered, his hands moving down her body to spread wide against her derriere. "I tell you lately you got a beautiful—"

"Ask me again, Con," she breathed. "Ask me again if I like it. Ask me to tell you how you make me feel."

"I know you like it." He'd withdrawn slightly. Now he moved into her again, and a long sigh escaped her. Con tightened his hold, his capable gambler's fingers pressing into the softness of her rump. "I think you love it. How do I make you feel, Mar'lyn?"

"Like…like I'm being ravished." She sighed again, and mingled with the breathy exhalation was a low groan of pure pleasure. "Like I'm a princess and you're the intruder who's slipped past the castle walls. How do I make you feel?"

Every time he moved into her he pulled her to him. When he withdrew, his fingers spread open on her flesh. He was controlling his motions, Marilyn thought dazedly, unerringly rocking her higher and higher, pushing her closer to the point where she would have to cry out for release.

"I feel like I'm going out of my mind, sugar." His voice was strained. Through her lashes she saw the gleam of candlelight gilding his cheekbones, touching his parted lips. "And I love it, honey. Tell me I can bring it on home to you now, okay?"

He clasped her to him and she received him, he withdrew and her head arched back on her neck. "Yes, Con," she breathed. "You can—you can bring—"

The heat that had been mounting in her exploded shockingly into flame as Con thrust into her one final, overwhelming time. Marilyn heard her own voice, cracked and ragged, calling out his name, heard his voice rasping out incoherent endearments, felt the shuddering rush inside her as he pulled her to him and this time kept her desperately, inseparably close. She felt as if she was being buried in black roses, felt as if she was flying through black stars—

—felt as if there were no longer two separate beings called Con Ducharme or Marilyn Langworthy at all, but just a single heart beating, a single soul blazing through the dark into new existence.

IT SEEMED an eternity later that she opened her eyes, but as soon as she did the realization slammed into her like a blow. It was no more than the truth. Con and she *had* become one being. Even now that tiny being was nestled safely in his mother, was wrapped securely in the strong arms of the father who didn't know he'd created him.

She'd done her child's father a terrible wrong, Marilyn thought dazedly. And no matter what the outcome, she couldn't continue to perpetuate that wrong a second longer.

She raised her head. Con's eyes, brilliantly gold-green and still holding the residual heat of passion, met hers.

"Aw, *cher',*" he whispered. "You take my breath away."

The simple vulnerability of his words pierced her. For a moment she faltered. Then she gathered her courage.

"My baby, Con," she said in a low rush. "The baby growing inside me. He's not just mine, he's—"

Chapter Eleven

A shrill buzzing ripped through the quiet like an alarm, shocking Marilyn into an abrupt silence that left her sentence unfinished. She stared at Con with startled eyes, and saw with disconcertion that the lover of a second ago had been replaced by a coldly alert professional.

"You usually get callers this time of night, heart?" he asked tersely.

"I seldom get callers, period. Unless—" Her brow smoothed. "It has to be Jim and Dan. It wouldn't be the first time they've gone out for the evening, each assuming the other has a pass-card to get back into the building."

The buzzer sounded again, and Con swore under his breath. "DeMarco's boys wouldn't announce themselves, but whoever it is, they've got lousy timing. No, *cher'*, I'll check it out."

This last was added as she made a move to sit up. Getting to his own feet, unhurriedly he pulled on his pants, zipping the fly just enough that they rode low on his hips. He started to step across the small barrier of candles, and then turned and bent swiftly to her.

"*Real* lousy timing," he muttered, planting a brief, hard kiss on her parted lips.

With lazy grace he padded barefoot to the intercom panel by the door. Pushing the button that opened the speak channel, he raked a hand back through his hair.

"Yeah?"

There was silence. He looked over at her and then switched his attention back to the intercom, but before he had a chance to say anything further a woman's tentative tones crackled over the speaker.

"Marilee? Marilee, are you there?"

Marilyn closed her eyes in disbelief.

Holly had *never* visited her before. Why had she chosen tonight of all nights to do so? She opened her eyes and looked around her. If the big, half-naked man by the door and her own dishabille wasn't evidence enough of what had just transpired here, the clothes flung haphazardly over the furniture and the collection of candles on the floor were more than a tip-off.

Not to mention the bowls of chocolate and strawberries, she thought in dismay as she caught sight of them.

The buzzer shrilled again. Con looked over at her, his eyebrows raised in inquiry.

"I thought Holly was supposed to be at the Langworthy lodge this weekend with Celia," she said in low-voiced desperation. "I can't let her—"

"Marilee, if you're there, answer me." Holly's voice, even distorted by the speaker, sounded thin and quavery. "I need to talk to you. It's important."

She'd had news of Sky. Even as the possibility tore through Marilyn's mind like an electric shock she was scrambling up from the rug. "Let her in," she commanded Con urgently as she frantically grabbed up her clothes. "Let her *in*."

But already he was pressing the button that released the main door. Distorted or not, it was evident by the sounds emanating from the lobby that Holly was unaccompanied by anyone else and that she had succeeded in gaining entrance.

Even now her half sister would be waiting for the elevator, Marilyn thought. She spied her thong panties wedged between two sofa cushions and hastily snatched them up. The chocolate and strawberries—she *had* to hustle them out of sight. Except that left the candles, and removing them was a priority. Or should she forgo everything else and race upstairs to have a three-second shower?

She froze in indecision. If the relationship between her and her half sister had been halfway normal, this unannounced visit wouldn't be cause for panic, she thought bleakly—slight embarrassment, maybe, but not panic. But as it was—

"I'll take care of this." Unhurriedly Con ambled over, the expression in his eyes as he looked at her tenderly amused. "Gawd, we can't have her suspecting big sis might have been foolin' around, can we, *cher*? Go jump in the shower, brush your hair, whatever it is you feel you need to do. But, Mar'lyn?"

She was already gathering up the rest of her clothes. "Yes?"

His gaze was shadowed. "I know what you're thinking. Don't get your hopes up too high. The Confidential organization has my cell number, and I would have been informed if there'd been a break in the case."

He was probably right, she thought as she stepped out of the shower a few minutes later and hurriedly selected another recent purchase from her wardrobe—this one an old-rose stretch velvet gown that fell to just above her ankles. But for almost five months she'd forced herself to keep hoping that Sky would be returned, and she wasn't about to stop now.

Shoving her feet into a pair of velvet mules, she glanced quickly at herself in the mirror. Long-sleeved and with a key-hole neckline, the gown was comfortable enough to lounge around at home in, as the saleswoman had assured her, but pretty enough so that with heels and earrings it wouldn't look out of place at an evening function. The only reason she hadn't worn it to the club with Con the previous night was that the stretch velvet made no attempt to skim her pregnant figure, but instead clung lovingly to every curve, as her reflection right now made obvious.

But that was the very reason Con would love her in this. He thought her butt was sexy. He thought her breasts were sexy. He thought her *pregnancy* was sexy.

He would, she thought, unable to repress the quick heat that ran through her. Con had once told her he wanted a whole houseful of children with a mama to go along with them. She'd better get used to being pregnant, because she had the feeling that with him she'd be more often in that state than out of it during the next few years.

Even as she began to turn from the mirror the realization of what she'd just been contemplating struck her and she stopped dead. Was she really considering a future as Con Ducharme's wife? And did she really think it was possible he might propose that future to her?

Yes, and yes, Marilyn thought shakily. Which made it even more imperative that she tell him the truth. But maybe it was just as well Holly's untimely arrival had prevented her from blurting out such a bombshell to a man who believed he was incapable of fathering children, she thought as she left the bedroom and hastened down the hall. She needed to prepare him for what would definitely come as a shock, albeit a welcome one for a man like—

Her thoughts screeched to a halt. Her foot on the top step of the stairs, she stared in dismay at the scene below.

The chocolate and strawberries were nowhere in sight. The candles had been similarly whisked away. In the scant moments he'd had before Holly's appearance, Con had miraculously managed to remove all evidence of their recent lovemaking.

All evidence except himself, Marilyn thought hollowly. There was no way Holly hadn't guessed at the situation she'd come close to walking into, when the man she was talking to was barechested and barefoot.

"…don't think Daddy meant to tell us, for fear of worrying us, but naturally when Antonia mentioned Marilyn had dropped by Mother and I bullied it out of him."

Seated on the sofa below, Holly spread her hands in a helpless gesture. "Marilee could have been *killed*. I just had to come and see for myself that she was all right. I didn't realize she had someone here to look after her, Con—in fact, I didn't realize she was seeing anyone at all. But that's my fault. I'm sure if I hadn't been so wrapped up in my own worries these last few months Marilyn and I would have had more of a chance to get to know each other."

It was exactly the kind of Pollyanna-ish sentiment she might have expected from her half sister, Marilyn thought. And once upon a time Holly's blithe assumption that her father's other daughter would want to forget a sisterly relationship with her, complete with intimate little chats about men, now that she was living in Denver might have seemed exasperatingly obtuse.

Now it didn't. Now it just seemed achingly sad. If Holly's vision of them becoming close had come true, she told herself with sharp regret, Sky might never have been kidnapped. At the very least she would have been more of a support to Holly during this terrible time.

As it was, she'd been no support at all. And still Holly had rushed over here tonight to reassure herself that her big sister was unharmed.

"Just one of those freak accidents, or so building management assured us. There'll be an investigation into how it could have happened."

From Con's words, it was obvious Samuel had vouchsafed nothing more than the barest facts to Holly. He looked up as Marilyn belatedly began her descent and gave her a slow smile that took in the form-fitting velvet dress she was wearing before he went on.

"*Cher'*, tell your little sister you're all right. I tried to, right after I introduced myself, but I'm not sure she's convinced."

"I'm fine. Just a little sore in the shoulder muscles, but otherwise none the worse for wear." Marilyn was taken aback to see tears sheening her younger half sister's luminous green gaze, as Holly crossed the floor toward her.

"Thank God. Oh, Marilee, when Daddy told us, both Mama and I couldn't believe he hadn't phoned us at the lodge right away. Have you seen a doctor? Is the baby all right?"

There was real fear in her question. Marilyn hastened to dispel it. "The baby's perfectly okay. Dr. Roblyn said there's nothing to worry about." She hesitated. "It—it was sweet of you to come, Holly. Do you have time to stay and have a cup of tea?''

After all the times she'd rebuffed similar invitations from Holly, she wouldn't have blamed her if she'd declined, she thought. Instead, Holly's face lit up.

''Tea would be wonderful.'' She shot a sudden mischievous glance at Con's bare torso. ''Are you sure this is a good time?''

''Of course it is,'' Marilyn said, too swiftly. ''Con and I were just—were just—''

''Were just watching a documentary on tree frogs on television,'' Con supplied, a corner of his mouth twitching. ''But don't worry, it ended a couple of minutes before you arrived. Mar'lyn, honey, I got to make a couple of phone calls,'' he went on, taking in her flaming face with wicked amusement. ''I'll use the phone upstairs so I won't disturb you ladies, okay?''

There wasn't a trace of repentance in the man's tone, Marilyn thought in exasperation as he took his leave of them, his exaggeratedly serious gaze and Holly's dancing green one almost carbon copies of each other. She gave him a quelling look as he passed by her on the way to the stairs—a mistake, she realized as he planted a careless kiss on her mouth.

''Don't be mad, sugar,'' he murmured. ''Somehow it didn't seem right, sweeping what we'd just had together under the rug as if it was something to be ashamed of. Count yourself lucky I'm not taking out a full-page announcement in the *Denver Post*.''

''Tree frogs, huh?'' As Con made his way upstairs and Marilyn plugged in the electric kettle, Holly sat down at the kitchen table, her tone musing. ''I think I watched that documentary once myself. Nine months later Sky was born.''

"Well, since I'm already pregnant I don't have to worry about that, do I?" Marilyn replied, her tartness automatic. She whirled around in instant contrition. "Oh, Holls, I'm sorry. I didn't mean to snap."

"Holls?" There was an odd expression on Holly's face. "Did you just call me by a *nickname*, Marilee?"

She looked like she'd just been given a priceless gift, Marilyn thought testily. Those green eyes—heavens, they were like Con's—were again sheened over with incipient tears, and the corners of her upturned mouth were trembling.

Holly was twenty-three. She was thirty-one. It was awfully late for each of them to have gotten a brand-new sister, but it seemed that was exactly what had just happened, she told herself, blinking away the foolish prickle in her own eyes.

"So what if I did? For God's sake, we're *sisters*, aren't we? I guess if you're entitled to call me by that awful name Marilee, I get to call you Holls if I want. How do you take your tea?"

"Milk and just a third of a spoon of sugar, Marilee."

Marilyn snorted with a sister's lack of patience. Holly smiled shyly at her before knitting her brows in a thoughtful frown.

"Your Con Ducharme's certainly a hunk, Marilee. Where'd you find him?"

"We met at the office," Marilyn replied briefly, knowing how misleading her answer was and regretfully realizing that for now it had to remain misleading. Even if she had the right to tell Holly why Con was in Denver, bringing up the subject of Sky's kidnapping would shatter her sister's fragile mood.

She set two mugs of tea on the table and sat down, her expression softening. "And yes, he's a hunk, although that's not a word I ever thought I'd hear myself saying. It—it's pretty serious, Holls. On my part, anyway, and I think on Con's, too.''

"He's obviously good for you," Holly said softly. "You seem happier than I've ever known you to be." She looked suddenly worried. "He's glad about your pregnancy?"

Of course, Marilyn thought. Holly, like the rest of the family, was still of the belief that Tony had fathered the baby inside her. And although she had an almost overwhelming compulsion to proclaim the truth about her child's parentage to the world, it was unthinkable that anyone else should hear the news before the father himself did. She shook her head.

"Con doesn't have a problem with that at all. He doesn't have a problem with me being pregnant, period. He thinks I'm beautiful like this." She gave an embarrassed little laugh. "Maybe the man should have his eyes checked."

"Marilyn Langworthy, you just take that back!" Marilyn was surprised to see a flash of anger in her sister's gaze. Holly went on, her tone fierce. "You *are* beautiful. If you ask me, you're even more beautiful now as an expectant mom than you ever were as a model-thin fashionista. Just looking at you used to make me want to haul a carton of ice cream out of the freezer and scarf down the whole thing in one go."

Her glaring green eyes held Marilyn's startled blue ones for a long moment. Then, as if on cue, they both dissolved into laughter.

This felt so good, Marilyn thought, her shoulders shaking helplessly as yet another gale of the giggles swept through her and her sister. Why had she deprived herself of this for so many years?

Because you were afraid to come out of that ice castle you built around yourself. The answer came to her promptly. *But then you met a man who blowtorched his way inside, and everything changed. All that matters now is that in the past three months you've somehow gotten yourself a baby, a sister and a sexy hunk of a lover. You got dealt a winning hand when Con Ducharme came into your life, so just be thankful and enjoy your good fortune.*

"I thought I'd forgotten how to laugh, Marilee." As their giggles subsided, Holly wiped her eyes and gave her sister a suddenly shaky smile. "Thanks for helping me remember. I tell myself it won't do Sky any good to come home to a mom who only knows how to burst into tears, but sometimes it's—" Her voice shook, and she steadied it with an obvious effort. "Oh, Marilee, sometimes it's so *hard*," she said hoarsely, her gaze brilliant with pain. "My little boy's been gone four and a half months now. Everyone tells me not to give up hope, but what if—what if he—"

Her haunted eyes finished her sentence for her. Swiftly Marilyn pushed her chair back, and went to her sister's side, her hands tightly gripping Holly's shoulders.

"Holls, listen to me," she said with the same fierceness her sister had displayed only moments before. "Sky's coming home, do you hear me? Good people—people who *care,* people who know how investigations like this work—are out there even now doing everything they can to bring your son back to you. I can't say more because I don't know more, but I know he's coming home. Do you believe me?"

Tears spilling down her cheeks, Holly nodded. "I believe you, Marilee. I know you're not the type to make up a comforting lie just to reassure me. Do you think he'll be home in time for Christmas?''

"I don't know, sweetie." Marilyn relaxed her grip. "But I fully intend to buy and wrap a present to put under the tree for him. And this time it won't be a dumb silver rattle too heavy for him to lift.''

Holly gave her a watery smile. "Agreed—no silver rattles. Along with the usual toys, I'd already decided to get Sky something that would reflect the other side of his heritage. It was never my intention for him to grow up feeling he should be ashamed of the part of him that comes from his father, even though—'' She bit her lip, effectively cutting off her words.

A terrible suspicion filled Marilyn. It couldn't be true, she thought slowly. It just couldn't be. And yet…

It would explain her silence, wouldn't it? If she got pregnant as a result of Tony forcing himself on her the way he tried to do with me, it's no wonder she's refused to tell anyone. No child needs the burden of growing up knowing his conception came about as a result of violence, not love. The heritage thing fits, too—when Sky's old enough to learn the truth Holly wants him to be proud of his Italian lineage, not to think his father's in any way representative of the majority of Italian-Americans who helped make this country great.

Holly had just demonstrated that she still wasn't ready to break her silence on the subject—not even to a sister. But maybe to a sister she could bring herself to hint at the truth, Marilyn thought worriedly.

"I'm not prying, Holly," she said carefully. "I know you have your reasons for wanting to keep the identity of Sky's father to yourself. But tell me one thing—other than having the same grandfather, is there any relationship between the child growing inside me and your Sky?''

She knew as soon as she'd spoken what her sister's reaction was going to be. Holly's green eyes, normally a mirror to her every thought and mood, turned instantly blank. Her features seemed suddenly pinched.

''I don't know what you're talking about, Marilee,'' she said distantly. She took a final polite sip of her tea, pushed her chair back, and stood.

''I'm afraid I don't know what you're talking about at all,'' she said softly.

Chapter Twelve

"Henri, thanks for recommending that Burgundy the other evening." Con touched the black-clad wine waiter lightly on the arm as he paused by their table. "You obviously know your wine."

So this was the contact Con had telephoned last night during Holly's visit, Marilyn thought, taking a sip of her Perrier and lime and letting her gaze drift with assumed aimlessness around the gambling club's intimate little lounge. Its decor had been chosen with an eye to a Roaring Twenties theme, with art deco–styled furniture set around the horseshoe-shaped mirrored bar. She allowed her attention to wander back to the conversation.

"My pleasure, Mr. Ducharme. Are you playing tonight?"

"Maybe a little flutter at the poker table later," Con drawled. "If there's an interesting game, of course."

"Ah." Henri nodded in comprehension. "I believe the gentleman I alerted you to who made the reservations for this evening will be starting a game within the next half hour, sir. No limit to the stakes. Shall I put your name in to play and have your house chips sent along to the Red Room?"

"Yeah, if that's where the game's being held." Con

exchanged a glance with the man. "We're talking fast company? I don't want to walk in and find a roomful of fish, Henri."

"All very experienced players, Mr. Ducharme. The club makes every effort to steer novices to games more on their level," the waiter assured him.

As Henri left their table Marilyn toyed with the miniature silver spear impaling her slice of lime, hoping her outward manner displayed none of her inner turmoil, but when she spoke her voice held a nervous edge.

"So this is the night?"

"If my money just bought accurate information." Con's own tone was uncharacteristically clipped. He frowned across the table at her. "Tell me again why you're not back at the apartment with the bodyguard I asked Colorado Confidential to provide for you, *cher'*?"

She lifted her chin. "Because we don't want Tony to suspect this is a trap until he walks into it. And if my presence can allay his suspicions one iota, then I want to do my part. Next question?"

For a moment Con held his scowl. Then he gave her a rueful smile. "My next question? How about why did you choose that outfit to wear when you knew I'd need all my wits about me tonight?"

She looked down with feigned surprise at the dress she'd bought earlier that day. "Why, this old thing? Heavens, I just chose it because it was comfortable."

"Comfortable for you, maybe." His gaze took in the midnight-blue jersey neckline swooping low to reveal more than a glimpse of creamy breasts. "But it's got me feeling damned uncomfortable, heart."

"Poor baby." She glanced teasingly upward at him through her lashes. "I guess we'll just have to find something to do about that when we get home, won't we?''

"I guess we will," Con said huskily. "But that doesn't help me much right now."

And it didn't do much to help her, Marilyn admitted shakily as their gazes met and the temperature in the room instantly seemed to go up by about fifty degrees. The man sitting across the table from her looked every inch the riverboat gambler tonight. Perfectly tailored black broadcloth spanned those broad shoulders and chest, then moved in very slightly at the waist in a cut and length old-fashioned enough that Rhett Butler might have worn it. Pistols at dawn, indeed, she told herself faintly—right down to the string tie that was a southern variation on the western-themed silver-and-turquoise bolos she'd spotted on a few ranch and oil-baron types around the room.

A thought struck her. "What do you mean, if your money bought accurate information? I didn't see any money changing hands between you and Henri just now—oh!" Her eyes widened. "But Con, I was *watching* you. How did you do it?"

"Trade secret, *cher'*." A quick grin flashed across the tan of his face. Leaning across the table toward her, he lazily plucked something from the bodice of her dress. He sat back, the silver coin glinting between his fingers. "Now, sugar, you should know better than to slip a man's lucky piece away from him like that," he said in mock reproval.

A low ripple of laughter escaped her. "You'll have to demonstrate that 'the hand is faster than the eye' trick when we're alone sometime," she murmured, still tingling from the touch of his fingers on her skin.

He shook his head, his gaze on hers. "Ain't no good

fast, Mar'lyn, honey. What I'll do is keep my hand real slow and easy, so you get the chance to see how I work it.''

Just like that he could make her melt, Marilyn thought dazedly. If he took her wrist right now and led her from this table to a secluded hallway—

Hastily she brought her drink to her lips and took a sip. She set the glass down and fixed Con with what she hoped was a steely glance.

''Stop that, Ducharme.'' Her voice didn't sound stern, it just sounded breathy, she noted. She cleared her throat and tried again. ''Let's concentrate on what's going to happen tonight. Why won't you tell me exactly how you plan to get Tony to divulge his uncle's whereabouts to us?''

''Because I'm not sure what the plan's going to be.'' He shrugged at her raised eyebrows. ''Look, heart, this is where ColCon and I part company.'' His truncation of the organization's name seemed dismissive. ''Colleen Wellesley, the woman I told you about who runs the outfit, is big on rules and procedure and planning an operation right down to the last damn detail. I don't like rules, I figure procedure's just a way of letting someone else make the decisions for you, and I know that the best-laid plans can get all shot to *merde* as soon as the other guy does something unexpected.''

He inhaled tightly. ''Sorry. This team-playing stuff was a bone in my gullet right from the start. What I'm trying to say, *cher'*, is that my only plan tonight is to wing it with Tony—size him up as we go along, try to figure out what makes him tick, and then take it from there. That's the way I play poker and that's the way I handle an investigation.''

''I guess I can see your point,'' Marilyn said slowly.

"There was no way we could have foreseen Holly's visit last night, and my suspicion about Tony being Sky's father came right out of the blue. If it's true it could change everything, Con."

"Not quite everything." His expression was grim. "DeMarco won't want to let anything get in the way of his plans for that virus. But I know what you mean—if you're right about Corso it puts a whole different slant on whether or not Sky will ever be returned to his mother."

"I don't think Tony's capable of bonding with Sky the way an ordinary man would with his child. But it might appeal to his ego to have a son he can raise to follow in his footsteps, the way he's followed in his uncle's," Marilyn said worriedly.

"And seeing you tonight could set him to wondering whether two sons following in his footsteps might be better than one," Con said tightly. "Dammit, *cher'*, why don't you let me call Colleen Wellesley right now? Along with ColCon, she runs a security agency right here in Denver called ICU. They could have someone here within minutes."

"I'm not about to trot meekly back to the apartment with a hired bodyguard breathing down my neck while you're doing something to bring Sky home, and that's final, Con." She picked up her drink again. "You know as well as I do that Tony wouldn't try anything here. I'd rather talk about why you don't seem convinced about Holly and Tony having a one-night stand."

"You sure you never played poker, shug?" His question was sharp. "'Cause I get the feeling you did some pretty fancy shuffling of the cards just now. What are you trying to distract me from?"

Not for the first time since Holly's inopportune visit

the night before, Marilyn found herself wishing that her sister had buzzed for entrance just thirty seconds later. Those thirty seconds would have made the difference between still carrying around the burden of a lie—a burden, she thought hopelessly, that was getting heavier hour by hour—and having everything straight between her and the man she loved. Three times today she'd screwed her courage up to tell him, and three times something had happened to derail her intentions—Jim and Dan had dropped by to see how she was, her mother had phoned from Boston, Con had decided she looked pale and had hustled her out of the apartment for a few hours of shopping and a leisurely ramble around Denver's eclectic and offbeat Larimer Square.

Tonight, she told herself desperately. *No matter how late we get in, no matter how it turns out with Tony, tonight I'm going to tell him that whatever erroneous medical information he's received about his ability to father children, the baby inside me is his. And after he gets over being furious that I've kept this from him so long, he's going to be delirious with joy.*

Except right now it was important she keep her secret just a little longer. Right now Con didn't need anything that would take the edge off his upcoming confrontation with Tony Corso. She raised her eyes to his.

''I'm not trying to distract you from anything. I'm just nervous, Con.'' That much was true at least, she thought guiltily. ''As far as I'm concerned, with Holly's reaction to my question last night, the stakes just got a whole lot higher. Like I said, what if Tony's decided to keep his son for himself?''

Con's gaze remained narrowed a second longer, as if her explanation still rang slightly false to him. Then he sighed, and sat back in his chair. ''It's the Silver Rapids flu thing, *cher'*. If he knew Holly was carrying his child, how could he have arranged for you to take her there the day the virus was released? I just can't—''

"Mr. Ducharme, sir?" Henri was at Con's elbow. "The game you're signed up for will be starting any minute. The gentleman we discussed is already there, along with a few of the other players."

"Thanks." Con's voice was level. "And Henri—I'll be drinking bourbon on the rocks during the game. Inform the bar staff that cola with dash of bitters looks just like bourbon in a glass, and tell them that's what I expect them to serve me, no matter what my order is."

"Je comprends, monsieur." The waiter's dark gaze sharpened as he lapsed into his native French. *"Bonne chance."*

Con grinned. "Good luck? I was born with it, Henri," he drawled. "Just like you were born on the bayou, not in Paris."

Startled, Marilyn looked up in time to see first disconcertion, then chagrin, chase across the other man's features. Looking around, he bent to their table.

"You called it, Cap—Cajun through and through and proud of it. But French goes with waiter like Zataraines goes with hot sauce, right?" His grin was accompanied by a slow wink. "You don't need my luck, how 'bout takin' a li'l bit of Louisiana into that poker game with you? *Laissez les bons temps rouler,* Ducharme."

"Laissez les bons temps rouler," Con repeated with a slow smile as he pushed back his chair and got lazily to his feet. "Yeah, I'll go along with that."

"Care to translate?" Marilyn asked tartly as they made their unhurried progress through the lounge.

"Translate?" Con looked blank for a moment, and then gave a low laugh. Lightly grasping her by the elbow as they entered a plushly carpeted hall, he nodded toward a discreet sign above a gold-handled set of double doors and steered her toward it. He pushed open the doors and stood aside to allow her to enter.

"*Laissez les bons temps rouler* means let the good times roll, *cher'*. Down home we say that before a party or a fight." His smile tightened, and he narrowed his gaze on a man standing by the other side of the room, highball glass in hand and a cowed-looking blonde by his side. "And me, I think I'm spoiling for a good fight," he said under his breath. "There's Corso. He hasn't spotted us yet."

Marilyn followed his glance reluctantly and almost immediately looked away again. Why was *she* suddenly so nervous? she wondered. She wasn't going to be the one sitting at a poker table for the next few hours, trying to read what lay behind the closed expression and emotionless eyes of a man who was almost certainly implicated in a proposed scheme to unleash a biological weapon on innocent people.

"How 'bout we go over and introduce ourselves, sugar?" Con's flatly voiced suggestion broke into her thoughts. "It's never too early to get the other guy off-balance, I say."

With its crimson and gold wallpaper, dark carpeting and cut-velvet upholstery, the Red Room's decor was obviously meant to convey a sense of opulence, she realized as, with Con's hand lightly on her back, they made their way through the scattered knots of players and their guests. To her the room and its furnishings felt heavy and oppressive, the mood undoubtedly exacerbated by the unusual lighting setup. Gold sconces set at intervals along the walls gave off a weak and unpleasantly sallow light, but in the middle of the ceiling a massive fixture, suspended on chains, shed a cold and shadowless illumination on the round, felt-covered table below.

· The shiver that ran suddenly through her had nothing to do with the temperature. She glanced at Con, knowing he couldn't have failed to feel the tremor and expecting him to comment on it, but his gaze was on a young man standing a few feet away.

"Dude Walker." Finally Con had realized she was looking at him. He spoke out of the side of his mouth, his eyes again scanning the room. "M.I.T. grad, mathematical genius, a rounder like I used to be."

"What's a rounder?" It was a little annoying to hold a conversation with someone whose attention was so obviously elsewhere, Marilyn thought.

He frowned. "What? Oh. A guy who makes his living playing poker, *cher'*. On the other hand—" he inclined his head unobtrusively toward a fleshy, balding man already sitting at the table "—there's someone who stopped worrying about making a living a couple hundred million ago. Sandoval Malaga, once a gunrunner, now a European business tycoon who can't say no to a deck of cards. Don't matter if it's Texas hold-em or Go Fish, he plays like he's spilling his blood on the table instead of chips."

"I don't get it." Marilyn blinked. "Are you telling me you've played with everyone here in this room, Con?"

"All except for Corso," he answered distractedly. "High-stakes poker's a pretty small world, and although I don't play for a living anymore I keep my hand in."

"High-stakes," she repeated. "How high?"

"This game?" He exchanged nods with a leathery-faced man Marilyn recognized as being one of the bolo-wearers from the lounge. "Minimum buy-in's twenty-five grand. My personal opinion is that before the night's over young Walker's going to lose that fancy condo in Aspen he bought a few months ago. But then again, maybe I'll be the one who signs over a deed when the last hand's played. Well, I'll be damned."

Raising his brows, Con gave an almost inaudible whistle. "See that gray-haired woman in the glasses over there? She's Molly Otis, one of the best—"

"Twenty-five grand? Just to get into the game?" Marilyn had stopped dead. Now she pulled sharply enough on his jacket sleeve to get his full attention. "Are you *kidding,* Con? Where are you going to get—"

She looked around and lowered her voice to an appalled whisper. "Where are you going to find that kind of money? Come on, let's get out of here." Again she tugged at his sleeve, this time frantically. "We can phone Colleen Wellesley, alert her to the fact that Tony's here. Colorado Confidential will just have to come up with some other plan to get the information we need out of—"

"Firstly, *cher',* the membership fees here include a substantial purchase of house chips that can't drop below a certain minimum amount, and secondly, the last time I walked into a game with no more than a set of steel ones and not enough front money I was thirteen years old. When the other players found out they took me to a back alleyway and read me from the book, chapter and verse. I didn't look too pretty for a few weeks after." He smiled briefly. "I don't walk into games I can't afford to play. Luckily for me, there aren't too many games out of my price range these days."

"I don't—" Marilyn began, but he didn't let her finish.

"I'm filthy rich, *cher'*. I got an inheritance from a great-uncle and the rest I made myself during my serious playing days."

"Long time no see, Marilyn."

Suddenly Tony Corso was standing in front of them. Without looking at his blond companion he handed her the glass he'd been holding and tipped his head to one side.

"There's something different about you. No, don't tell me, let me guess—new hairdo? Different lipstick shade? Nah, that's not it."

"Hello, Tony."

Even in her ice-queen prime she couldn't have done better, Marilyn thought gratefully. Her voice was steady, her tone frigid. With cold eyes she appraised the man she'd once dated.

He wasn't physically unattractive. About her age and height—she hadn't worn heels when she'd gone out with him, she remembered—he was compactly and stockily built, although his suits were expertly cut to camouflage the slight softness around his belly. It was a telltale sign of his vanity, as were the manicured cuticles and buffed nails on his fingers.

Her fragile composure fled. The last time she'd seen Tony Corso one of his fastidiously manicured hands had struck her across her face, Marilyn recalled leadenly. It had been his reaction to her request that he leave her apartment after he'd tried to turn what was supposed to have been a good night kiss into a wrestling match on her sofa. Only the fact that Jim and Dan had knocked at her door as Tony had been drawing back his hand for a second vicious slap had put an end to the incident.

"Bun in the oven?" The crudeness of his words seemed even more out of place in such a setting. "Yeah, that's what's changed. And you used to have such a good figure—''

''Tony Corso? Con Ducharme.'' Stepping forward, Con held out his hand, and automatically the other man grasped it. ''I hear you're the one we have to thank for setting up this game. Good group of players, wouldn't you say?''

Marilyn heard a strange whistling sound coming from Tony's half-open mouth. Her gaze sharpened on him, and she saw that his eyes had widened in pain and there was an ashy undertone to his skin. Looking down, she saw Con's handshake tighten, saw those manicured fingers slowly start to turn purple.

''Texas hold-em. Cadillac of poker games, as they say,'' Con noted blandly, still crushing Corso's hand. ''Well, I won't keep you, but Marilyn's told me so much about you I just had to shake your hand. Come on, *cher'*, let's get you settled with the rest of the guests before I take my place at the table.''

His smile still in place, with a final cruel squeeze Con released Tony's hand. Stepping back, he started to walk away, but then he turned back to face the mobster once again.

''You don't know it yet, but this is how it's gon' play out, Corso,'' he said, his tone so low that only the man he was speaking to and Marilyn could catch what he was saying.

''Jasper, there—'' he glanced at the bolo-tied man ''—he'll drop out first, probably about three hours into the game. Not long after, Molly's going to fold. The cards just aren't going to be runnin' her way tonight, for some reason. Young Walker's going to hang on longer than Sandoval, but sooner or later it's just gonna be you and me. And at some point after that you're going to realize you've gone way over your limit.''

''What the *hell* are you talking about?'' Some of the color had seeped back into Tony's face. Behind him the blonde flinched at the fury in his voice. Con shrugged, and Marilyn saw the flash of silver appearing and disappearing between his fingers.

''Just telling you your fortune, Corso. Reading your cards. Like I was saying, you're going to ask me if I'll take your marker, and I'm going to turn you down. That's when the stakes are going to get interesting…because even though by then I'll have taken all your money, you'll still have something I want.''

Some of the outrage left Tony's expression. He gave a sharp bark of laughter. ''I get you now. Well, buddy, if it comes to that it won't be the first time I've run out of glimmer near the end of a game and had to put Crystal up for collateral. Maybe we can swing a trade—you take her and I'll take—''

''You don't want to finish that sentence, Corso.'' Con's tone was flat with menace. ''And I'm not talking about the lady, although if she decides she wants to walk away from you after tonight me and Mar'lyn would be pleased to help her arrange it. It's your uncle you're going to hand over. If you lose, you tell me where I can find DeMarco.''

''Helio?'' Watching him closely, Marilyn was sure she saw fear flash through Tony's startled gaze. ''What makes you think I know where to find him? And what do you want with—''

He stopped. His eyes narrowed. ''You're the Marshall, dammit. You're Con—''

''Ducharme,'' Con said tonelessly. ''If you want to go through the introduction and handshake thing all over again I'd be glad to oblige, Corso. But I don't think that's necessary, do you?''

Tony's right hand was already tucked safely away in his pocket. ''No, that's not necessary, Ducharme,'' he said slowly. ''But tell me something. If everything turns out the way you say—'' his lips twisted in a disbelieving smile ''—and before we play that last hand I put up what I know of my uncle's whereabouts, what's your stake going to be? What are you willing to risk on that final river card?''

She didn't need to understand the slang to realize what he was saying, Marilyn thought uneasily. Tony was accepting Con's challenge—and throwing down one of his own. An indefinable feeling of dread suddenly rolled over her like a fog, and when she looked fearfully at Con she saw there was no expression in those emerald-green eyes at all.

He shifted. Her hand fell away from his sleeve, but he didn't seem to notice.

''What am I willing to risk?'' he said softly. ''To get DeMarco, I'm willing to risk everything, Corso. If you lose you hand him over to me, and if I lose…''

The Con Ducharme who'd held her in his arms last night was gone. In his place was the gambler she'd seen once or twice before, the man who was willing to pledge everything he held dear on the turn of a card. That man gave Tony a thin smile.

''If at any point in the game I lose, you'll never see or hear from me again, Corso. I'll turn my back on this city and everything in it forever.''

Chapter Thirteen

"I'm dusted, boys." The young man Con had called Dude Walker grinned crookedly and pushed his chair away from the poker table. "Anyone spot me ten for a cab ride?"

"In your jacket pocket."

Already shuffling a newly opened pack of cards, Con didn't raise his eyes from the table as he spoke. Walker unslung his jacket from the back of his chair, partially withdrew a sheaf of bills from its breast pocket, and shot Con a confused look.

"When'd you put this here?"

Con looked up as if he was surprised to see the younger man still in the room. "During the break three hours ago."

"But three hours ago I was still on fire. How did you—" Walker stared at Con with rueful respect. "This one's been a berry patch for you right from the start, hasn't it?" He shook his head. "Think I'll ask the cabbie to drop me off at an old folks' home, maybe see if I can sit in on a game of penny a point pinochle. I was out of my league here tonight."

She might not know anything about poker, Marilyn thought dully, but she knew enough to realize that Wal-

ker was right. He *had* been out of his league, as had the
others who had one by one dropped out over the past—
with little interest she checked the diamond-studded face
of her watch—over the past five hours.

They'd left in the order Con had predicted. So far
everything had gone as he'd predicted. And none of that
took away any of the pain she'd felt when he'd made
his deal with Corso.

*"I'll turn my back on this city and everything in it
forever..."* Coming from any other man that bet would
have been recklessly dangerous, but coming from Con
it was coldly arrogant. He had no doubt about the even-
tual outcome of this game, and when she'd tried to con-
front him during the break he hadn't seemed to realize
what he'd done.

"Hell, *cher'*, he needed to hear something extravagant," he'd said with a distracted frown. "What does it
matter what I said to reel him in?"

Even while he'd been talking with her his gaze had
flicked from Sandoval Malaga to Walker. It had narrowed with interest as the former arm's dealer had
downed a stiff drink and then signaled the circulating
waiter for another, and had lingered on Walker as the
younger man had rolled his shoulders and rubbed the
back of his neck like a fighter who was wearying. Finally
he'd allowed himself a veiled glance in the direction of
Tony, standing with a silent Crystal. Marilyn had been
close enough to see the flicker of satisfaction in Con's
eyes.

"DeMarco's a dead man, heart," he murmured. Despite the endearment, it seemed to her that he was talking
to himself. "He doesn't even know it yet, but I've won.
I always knew the only way to bring that bastard down

was to go after him myself, despite what Wellesley and Longbottom said.''

The darkness had won, Marilyn thought now. Con Ducharme might believe he had, but in reality he'd lost everything that should have mattered to him. She'd been right two nights ago—against his hatred of DeMarco, she didn't stand a chance. And whether another Helio DeMarco came along in the future or not, she would never feel secure in Con's love again.

''Just a minute, Ducharme.''

The few remaining nonplayers in the room, including the older man with the bolo tie Con had called Jasper, had taken advantage of the brief interval while Con had been shuffling the cards to exchange low-toned conversation with each other. Tony's curt interjection drew everyone's immediate attention to the table and the last two men sitting there.

''Steward, get us another deck.'' Tony kept his gaze on Con. ''Ducharme, I'd feel a whole lot better if I was the dealer for this final game. You got a problem with that?''

''I've got a problem with you implying I'm a mechanic, Corso.'' Con's voice was toneless. ''You know how it works in hold-em. Dealer keeps changing from player to player, moving round the table. It's just the luck of the draw that it's my turn again.''

''You with Burke, sweetheart?''

Marilyn looked up in confusion as Jasper McMurtry, his leathery features crinkled in concern, sat down beside her. Why didn't anyone seem to speak English in this game? she wondered edgily. Berry patch, burke, mechanic…some of them she'd managed to figure out, but most of the slang was just downright baffling.

"I'm with Con." She frowned. "Did Corso just accuse him of cheating? What's a mechanic?"

"A player who shades when he's the dealer." McMurtry stroked his shaggy moustache with a liver-spotted hand. "In other words, yeah, honey, that little prick just called your man a cheat. When I used to play the Panhandle circuit back in the old days that kind of accusation could only end in gunplay. But Con's got alligator blood."

He chuckled at the flash of irritation that crossed her features. "Cool under pressure, like all the legendary players."

"But if it means so much to you, Tone, I'll pasadena this time." Con's drawl held a hint of laughter. "Carl, hand my friend another railroad bible, will you?"

"What'd I tell you, honey? Cool as a cucumber." Jasper's watery blue eyes were lit with amusement. "Pasadena means pass. He's letting Corso deal. Railroad bible, that's a deck of cards."

"It's not just the lingo, I don't have a clue how the game itself works, or what makes one player better than another." Marilyn bit her lip. "Is—is Tony on Con's level? Could he win?"

"No, he's not—and sure, he could." The old man smiled at her. "Rank amateurs win against sharps in individual games all the time. But skill eventually beats out dumb luck." He nodded toward the table. "Okay, each player's got his two cards now, honey. Since Tony dealt, your man bets first." Watery blue eyes blinked. Marilyn looked anxiously at him.

"What's the matter? Con bet a hundred and seventy-five dollars just now, right?"

"A hundred and seventy-five thousand," Jasper muttered. "I'm glad I got out when I did."

"I'll see your one seventy-five and raise you five hundred."

Was she imagining it, or had she heard a slight hoarseness in Tony's voice? Despite everything, Marilyn found herself getting caught up in the tension all around her.

"Okay, those three cards that just got dealt in the middle of the table are the flop," Jasper said, quietly enough that only she could hear. "Any player can use them to make the best possible hand. After the next round, another card goes in the middle. It's called the turn. Another round again, and then the river card gets dealt out. Fortunes are won and lost on the river card, honey."

Some of her nervousness must have communicated itself to him, because he shot her a keen glance and patted her arm reassuringly. "But you know what? When you come right down to it, it's only money. Like they say, if you can't walk away with the girl, the gold watch and everything, choose the girl and you'll never regret it. There's a heap more important things in this old world than winning a damn poker game."

He raised bushy brows at her. "The way it is between two people in love, for instance. And the babies that come out of that love. Based on that, you're the richest person in this room, darlin', and don't you ever think different."

She *was* the richest person in this room, Marilyn thought, giving the old man a shaky smile before turning a tear-blinded gaze back to the table. Another hand was dealt, but she was no longer watching the action. She'd lost Con—lost him to the driving determination he had to exact vengeance on an evil man at whatever cost to his own soul—but she still had his baby inside her, safe by her heart.

He would never know that.

It's not only that you gambled with what you and I had, Con, she thought hopelessly, *and with what we could have had together. It's that you've allowed Sky's fate to hinge on a—a game. If you can do that, how can I ever trust the life of our own child to you?*

"Hell, let's let the dogs out, Corso. I'm putting it all in. That's one seven, by my calculations." Shoving the still-impressive pile of chips left in front of him to the center of the table, Con leaned back, one shirtsleeved arm draped lazily over his chair, his cards hidden in the palm of his other hand.

One seven. That was—

"One point seven mil." Under his moustache, Jasper pursed his lips. "Corso can't call that, let alone raise."

Oh, yes, he can, Marilyn thought sickly. *And he's going to. But not with money.*

"Seems you saw this moment coming all night long, Ducharme." Tony shook his head almost admiringly. "You know I'm down to the felt. I should have come into this with deeper pockets, but I guess I just didn't know what I was up against. That other deal still on the table?"

"I never welsh on a bet, Corso." A corner of Con's mouth lifted, but his eyes remained coldly appraising. "F'sure, the deal's still on. You takin' me up on it?"

Beside Marilyn, Jasper McMurtry frowned. "Don't ask me what they're doing now, hon. As far as I know, those two ain't playing poker anymore. Con isn't, anyway."

"You're right, he isn't." She heard the harsh rasp in her own voice and was surprised she was able to speak at all. "He's playing God. And I think Tony was counting on that."

The earlier signs of agitation Corso had revealed, slight as they'd been, had now completely vanished. A broad smile appeared on his face, and he nodded. "Helio's whereabouts if I lose. You drop this whole thing and walk away if I win. I'm raising you to that, Ducharme."

"And I'm matching you. Cards on the table time, Corso." Negligently Con dropped his cards face up on the green felt surface. "Ace and a nine."

Tony did the same, his grin widening. "Ace and a queen. That gives me what? About a seventy percent chance of beating you?"

"Seventy-one." Con's expression was unreadable. "But we've still got five cards to go."

"He's turning over the flop—those first three cards that got dealt in the middle," Jasper said worriedly. By now he was standing, as were the rest of the nonplayers. Slowly Marilyn got to her feet beside the old man.

"A deuce, a king…and a four. That's not good, honey. That just helps Tony." Jasper scrubbed his hand across his mouth. "Let's have a look at the turn card. Uh-oh."

"That's a king, isn't it?" She hardly noticed she was clutching Jasper's arm until he laid a big hand over hers.

"Well, Ducharme, I hope you've got your bags packed." Tony spread his cards expansively. "With the turn I've got two kings. I don't see you beating that anytime soon."

"I didn't hear the fat lady sing, Tone. That means it's not over yet."

Although his voice was even, for the first time since he'd sat down at the table Marilyn knew Con was shaken. At the side of that tanned throat she saw a pulse beating. He reached forward, but before he could turn over the river card he was touching Tony's hand shot out to grab his wrist.

"Let a third party do it," he commanded. "I just don't trust you, Ducharme."

"That's the second time you've called him a cheat. You either make an official complaint to the club, or retract what you just said." Stepping forward, Jasper turned a scowling face on Con's opponent. "Well, Corso?"

"Forget it, McMurtry." Con sounded suddenly weary. "If he doesn't trust me, he doesn't trust me. You turn the river card over for us."

McMurtry held his glare for a moment longer. Then, with a disgusted snort that lifted the trailing ends of his moustache, he quickly reached over and turned the card. He stood back.

"Hello, li'l darlin'," Con said softly. He plucked the card up, inserted it in with the others in front of him, and spread them for Corso to see. "A nine. That gives me two pair. And that beats your two kings, Tony. While I'm unpacking my bags, how about you let me know where I can locate—"

"You freakin' *cheated!*" Corso was up and on his feet so abruptly that his chair tipped backward. He lunged across the table at a still-sitting Con, his face distorted with rage, and only the quick action of two of the club stewards restrained him. "I don't know how you did it, damn you, but you rigged this game right from the start, you bastard!"

"Right from the start." Con sounded bored. "Yeah, they were all secretly working with me, Tone—Dude and Sandoval, Molly Otis and even Jasper here. Hell, I've seen a few sore losers in my time, Corso, but this is the first time anyone's come up with a conspiracy theory to explain—''

"The bet's off." Tony pointed a shaking finger at Con, the two stewards holding him back with difficulty. "The bet's off because this game wasn't straight. If you think I'm going to hand over my uncle's whereabouts to you just because I gave you my word, you're out of your mind."

"You know you're going to be blackballed from every club you ever try to walk into, don't you, Corso?" McMurtry, his face grim, confronted the other man. "Whatever the hell your deal was with Ducharme, pay up."

"Ducharme?" Tony laughed humorlessly. "That's not even his name, for God's sake. In my book, only a cheat needs to play under an alias. Or are you still insisting this was a straight-up game, *Burke?*"

As if through a haze Marilyn saw Con get to his feet. She saw his face darken, saw his eyes searching the cluster of onlookers, saw that emerald gaze seem to shatter into a thousand pieces as it met hers. She stumbled forward, and felt Jasper's grip on her arm as she swayed against the raised mahogany edge of the table.

"What's he saying, Con? What does he mean, your name's not Ducharme?" Without waiting for his answer, she whirled to face Tony. "Of course his name's Ducharme—Connor Ducharme! Don't you think I'd know if he was using an alias, for heaven's sake?"

"He's Conrad Burke." Tony stared at her, a disbelieving grin playing around his lips. "Poor, frigid Ice Queen—he didn't even give you the right first name, did he? Hell, babe, if I'd known that's the way you liked it I would have given you a phony identity myself. I probably would have gotten into your bed at least once, anyway.''

Appalled, Marilyn swung around. Con, his expression blank, met her stricken gaze.

''You never slept with him?'' He shook his head. ''I don't get it, *cher'*. Why would you tell me you had? And if he's not the father of your—''

As if he'd suddenly realized they weren't alone, he stepped toward her and took her arm in a firm grasp.

''We need to talk somewhere private,'' he rasped. ''Come on, let's—''

''Before you go, tell me, Burke.'' Tony rocked back on his heels, his hands in his pockets and his smile not reaching his eyes. ''What's the Ice Queen like when she melts? Did I miss out on anything—''

He never got to finish his question. With a muttered oath Con let go of her arm and wheeled around to face the other man. Even as his fist drew back Corso yanked Crystal in front of him as a shield.

Con checked his swing. His arm fell to his side.

''This isn't over between us, Corso,'' he said harshly. ''And the next time we meet I'll make damn sure you don't have a woman around to hide behind.''

It was strange, Marilyn thought disjointedly. Her legs still seemed to work—or at least she assumed they were working, because she could see shocked and curious faces blurring by and the double doors of the Red Room were getting closer. But she couldn't feel her feet at all. She couldn't feel any part of her. She realized they were in the hall only when Con spoke.

''Down here. I saw an empty meeting room on the way in.''

She supposed she could still call him Con. It just wasn't short for Connor, as she'd thought, but for Conrad. Somehow that name seemed vaguely familiar, although she couldn't think of any reason why it should be. Unless...

"No." She shook her head and gave him a bright smile. "I don't know any Conrad Burke, do I? I don't know you. For a minute there I thought I did, but I—"

He'd lied to her. He'd lied, and then he'd assured her he was telling the truth, and he'd kept on *lying*. He'd lied while he was making love with her, he'd lied while she'd poured out her heart to him, he'd looked deep into her eyes and he'd lied.

All at once the fog around her was driven away by a cold, clear anger. Everything jumped into sharp focus.

"We won't be disturbed here." Con ushered her ahead of him into the small meeting room. He closed the door behind them and turned to face her, his features etched with strain. "I want you to hear me out, *cher'*. I know what I did was unforgivable, but—"

"Unforgivable?" She stared at him. "Unforgivable's for standing someone up and making them worry that you've gotten into a car accident. What you did goes way beyond unforgivable, because what you did forces me into the position of having to ask you unthinkable questions." Her voice shook with fury. *"Who the hell are you?* Who's Connor Ducharme? Who's Conrad Bur—"

Her hands flew to her mouth. She could feel the blood draining from her face. A few feet away she saw a partially open door, and she spun around and ran toward it.

It was a bathroom, as she'd hoped. She made it to the toilet just in time, falling to her knees in front of it and retching dryly.

"You remember." As she raised her head, Con was there, a wet paper towel in his hands. He drew her to her feet and wiped her mouth, his gaze tortured. "You remember, don't you?"

"I was five. You were visiting your Aunt Celia and I was visiting Father. Your mother is Celia's sister." She moved away from him and pulled another towel from the dispenser. "You never were a stranger, were you? You knew who I was that first night at my office."

"That night at your office shouldn't have happened, *cher'*. I didn't mean for you to—"

"Don't call me that, Burke." Oblivious to his presence, Marilyn bent to the cold water tap and rinsed the taste of bile from her mouth. She straightened, and met his gaze in the small mirror above the sink. "No, really," she said conversationally. "You just don't have the right anymore. So why this insane deception? What was the point?"

"I wanted to better the odds." His reply was barely audible. "I wanted a chance with you, and I knew I wouldn't have one if you realized who I was. I knew it was a gamble, but I thought—"

"A gamble. Bettering the odds. Tell me, Con, was this all a game to you? Is *everything* a game?" They'd moved into the main room again, and she turned to him, her fists clenched. "But of course, it is, isn't it? Tonight was proof of that. You didn't even let the fact that a child's life hung in the balance stop you from making a criminally reckless bet with Tony—"

"That wasn't a bet. It was the nearest to a sure thing I could set up in the time I had." Con's jaw tightened. "Corso's conspiracy theory was right—they were all in on it, from the start right up until the end, when Jasper finessed the river card."

He rubbed his jaw. "Like I said, the world of high-stakes poker's pretty small, and those four there tonight have known me for years. Even Sandoval played along when he knew what it was about. Corso didn't have a snowball's chance in hell of walking away from that table a winner.''

"It was rigged, just like Tony said? And you didn't see fit to tell me that either?''

"Corso's a poker player. Not a great one, but an adequate one. I couldn't run the risk of him reading your reactions and wondering why you weren't as tense as you were supposed to be.'' Con took a step toward her. "It wasn't a game, it was part of the job I was brought here to do, Marilyn. Rightly or wrongly, I felt I needed to play a lone hand on this one.''

She shook her head. "I don't think so. You go ahead and tell yourself that for the rest of your life, if you have to, but that's not the way it was. The truth is, you came to Denver wanting two things—Helio DeMarco and Marilyn Langworthy. When you had to make a choice, part of you wanted DeMarco more.''

As suddenly as it had filled her, the anger left. In its place was an all-enveloping sadness. "And part of me knew that all along,'' she said softly. "You're a gambler. I'm not. I couldn't take the risk of telling you the baby inside me is yours.''

A muscle moved at the side of his jaw. "Whatever you're basing that on, you've got it wrong, heart. Your calculations have to be off by a week or two—''

"Try a year or two, Burke.'' Her tone brooked no argument. "I had a brief—a *very* brief—relationship in Boston about eighteen months ago. You've been the only man since. I don't care if a hundred doctors told you in the past that it's impossible for you to be a father—this baby's yours.''

She exhaled tightly. "If it was a childhood case of

the mumps, from what I've read it doesn't always totally eliminate your chances of having children. Sometimes it just lessens them. That has to be what happened in your—''

''It wasn't a childhood illness. That was another lie.'' His gaze was shuttered. ''Celia was married to a Dr. Edward Grace before she met and married your father. Teddy's passion was biological research, and during one of my visits with them he used me as a guinea pig to test a new vaccine he'd developed. I had a bad reaction to it, got very sick. That's what drove Celia to leave the marriage—she discovered what he'd done to me.''

''Your own uncle experimented on you?'' Horror washed over Marilyn, for the moment blotting out everything else. ''Dear God, Con—was the man mad?''

''Certifiable,'' he said simply. ''But he was also a brilliant scientist. His unethical practices were uncovered not long after that—I think Celia had something to do with blowing the whistle on him—and his credentials were revoked, but although no legitimate facility would employ him I've always suspected he ended up working for an employer with fewer scruples.''

''An employer like Helio DeMarco,'' Marilyn said in slow comprehension. ''That's why you hate him so, isn't it? That's why this is so personal for you. You see him as the kind of man who would employ someone like Teddy Grace—provide him with the money and the support to continue his evil research.''

Her eyes widened. ''You don't think—''

''That Teddy's actually working for DeMarco?'' Con shook his head. ''No. He's crazy, but even he wouldn't be insane enough to have continued operating in this country when there are plenty of corrupt governments in every corner of the world that would be glad to take him in and give him what he wants.''

Except maybe what Dr. Teddy really wants is right here in Colorado. Marilyn frowned as the stray notion drifted through her mind. It didn't make sense, she decided. Con was probably right, and Grace was living as the honored guest of some crackpot dictator with delusions of world domination. But none of that changed what she'd originally set out to tell him.

"What your uncle did to you all those years ago robbed you of the opportunity to live a whole life, Con," she said, her tone low. "Just not in the way you think. Get yourself tested again if you're still not convinced, but whatever the lingering effects of Teddy's research might have been in the past, they've been reversed."

She looked down at the noticeable curve of her pregnancy and attempted a smile. "Who knows, maybe more than reversed. I'm beginning to look like I'm carrying twins, for heaven's sake."

"A whole houseful of children, with a mama to go with them." Con's voice cracked. "I never wanted anything else. I never wanted anyone else but you, *cher'*. I know I hurt you, but if you'll only give me the chance I'll spend the rest of my life making it up to you."

He was everything she'd ever wanted, too, Marilyn thought as she met his desperate gaze. And that was why his answer to her next question was going to tear her in two.

"If I say yes, can we leave tonight?" She didn't allow the slightest tremor to enter her voice. "Catch the next flight out of Denver going to New Orleans, and leave all this behind?"

She made an impatient gesture. "Oh, I know you'll have to be debriefed by Colorado Confidential, but once you fill them in on what we've learned and hand the case back to Colleen Wellesley, we could be—''

"Hand the case back to ColCon?" A flicker of astonishment crossed his features. "The case against De-Marco? You don't understand, honey—this is *my* case. I'm bringing DeMarco in, whatever it—''

"Whatever it takes." She finished it for him, her smile crooked. "You know, Con, I met a very wise man tonight. He told me that fortunes could be won and lost when that last card was turned over."

"The river card." He nodded, those emerald and gold eyes she loved so much shadowed with incomprehension.

"The river card," Marilyn agreed softly. She stepped forward, pressed a light kiss to the side of his mouth, and stepped back, her own gaze suddenly swimming.

"You just turned over the river card, Con," she whispered unsteadily. "And you just lost me and the life we could have had together with our child."

Chapter Fourteen

Life wasn't well-scripted, Marilyn thought unhappily as she waited for Con to collect her wrap from the coat-check. Real life was filled with awkward silences, dreary inconveniences, farewell scenes cluttered by trivial but necessary delays.

It was three in the morning. When they'd driven to the club hours earlier they'd used Con's rental SUV, judging it a better choice than her small import to handle the slippery roads that were always a possibility during a Denver November. Short of calling a taxi to take her to the same building Con was heading for anyway, she needed a ride home.

So here she was, her makeup smeared from the tears she'd shed, waiting for Con while he in turn waited for a young woman to match up a coat-receipt to a coat.

The cloakroom racks were still full, in spite of the hour. This wasn't a world she was used to, Marilyn acknowledged. In this world people got a thrill out of throwing away money, gave too much importance to black and red painted symbols on rectangular pieces of stiff paper, couldn't tear themselves away from a round, felt-covered table even though it was only hours before dawn. Con had told her this wasn't his world anymore, but he certainly seemed at home in it. She couldn't help wondering if he might not return to it one day.

He'd tried to get her to change her mind. He'd stopped when she'd abandoned any attempt at reiterating her decision and had simply stood there in his arms, the silent tears slipping down her cheeks.

"Aw, don't cry, p'tite," he'd said hoarsely.

He'd pulled her to him, and she'd felt his hand roughly stroking her hair. She'd squeezed her eyes shut, her face pressed against his shirt, and heard him inhale.

"You don't know how many times I pictured you in New Awlins, heart. Saw you drinkin' chic'ry coffee and eatin' beignets in bed of a Sunday morning, saw you laughing and catchin' the doubloons they throw from the Mardi Gras floats, had a snapshot in my mind of you and me sittin' in a courtyard restaurant, you with a big pink flower tucked behind one ear."

She'd felt his lips brush the top of her head. He'd put her gently away from him. "You know what, *cher'?* I'm just going to tell myself that still might happen," he'd said softly. "I'm going to pretend like I didn't screw everything up between us. That all right with you?"

She hadn't been able to reply. He'd held her tear-blinded gaze for a long moment, his own eyes dark, and then he'd nodded as if she'd agreed.

"The manager's got something of mine in the safe." Marilyn blinked. Apology crossed Con's features as he held her coat for her. "The girl's gone to find him. It shouldn't take but a minute, hon."

"What do you need from the club's safe?" she asked listlessly. "Is it something you can pick up tomorrow? I—I'm tired, Con. I just want to leave."

It was true. She was bone-tired, and not all her exhaustion was emotional, Marilyn realized. Despite the iron supplements she took faithfully on Dr. Roblyn's orders, since her second trimester had begun she'd found herself needing a good ten hours of sleep every night. Right now her body was telling her it had had enough for one day—her back ached, her feet hurt and, as usual, she had to go to bathroom.

"I didn't want to wear my gun into the game." From the brevity of Con's explanation, she knew he hadn't wanted to bring the subject up. He went on with obvious reluctance. "I could have, I suppose, since I'm federal law. It just didn't seem like the greatest idea, so when we arrived I had it locked away for the evening."

She glanced down the hall past the bank of elevators. "I might as well use the ladies' room while you're waiting, then. I'll be back by the time you're finished up here."

He still didn't understand, she told herself a few moments later as she dried her hands under a stream of hot air. She could see it in his eyes, she could sense it from his actions—he still hadn't accepted that he couldn't somehow change the situation, couldn't walk out of this with the girl, the gold watch and everything, as Jasper had said. Con still thought that after he brought down DeMarco, he would be able to win back that life he'd told her he'd pictured them having. Seeing the fugitive hope in his eyes every time he glanced at her was tearing her apart.

"Mr. Ducharme's signing for his property in the manager's office." As she approached the coat-check, surprised to see no sign of him, the young woman behind the counter provided the explanation for his absence. "It's the open door just down the hall if you'd rather join him than wait here."

Marilyn turned indecisively, but the jingle of keys in

her coat pocket as she did decided her. "No, I think I'll take the elevator down to the parking garage and get the car warmed up. Let him know that's where he'll find me, would you?"

Tomorrow she would have to make it clear to him just how impossible it was for her to continue seeing him on the twenty-four-hour basis he felt she needed for protection, she thought as she entered the elevator. He'd mentioned Colleen Wellesley's Denver people—surely there would be no problem in having an agent from ICU assigned to her for as long as necessary.

At most, that would only be another six days, if their fears about DeMarco's desire to engineer a viral outbreak to sabotage Josh's chances were right. By Thanksgiving—Dear God, that was this coming weekend, Marilyn thought as the elevator doors slid open and she stepped out—everything might all be—

"You were in on it, weren't you, bitch?"

Her shocked scream was abruptly cut off as Tony Corso's forearm tightened brutally across her windpipe, his action nearly jerking her off her feet.

"Burke set me up and you were part of it, damn you! I thought I made it clear the last time I saw you that nobody plays me for a fool and gets away with it, but it looks like you need another lesson. *Move!"*

Even as Corso grunted out the furious command he released her. Marilyn stumbled, and before she could securely regain her balance she saw his hand blurring toward her.

She tried to dodge the blow. It caught her high on one cheekbone, with a heavy, smashing force that couldn't have come from his fist alone. She fell to her knees on the concrete floor.

Pain, like the jaws of some terrible beast, seemed to

take her in its jaws and crush violently down. The first wave rippled all through her body, and then a second, greater wave of pain seemed to race back until it was concentrated once more on the place where he'd hit her. Marilyn's hand flew to her cheekbone. It came away dotted with blood.

"Ever been pistol-whipped, Ice Queen?"

Tony's voice was thick with rage—rage, she noted fearfully, and a sickeningly obvious arousal. Her skin felt suddenly as if there were dozens of loathsome bugs crawling over it, and she fought against the nausea that rose in her.

"Please—" She gasped the entreaty out. "My baby. You can't want to do this to a pregnant woman, Ton—"

"Burke's unborn brat?" Corso reached down impatiently. He jerked her to her feet. "You don't think that's a freakin' bonus, as far as I'm concerned? My car's over there. You and I are going for a little joyride, Marilyn."

He shoved her in front of him, and this time she kept her balance. Tony jerked his head toward a corner of the garage and she turned her stumbling steps in that direction.

As soon as he got her into his car her and her baby's chances of survival would take a sharp downward turn, she thought in terror. She had to stall for time and pray that Con was already on his way down here.

"What—what does Helio intend to do with the virus you stole from M & G?" she asked shakily, risking a quick glance over her shoulder at him. She saw the flicker of disconcertion that passed over his fleshy features and pressed her advantage. "He's going to release it just before the election, isn't he? That's mass murder, for God's—"

"Shut up." Unlike his previous command, this one

held an edge of angry desperation. "There's nothing to prove I was responsible for the theft of that stock and even if there was, once I handed it over my part in this was finished. I don't know what it's going to be used for. I don't want to know."

"That defence isn't going to get you off at trial." They'd reached his car. Marilyn turned to face him, her back against the vehicle. "And they are going to catch you and put you on trial, Tony—don't you see that? You'll be considered an accessory to terrorism. The authorities will never stop looking for you."

"Then I'll just have to start covering my tracks as of now, won't I?"

She'd pushed him too far, Marilyn realized, dread slicing through her as she saw his face contort in fury and the gun in his hand start to come up. Her frantic gaze swung past him, hoping against hope to see—

"Con!"

Even as she saw him burst through the service door from the stairs near the elevator, gun in hand and his features so grimly carved they were almost unrecognizable, in front of her Tony spun around, his finger tightening on the trigger of his own gun.

"Get *down, ch*—"

As Marilyn fell to her knees the rest of Con's hoarse shout was obliterated by the explosion that echoed deafeningly through the underground garage—the *double* explosion, she realized a heart-stopping moment later. She saw Tony slam backward against his car in the very spot where she'd just been standing, saw the still-smoking gun fly from his hand to clatter across the concrete, saw but at first didn't fully comprehend the meaning of the red smear on the white paintwork of his vehicle as his body slid slowly and gracelessly sideways.

With shocking abruptness, he suddenly fell the last few feet onto the oil-stained concrete. Only then did she realize he was dead.

"*Cher'! Cher'*, are you hurt?" Con's arms were around her, his embrace crushing. Almost immediately he put her slightly away from him, and his strained eyes searched her face. Devastation shattered his gaze. "Your face, heart." His voice was a rasp. "He hit you, damn him. We've got to get you to the hosp—"

"So Tony won't be beating up on women anymore. I'm glad about that."

The toneless comment came from a woman standing a few feet away. As Con lifted Marilyn to her feet and moved so that the front of the white car blocked her view of Tony's lifeless body, Crystal gave her former companion one last glance.

"He was a sadistic bastard. I think he hated women." She shrugged emotionlessly. "Maybe because he saw them as a reminder that he wasn't fully a man, to his way of thinking, but all I care about is that I don't have to be afraid of him anymore."

"What do you mean?"

The blonde's shoulders lifted. "The son-of-a-bitch shot blanks, honey. He couldn't have kids. He saw that as being less than a man." Her laugh was bitter. "It didn't occur to him that hitting women was what made him that."

She walked away and Marilyn didn't stop her. She turned to Con in agitation. "That means he couldn't have been Sky's—"

"I nearly lost you." His interruption was harsh. "Dammit, *cher'*, I nearly got you killed."

His tone was sharp with self-accusation, but her attention was fixed on something else. Her eyes darkened in horror as she saw the stain of crimson on his shirt, half-hidden under his jacket.

"Con, you're bleeding!" She recalled the sound of the double explosion, and her voice rose. "He shot you, Con. How bad is it?" Her trembling fingers tried to push aside his jacket, but he caught her hand with his.

"Flesh wound," he said tightly. "It should have been straight through my heart, for allowing you to be put in danger tonight, *che*—"

He didn't complete the familiar endearment. His jaw clenched. At the back of his eyes Marilyn saw something flicker and die.

"Like you said, I don't have the right to call you that anymore," he said leadenly. "Maybe I never did. I'm calling Colleen Wellesley and telling her to send a body-guard from ICU over here immediately."

He released her hand and took a step away from her. "I came down here with my mind made up to walk away from this case like you wanted me to, heart." His smile was bereft. "You were right—I can't go after DeMarco and still hold on to you. But now I realize I'd rather lose you than live with the possibility he might come after you to revenge himself on me for Tony's death."

He reached out and touched her hair. His hand fell to his side.

"I let myself hope this wasn't the way the cards were going to play out, sugar," he said softly. "But I think I knew from the start I wouldn't walk away a winner from this one."

THE MORNING after Con had walked out of her life the bruise on her cheek had bloomed into an ugly saffron-and-purple swelling that had seemed to take up half of her face. Marilyn looked into the mirror. It had been four days now and the swelling had disappeared, as had most of the livid purple, although there was still a large, sallow mark where Tony had hit her with the butt of his gun.

She could touch her cheek now without flinching, but the pain in her heart was still as fresh as it had been that night. Today was the day she was going to do something about that.

If she could shake Lexy Kanin, the ICU agent assigned to watch over her, she told herself in frustration as she walked out of the bathroom.

"Nearly ready, Mair?"

Lexy was the type who shortened names. She was a hearty, husky young woman of about twenty-five, and although undoubtedly extremely qualified for her job with ICU, her personality was like one long fingernail-scratch down a blackboard, Marilyn thought tiredly. The woman alternately behaved as if Marilyn was a none-too-intelligent child who'd been entrusted into her care, or brightly expressed admiration for the fact that she'd risked pregnancy at her age.

"Just about." Marilyn stifled her annoyance as Lexy followed her into her bedroom. "I hope this doesn't seem terribly frivolous to you, but I have to get out of the apartment today," she went on, collecting her jacket from the bed and putting it on. It was a below hip-length black boucle, cut in a swing style and with roomy slash pockets. She'd chosen it last night as being the best suited for her mission today.

"An afternoon of window-shopping?" Lexy wrinkled her freckled nose. "I pretty much live in slacks and shirts myself, but I usually have a pretty good idea of what looks good on my friends. Who knows, I might just save you from walking out with something that doesn't suit you.''

She gave a jolly laugh. "Like those boots you're wearing," she pointed out kindly. "I guess they're in fashion right now, but how practical are they, with those teetery little heels?''

Marilyn counted to ten. "You're probably right," she said with assumed mildness when she trusted herself to speak. She slipped off the kitten-heeled Italian ankle boots, replacing them with a chunky pair of flat zip-ups she'd never liked. "Heavens, if you and I were in a foot-race I'd come off a pretty poor second wearing those, wouldn't I?''

She forced herself to add her own peel of laughter to Lexy's hearty amusement, but as they left the apartment and drove to the Tabor Center, she closed her ears to the other woman's steady stream of conversation, her mind racing.

He'd said he'd decided to walk away from the case. Recalling Con's words, her heart gave the same foolish little somersault of joy it had performed that night in the garage, and then began the same downward plunge it had taken at his following sentence.

"I'd rather lose you than live with the possibility he might come after you to revenge himself on me for Tony's death...."

None of her arguments had been able to sway him, Marilyn remembered unhappily—not her insistence that Colorado Confidential would eventually find DeMarco and put him behind bars, nor her desperate assertion that she would take every precaution, follow any rule he and ColCon might deem prudent to ensure a situation like the one that had just taken place with Tony could never happen again.

"You don't know him," Con had answered, his tone splintered. "I don't think Wellesley's crew even realize just how far he'll go to accomplish what he wants. Remember I told you he was like a gator?"

She'd nodded, and he'd gone on. "I saw one once that was said to have killed at least three men. It was the prime attraction in a little swampside private zoo some smart Cajun had rigged up next to his gas station. That gator's eyes had the same cold, dead look in them that DeMarco's have. If he has to bide his time for five years or ten years, he will, but one day he might decide to come after you, and I just can't let that happen."

She hadn't had a chance to tell him *her* greatest fear—that Helio's cold eyes would more likely be fixed on the man who had actually killed his nephew than the woman who'd been incidental to the occurrence. She'd lain awake for hours that night, coming up with and discarding a dozen insane schemes to bring Helio to justice without involving Con.

Her only hope had been that Colleen Wellesley would remove him from the case, but Lexy had dashed that possibility when she'd confided that the upcoming election had Colleen's manpower strained to the limit. Heartsick and fresh out of ideas, she'd been close to the breaking point when she had discovered the cell phone in her purse.

She'd realized immediately that it wasn't hers. It had taken a second's further puzzled thought to figure out that it had to have been Tony's, fallen from his jacket as he'd been shot and picked up in error by herself along with the spilled contents of her purse before she'd left the garage.

She'd set it aside without interest, intending to inform

Lexy about her discovery, but then an idea had struck her and she'd hurriedly grabbed the phone up again.

He hadn't been listed under "Helio" on the speed-dial feature, nor under "DeMarco" or even—by then she'd been clutching at straws—"uncle." But when in frustration she'd scanned every listing and found an un-identifiable number under the letter *X*, she'd known with a little chill of excitement that it had to be the one she wanted. Before her suddenly failing courage could desert her completely, her trembling fingers had punched in the number.

That conversation had been brief. The one she'd made immediately after had been longer, and at first more frus-trating.

Con had said that ninety-nine percent of the Denver police force was trustworthy, Marilyn recalled now as Lexy, still talking without seeming to require much in the way of a response from her, nosed the car into a parking slot on the upper level of the mall's garage. She'd been determined not to tell her story to one of the few who might be in DeMarco's pay, so she'd insisted on speaking with a higher-echelon officer. Only when she'd used the Langworthy name had she been trans-ferred to a man who'd impatiently identified himself as Captain Breen and crisply asked her what she wanted.

His impatience had dissipated with her first few sen-tences. His crispness had taken longer to fade.

"From the start we've been shouldered aside in this investigation by the feds," he'd grunted. "Corso's shooting was on our turf, and yet the U.S. Marshalls—the *Marshalls,* for God's sake—were on the crime scene by the time I got there. I'm gratified at least one member of the public has come to us for help, Ms. Langworthy."

His tone had become thoughtful. "Here's how I want

to set this up. You'll be fitted with a wire, naturally—that can be done just prior to your meet with DeMarco, and with it we can monitor the situation as it develops. If at any time we suspect there's any imminent risk to you, of course, we'll cut the operation short and get you out of there.''

Breen had been more than willing to agree with her stipulation that the Marshalls—Con in particular—not be notified. Marilyn had realized his ready agreement stemmed more from his already-stated grievance over jurisdiction than any real desire to go along with her wishes, but as long as there was no chance of Con learning of her plan and putting a stop to it she didn't care what Breen's motives were.

He'll find out eventually, she told herself as she and Lexy entered the newly renovated Tabor Center mall and headed for the escalators. *And he's going to be furious with me. But when he realizes that I did it for us—for our future together—he'll just have to see that it was all for the best.*

"I hope," she muttered worriedly, stepping off the escalator and glancing at her watch.

"You hope what?" Beside her Lexy's unplucked brows arched curiously.

"I hope there's a washroom nearby," Marilyn lied quickly. She gave the younger woman a rueful smile. "I guess you're beginning to know me well enough by now to realize that's never too far from my mind these days."

"Oh." Lexy looked away, but not before Marilyn saw dull red mottle her complexion. "Well, if you need to find one right away I suppose we should check the mall directory."

She'd been counting on the ICU agent's obvious embarrassment at anything remotely connected with the human plumbing system, Marilyn admitted to herself with a twinge of compunction. She had to give her bodyguard the slip to meet up with Breen. When they'd agreed that the Tabor mall, with its walk-through access to the hotel adjoining it, would serve as Marilyn's rendezvous with the officers assigned to provide her with the wire she was to wear, this plan had immediately presented itself to her. But even Lexy's shyness on the subject hadn't prevented her from taking up her post outside a public ladies' room on a previous outing. Something more was called for, Marilyn knew.

And that something more would be my acting skills, she thought nervously. *I'm no Meryl Streep but here goes, anyway.*

"No time for that." She injected a note of desperate urgency into her voice and began making a beeline for the nearest store. "I'll ask if I can use the facilities here."

She saw Lexy's flush turn a deeper red, and went on heartlessly. "If they try to tell me it's just for staff use I'm going to make a scene, darn it. I'm sure if I kick up enough of a fuss they'll give in."

"I'll wait here, Mair." The other woman cast a quickly professional eye at the glass storefront only feet away. "I'll be able to see you as soon as you come out."

There'd been a plan B, just in case Lexy had overcome her squeamishness enough to accompany her, Marilyn thought as she sped into the store. But since plan A had worked, now all she had to do was to put the second part of it into motion.

"Hi, Giselle." The chic dark-haired young saleswoman who was already approaching her smiled with pleasure and recognition—as well she might, Marilyn thought, since up until three months ago she'd been one of the boutique's best customers. "Giselle, I've got a problem."

"You need a dress for a function tonight?" Dark eyes looked dubiously at her figure. "I don't think I have anything—"

"No, I know Cavalli doesn't design maternity clothes, Giselle." Marilyn made a discreet gesture at the mall walkway where Lexy, arms folded and feet planted apart, was waiting like a security guard. "I've run into a friend of my half sister, Holly's, and the woman's the most crashing bore. She's ruining my shopping day, and she hasn't taken any of my hints that I don't want her company. There's a back passageway for store deliveries, isn't there?"

"Of course." Giselle's perfect nose wrinkled. "My God, she dresses like a lumberjack," she said in distaste. "Follow me."

By now Lexy would be wondering what was taking her so long, Marilyn thought a few minutes later as she sped down the softly carpeted hotel hallway, her heart pounding. But if she'd gauged the agent's reactions correctly, her ruse hadn't been discovered yet.

And by the time it is, I'll be in Room 507 with some of Denver's finest, getting fitted with a wire, she told herself shakily. *After that, all I have to do is call Helio on the cell phone once more and find out where he wants to meet me.*

Breen had assured her she would never be in any real danger. If he hadn't been able to promise her that, Marilyn acknowledged as she glanced up at the number of the hotel room she was passing and kept going, she would have contacted Colleen Wellesley through Lexy and handed the matter over to her, however regretfully. *And Colleen would have passed Helio's contact num-*

ber on to Con, she thought, *along with a warning to him not to attempt to play a lone hand but to use ColCon as backup. My Creole gentleman would have given her his most rakish grin, sworn up and down that he wouldn't dream of going after Helio alone, and all the while he would have been lying through his teeth.*

"You were born a gambler, Con," she said softly. "I didn't know until I met you that there were some things worth taking a risk on. Helio thinks I want money to keep my mouth shut about Tony's theft of the virus, and I'm going to get him to talk on tape just enough so that the authorities have grounds to hold him for questioning. After that it's up to Colleen and Colorado Confidential, and you and I can start living that life you told me about—coffee and beignets in bed, walking through the French Quarter together, long New Orleans nights spent in each other's arms. I've just got to play this one last card for us to have it all, Con, and then—"

She'd reached 507. She halted so abruptly she nearly lost her balance. With a suddenly trembling hand, she tapped quietly on the room's door, and almost immediately it opened.

"Captain Br—"

The greeting died in her throat as she met the eyes of the man standing in front of her. They were cold eyes, with a curiously flat, dead quality about them.

They were eyes that wouldn't look out of place just inches above the murky waters of a swamp, watching unblinkingly as its foolish prey moved into easy reach.

Marilyn's bones seemed to turn suddenly to ice. She'd just turned over the river card, she thought with sick dread. And Helio DeMarco had been underneath it all along.

Chapter Fifteen

He'd had it with Colorado Confidential, Con thought furiously as he strode into the Royal Flush, the Confidential agents the Wellesley woman had sent to bring him in following him like casino goons escorting a cheat to the manager's office. He'd been ready to make his move when they'd waylaid him as he was getting into his car and told him that he could either accompany them to ColCon headquarters without causing a fuss or in handcuffs, whatever his choice.

"Thanks, Ryan, Shawn." Turning from the long pine bar, Wellesley passed her glance over him without pause and smiled thinly at her two employees. "Did he give you any grief?"

"Not much." Shawn was the chatty one, Con had discovered on the drive from Denver to the ranch. The rugged blond man was over the moon about some Doctor Kelley Stanton and her little daughter, so Con had heard ad nauseum all the way. And Ryan wasn't much better, prosing about some long-lost love he'd just reunited with. "Not after we cuffed him, anyway."

"You'd better give me the keys to those cuffs before you leave, then." Again acting as if he was beneath her notice, Colleen approached the two men, her hand held out for the key Ryan produced from his pants pocket.

Con snorted, and went behind the bar. Lifting down a bottle of bourbon and selecting a squat tumbler from the collection of glassware on the counter, he poured himself a shot and tossed it back. He set the glass back down on the bar.

"Catch, Shawn."

Even as the handcuffs arced past her Colleen reached out and grabbed them. She fixed him with a flat stare, but her words were directed to the two men behind her.

"I'll take it from here, gentlemen." Her tone was steel. "Thanks again for bringing him in."

"Bringing me in," Con repeated as the Confidential agents left the room. "Like I'm a criminal. In case you forgot, Wellesley, I'm working on the same side you are, so what's this *merde* about bringing me in, dammit?" His voice took on an edge. "Do you know what you screwed up when you sent those two after me?"

"You're not working on my side, Burke."

She reached for the scotch she'd obviously just poured before he'd walked in. Con's gaze narrowed on the slight tremor in her fingers, and immediately Colleen set the glass down again.

"You're not working on anyone's side," she said. This time it was her voice that shook. "You're a maverick, a lone rider, a hired gun. I called you in here to tell you there's no place for a man like you in this organization. You're off the investigation into DeMarco, as of now."

He stared at her disbelievingly. "Are you out of your mind, *cher'?*" He gave a short laugh. "I'm your best bet—hell, your *only* bet when it comes to catching that bastard. And as a matter of fact, if your people hadn't interrupted me when they did, DeMarco would probably be in custody right now.''

''If my people hadn't taken you in when they did you'd be a dead man by now, dammit!'' As if her slender reserve of control had been finally depleted, Colleen slammed her palm sharply down on the surface of the bar. She went on, her voice rising. ''What the *hell* were you thinking, going after him by yourself like that? Do you realize he was aware of every move you made after you left the morgue and followed him this morning?''

Con's gaze narrowed. ''The hell you say.'' He shook his head. ''I don't buy it. I took every precaution, from the time I left that parking garage three nights ago and arranged with the coroner to pose as one of the morgue attendants, to when DeMarco showed up this morning to claim his nephew's body for burial.''

''Every precaution but one. Captain Jack Breen saw you talking with the coroner that night. And the good police captain's as dirty as they come,'' Colleen informed him flatly.

Con was more shaken than he was willing to admit. ''Looks like I owe you one, Wellesley.'' Out of habit he extracted the silver dollar from his waistcoat pocket. A moment later the coin was slipping familiarly through his fingers. He frowned. ''I should have informed you of my plans when I reported Corso's death. It won't happen again—''

''No, it won't.'' Wellesley raked a slim hand through her cropped hair. ''Like I said, this is the end of the line for you with Colorado Confidential, Burke. You're booked on a flight out of Denver this afternoon, going nonstop to your beloved Big Easy. You'll be listening to decent jazz and scaring up a card game on Canal Street by tonight.''

''Does Wiley know about this?'' The coin between his fingers slipped and he caught it before it fell from his hand.

For the first time since he'd walked in Colleen's hard gaze softened. ''Yeah, Wiley knows, Con,'' she said quietly. ''He was the one who recommended taking you off the case.''

She sighed. ''Remember when we first met I told you I didn't like tricky? I found out you pulled a fast one on us right from the start. We know about your relationship with Marilyn, Burke, and we know you were involved with her even before we asked you to keep an eye on her for us. She's carrying your child, isn't she?''

Con met her gaze. He felt a dull pain in his palm, and realized he was clenching the coin in his hand so tightly that the worn edges were pressing into his skin. He tried to relax his grip and found he couldn't.

''There's no way I should have been able to give her a baby,'' he said hoarsely. ''But yes, Marilyn's carrying our child. Now do you understand why you can't take me off this case, Wellesley? If you know her baby's father is the man who's made it his mission in life to bring down Helio DeMarco, make no mistake, DeMarco himself knows. And he won't hesitate to go after her.''

''That's one of the reasons why Wiley and I don't want you on this case anymore,'' Colleen said with a return of her earlier hardness. ''You know as well as we do that it's a recipe for disaster when an agent has a personal stake in an investigation.''

Con frowned. ''You said that's one of the reasons,'' he said dismissively. ''If that's all you've got, you're holding a pretty poor hand. With my knowledge and experience of DeMarco, I'd say I'm still playing the high cards here.''

Wellesley's mouth quirked up into a one-sided smile. She reached for the drink she'd set aside earlier, and downed the scotch in one gulp, her gaze over the rim of the glass never leaving his.

"You just demonstrated the other reason, Burke," she said evenly. "This isn't a poker game, with every man for himself. Colorado Confidential is a team, and you just can't bring yourself to be a team player, can you?"

She shrugged. "The election's in two days. If De-Marco plans to release the virus, it will be sometime before midnight tonight so the media has a full day to hammer home the connection between Josh Langworthy and the dozens of deaths we expect will occur. We're in a race against time here—we've alerted state officials to put extra security on public buildings and we've recommended that all small planes be grounded for the next twenty-four hours, especially those outfitted with crop-dusting apparatus, but those are just two possible ways DeMarco could disseminate the virus. Our only guarantee of averting what could be the most devastating biological attack America's ever known is to find him before he can put his plan into effect."

She shook her head. Watching her, Con thought he saw a flash of regret in her dark eyes. "And we still don't have a lead on Sky's kidnapping. We can't afford to gamble on this one, Burke," she said with finality. "And since you're a gambler, we can't risk having you in on it."

"What if I go after DeMarco without ColCon's blessing?" Con allowed an edge of anger into his question.

Colleen looked confused for a moment. Then her brow cleared. "ColCon. That would be your private name for my merry band of undercover cowpokes, I'm guessing." She gave him a tight smile. "Your plane leaves in two hours. If you aren't on it the Marshalls themselves have orders to bring you in.''

He liked to tell himself he knew enough to fold his cards and leave the table when he was beaten, Con thought. Truth was, he wasn't always that smart. But this was different. He could see it in the ex-cop's eyes. She would carry through with her threat if he tried to finesse this any further.

He knew with sudden certainty that even if ColCon…Colorado Confidential, he corrected himself wearily, managed to thwart DeMarco's plan in time, the man himself would sink out of sight.

There's only one way you gon' keep her safe, Cap, he told himself bleakly. *You have to make a clean break with her—never see her again, never contact her, never be there for your child. If DeMarco thinks she was only a passing fling, he won't see her as a way to get to you and he'll leave her alone.*

''Your two agents can give me a ride back to the city?'' At his query, he saw Colleen exhale, and he realized she'd been holding her breath. He managed a smile. ''Naw, *cher',* I ain't gon' cause you no more trouble,'' he said in his thickest drawl. Her answering smile was uncertain, and he went on in a more subdued tone. ''That's the truth. You don't have to worry about me on top of everything else, Wellesley. Give my best to Wiley when you see him, will you?''

When she didn't answer he turned to walk away. He'd gotten halfway to the door when she spoke.

''Burke.'' Con looked back at her, taking in the tense set of her mouth, the faint shadows beneath those dark eyes. She met his gaze steadily. ''You could have been the best Confidential agent of all, you know—good enough to have headed up your own organization. Wiley thought so, and even though I couldn't see it at first, now I know what he was talking about. I wish things had worked out differently.''

Something twisted inside him. He forced a tight grin. ''Hell, *cher',* what makes you think I would have wanted that? Besides…Big Easy Confidential? It just doesn't have the right ring to it, now, does it?''

He should have wished her luck with the case, Con thought as he strode out of the Royal Flush and crossed the gravel drive to the idling vehicle and the two agents waiting beside it. But Colleen Wellesley wasn't the type to count on luck, he supposed. She was methodical, motivated and a good leader of good people, no matter what he'd said in the past. And against Helio DeMarco, she was going to need all those qualities.

''That handcuff trick—how'd you work that, Burke?'' It was Shawn who posed the question, and Con lifted a quizzical eyebrow.

''Years of dealing off the bottom of the deck gives a man an edge, Cap,'' he said mildly. Even as he spoke he realized he was still holding his silver dollar in his hand, and he tossed it carelessly into the air.

''Dealing off the bottom. That's cheating.'' The agent scowled heavily.

Con sighed. The coin reached the top of its arc and began falling again. ''Yeah, I guess in Colorado that's cheat—''

''Burke! *Burke!''*

He spun around, the coin tumbling unheeded to the ground behind him. Colleen Wellesley, her face a tight mask, was running lightly down the verandah steps. Con's heart lurched in his chest.

''It's Marilyn, isn't it?'' he rasped. ''What's happened to her, Wellesley? *Tell* me, dammit!''

"She gave Kanin the slip." The brunette put her hand on his arm. "But that's not all, Con. Right after Lexy rang off I got another call, this one from a buddy of mine in the police department. Tom's one of the good ones. I trust him," she added.

Con shook off her hand. "Cut and deal, Wellesley," he grated. "What's happened to Marilyn?"

Her eyes darkened. "Tom says he walked in on a phone conversation Jack Breen was having with someone. Tom didn't hear much before Breen realized he wasn't alone and shut up, but he got the impression Breen had scammed some woman into thinking she was helping the police in a wire operation. Tom said Breen called the person he was talking to 'Lio'."

"Helio. But we don't know for sure that the woman he set up was Marilyn." Con heard desperation in his voice, and saw compassion in Colleen's gaze.

"Not for sure, no. But Breen described her as a mama-to-be, Burke. That *has* to be Marilyn."

An invisible knife slashed between Con's ribs. It hacked a bloody circle around his heart, pierced it, and drew it, still beating, from his body. He looked down at his chest and saw that none of that had happened.

It just felt like it had.

"I'm hauling in every available Confidential agent to look for Marilyn. I know you're going to want to go after her yourself, Burke. I'll inform both my men and the Marshalls Service that you're to be left strictly alone."

She started to turn back to the house, and Con found his voice. "No." The single word came out as a croak. He took a deep breath. "No, Wellesley, this isn't a god-damn poker game. I don't want to play a lone hand on this one. Tell me how Colorado Confidential can use me as part of the team.''

Dark eyes widened in disbelief at him. Then they narrowed. "How the hell do you think we can use you?" she said briskly. "You're the expert on Helio DeMarco, aren't you?"

Wellesley stood back. "You're heading up this operation, Burke. Shawn, Ryan, come join us in the meeting room. Burke, Colorado Confidential's going to be behind you all the way."

"I'M NOT A MONSTER, I'm a businessman, it's as simple as that. Your friend the Marshall has been bad for business lately, and losing the woman he loves and the child he fathered is going to show him he can't win against me."

Helio DeMarco snapped impatient fingers, and obediently the thin man standing at the hotel room's door looked up. "Go check the lobby," DeMarco ordered. "The doctor should have been here ten minutes ago. Probably the fool's forgotten who he's supposed to be asking for."

The thin man smiled. "Right away, Mr. Cheesman, sir." His smile turned dubious. "Boss, you sure you're going to be okay here with—"

"With a pregnant woman who's tied to a chair and gagged, to boot?" DeMarco finished dryly. "I think so, Simons. Go on, see if you can find Halid. We want to be out of Denver before—" He glanced at Marilyn, apparently thinking better of completing his sentence. "Just get Dr. Halid up here. We're running out of time."

As DeMarco's man slipped quietly from the room, behind the strip of duct tape that covered her mouth

Marilyn managed a frantic, guttural sound. The mobster glanced at her.

"That's not going to happen. You could swear to me on your baby's life you wouldn't scream and I still wouldn't believe you. We don't have anything to talk about anyway, Marilyn." He looked bored. "This isn't a movie. I'm not going to conveniently tie up all the loose ends of the mystery just in time for the hero to crash through that door and arrest me."

Even as he began to turn away, Marilyn forced another desperate grunt from the back of her throat. DeMarco's lips thinned.

"You're going to keep that up, aren't you?" He shrugged, the movement tight with irritation, and walked across the room to the television set half-hidden behind an entertainment armoire's louvered doors. Picking up the remote, impatiently he turned it on and selected the display feature, scanning the pay-per-view movies available. He punched in a channel number and tossed the remote aside.

A chilling scream filled the hotel room. Marilyn jumped, her movement immediately constrained by the tape binding her to the chair she was sitting in. Slanting her gaze toward the television, she saw a hockey-masked and knife-wielding figure slashing at a victim while the soundtrack rose to a terrifying crescendo.

DeMarco stood in front of her. With one quick pull he ripped the tape from her mouth. Tears jumped to her eyes at the sudden stinging pain.

"Why is a doctor coming here?" Despite the pain her words spilled forth frantically. "What is he going to do to me?"

Helio hesitated. Something flickered at the back of

those cold, dead eyes, and to her horror Marilyn realized that it was a flash of amusement.

"Dr. Halid's going to give you an injection that'll turn you into a modern-day Typhoid Mary," he said carelessly. "Then we're going to let you walk out of here…and by the time you make it to a hospital you'll have spread the rogue virus we developed from M & G's stock to half the population of Denver."

He shook his head, the amusement plainly visible now. "Not that getting to a hospital's going to save you or any of your victims. There isn't an antidote yet. It's going to take the Disease Control authorities weeks to come up with one, and the virus kills within hours."

A modern-day Typhoid Mary. The terror that sluiced through her at DeMarco's words was as cold and as vile as the runoff from a sewer. She would be the carrier, Marilyn thought in numb horror. She was to be the instrument of death for hundreds, maybe thousands of people. Long after she was dead, the name Langworthy would be remembered with revulsion and dread.

That had been Helio's plan all along, of course, she told herself dazedly. As trivial as the outcome of any election seemed beside the loss of so many innocent lives, that was what this was about—making sure Josh's bid for senator had no chance of succeeding, and that DeMarco's man Houghton was reelected. Everything else was peripheral as far as Helio was concerned.

Sky's abduction had been as she'd suspected, a smoke screen to divert Colorado Confidential's resources. Even DeMarco's desire to revenge himself on Con by killing her could have been more easily accomplished—it nearly had been, Marilyn acknowledged, with the sabotaging of the elevator in her building. Injecting her with the virus was obviously a last-minute and sadistic refinement of the original plan.

He might have chosen a homeless man, a child snatched from a playground, one of his own thugs. But when she'd unexpectedly contacted him on Tony's cell phone yesterday and then confided in a police captain who worked for him, she'd both set the trap and walked into it willingly.

She closed her eyes. Immediately she saw the man she loved, the man she would die loving, green eyes alight with wicked humor, dark hair falling across his forehead, those skilled gambler's hands moving over her body, bringing her to an ecstasy she'd never known was possible…

DeMarco had made one miscalculation, Marilyn thought dully, opening her eyes and staring at the well-dressed and well-groomed man with the soulless and reptilian gaze. It was the miscalculation that would eventually bring about his own death. Con's grief would consume him, yes. Helio was right about that. There would be nothing left of the man who'd been willing to turn away from the hatred he had for an enemy and choose instead to make a life with the woman he loved with all his heart. That man would be destroyed by her death and the loss of his unborn child.

But in his place would be the man she'd caught glimpses of once or twice—the man who'd stood over the body of a dead friend and sworn terrible vengeance, the man who was willing to gamble away his soul for the chance to bring down a killer.

Helio DeMarco would look into the eyes of that man one day. They would be the last sight his own eyes would behold before his life was extinguished. And the thought gave her no comfort at all.

A subdued knock sounded at the door. It opened, and the thin man called Simons entered, a smaller man with thinning dark hair right behind him, his manner more than nervous. He had to be the doctor, Marilyn thought fearfully. How could anyone who'd ever taken the Hippocratic oath be a willing party to an atrocity like the one Helio was planning?

"It was like you thought, boss." Simons looked disgusted. "I found him wandering around in the lobby, drawing the attention of every hotel security guard in the area."

"Please, Mr. DeMarco—I did not mean—" Clutching a leather satchel in front of him with both hands, the small man swallowed. "I did not mean to bring attention on myself. I could not remember the name you told me to ask for. I am a professional man, not a gangst—"

Again he floundered to a frightened stop. DeMarco turned away. "Maybe once you were a doctor, doctor. But with the experiments you performed in those camps your country's leader set up before the U.N. was called in, you're going to find it hard to get a licence to practice here without my help."

Sick comprehension flooded through Marilyn. She should have realized, she thought hopelessly. A man like Helio DeMarco would know where to find the kind of doctor who would have no qualms about infecting a pregnant woman, and through her, a whole city. Halid was a war criminal, as much a monster as the mobster himself.

"Of course, Mr. DeMarco. I meant no offence by my remark." Halid set his satchel on a nearby table. "This is the woman you want me to inject with—"

"With the virus, yes." DeMarco's tone was short. "And here's the virus itself. Be careful with that, doctor,'' he added swiftly as Halid took the small glass vial from him. ''If it breaks open we're all going to be walking around spreading death and destruction, not just Ms. Langworthy here.''

''Death and—''

''This is what he was like in the lobby, boss,'' Simons interjected, his glance at DeMarco sharp. ''How hard can it be to stick a freakin' needle into a vein? Junkies do it all the time. Why don't you let me take care of the doctor here, and then I'll inject the woman myself?''

''No, no!'' Already Halid was unlatching his bag. ''I will do it, no problem, Mr. DeMarco. The language is sometimes still confusing for me, that is all, and when the guards were watching me I was very nervous. When I am nervous I—''

''When you're nervous you talk too much,'' DeMarco said flatly. ''And having someone around who talks too much is dangerous in my line of work. If you don't want me to go along with Simon's suggestion, Doctor, you'll shut up right now. Get that syringe ready, and like I said, be careful.''

He exchanged a glance with the thin man. ''Stay here and make sure this goes off without any more screwups from our nervous friend. The virus takes a few seconds to reach the respiratory tract, so as long as you leave as soon as Halid completes his injection you don't run any risk of being infected by her yourself. I'll get the car from the parking garage and be waiting for you out front of the hotel. I don't like needles.''

''He's going to hunt you down. And then he's going to kill you.''

She hadn't bothered to speak before because there'd been no reason to speak, Marilyn thought. Nothing she could say would save her and her baby. Nothing she could say would prevent Helio's insanely evil plan from being implemented through her. So she hadn't pleaded and she hadn't begged…but she didn't want him to walk out of here believing he'd won.

"Burke?" DeMarco had his hand on the door. "I don't think so. This is going to finish him off. Maybe you don't know your man as well as you think you do."

"I know him like I know myself," Marilyn replied. "And that's how I can be so sure he's never going to rest until he kills you." She met his coldly unconcerned gaze. "Because if it was me who survived and Con who was dead by your hand, DeMarco, I'd do the same thing."

He blinked. Then he frowned, switching his attention to the thin man. "If you're not standing by the curb when I drive up I'm not waiting around," he said curtly. "Get this over with fast."

Marilyn closed her eyes. She could hear Halid and Simons exchanging terse remarks, and then the sharp smell of disinfectant bit at her nostrils. She didn't waste her time wondering at the irony of Halid using an alcohol swab on skin he intended to inject with poison.

Truth. Beauty. Love… She wasn't even sure if she'd said the words out loud, but they rang like silver chimes in her heart. "I had them all," she breathed softly to herself. "I fell in love with a gambler. We made a baby together. Together we won it all."

She felt a suddenly cool patch on the inside of her elbow, and knew Halid had just swabbed the injection site.

I love you, Con. And I love the baby we created. I wish you could have shown us both your beloved Big Easy…

The needle slid in. Her eyes flew reflexively open. She

saw Halid depress the syringe's plunger, saw the color-less contents rush past the markings on its barrel, saw Simons bring the silencer-fitted gun in his hand up—

"Federal Marshall! Put down your weapons, we're coming in!"

At the shouted command—*Con's* shouted command, Marilyn realized, her wild joy turning immediately to fear—everything happened at once. Simons swung his gun from the still-unsuspecting Halid's head toward the door crashing back on its hinges. Marilyn heard her own voice screaming out a warning to Con and those with him, but even as her terrified words left her lips she saw Con fire at Simons. The force of the bullet slammed the thin man off his feet, his own shot going wild, and be-fore his body had completed its arcing fall to the floor Con was racing toward Halid, his face an unrecognizable mask of fury.

The doctor's hands went instantly up in a gesture of surrender. The half-full syringe dropped and shattered at Con's feet.

"Oh, *no!*" Anguish shafted through her. "Con—get *away!* Everybody get away! Evacuate the hotel, shut down the venting system. For God's sake, Con—that's the *virus.* Helio's plan was for me to be the carrier!"

The roomful of people froze, all except for Con.

"We're getting you to a hospital, *cher'.*"

From somewhere he'd produced a jackknife and was already carefully slitting the duct tape that bound her ankles together. He cut through the tape strapping her left arm to the chair and moved to her right arm, where the puncture mark still showed red. Con looked into her face, his features taut with unbearable strain and his green eyes sheened with pain.

"I won't let this happen to you, heart," he rasped

desperately. "If I have to carry you there in my arms and stand over the goddamn doctors with a gun, I swear I'm not going to let you die. I *can't* lose you, *cher'*."

"Please, Con—*get away from me*." Marilyn felt her own eyes fill. She went on in a broken whisper. "You don't understand. There isn't an antidote. I'm already dead. But maybe if I'm quarantined here other lives might not be—"

"Excuse me." Halid let his hands drop. They shot back into the air as a slim woman with cropped dark hair stepped forward and leveled her gun at him.

"Con, if what Marilyn's saying is true, then she's right. We might still avert the outbreak by—"

"It was water." Halid stated. "Distilled water. Mr. Cheesman tells me to come here with my medical supplies and frighten this lady by giving her a needle. That is bad, yes. I know I have broken a law. But there is no harm done to her, so maybe I can go now, no problem?"

"Water?" Con's face darkened. He bent swiftly and picked up the barrel of the smashed syringe. "If it's water, then you won't mind tasting it," he said hoarsely. "Go on, you bastard—there's enough left in there to prove whether you're lying or not."

Halid shrugged. He tipped back his head and stuck out his tongue, upending the broken cylinder above it. A few drops of clear liquid fell into his mouth.

"Con, we can't take any chances." The brunette's tone was brittle. "Who knows, this man might like the idea of dying as a martyr as long as he takes as many innocent citizens with him as he can, or maybe DeMarco told him this stuff was harmless just to get his cooperation. Until we get it tested we have to assume it's the virus—"

"Simons was about to kill Halid just as you arrived,"

Marilyn interrupted. A tiny flame of hope flickered somewhere deep within her. "If he'd succeeded, Halid wouldn't have had the chance to tell us anything and we'd all still believe I was injected with the virus. So DeMarco *wanted* me—wanted the authorities—to assume exactly that."

"But what would be the point?" The brunette's brows drew together. "We'd find out sooner or later you weren't a carrier, and then—"

"And then it would be too late," Con said flatly. "Because while we were evacuating this area of the city and getting Marilyn into a biohazard quarantine, we wouldn't be trying to find out where DeMarco's really planning to disseminate the virus. Who's Cheesman?"

"DeMarco," Marilyn answered absently, her mind still racing. "It's the name he's registered under at the front desk. Con, I think Halid's telling the truth, but Colleen—" the brunette had to be Colleen Wellesley, she thought, "—Colleen's right. Everyone in this room has to be quarantined, just in case. The search can still go on for—"

She stopped. Her eyes met Con's uncomprehending ones.

"What is it, *cher'?*" His hands grasped hers. "What's the matter?"

"That's it." Her voice was unsteady, Marilyn noted dispassionately. "That's how he's planning to do it. I was just a smoke screen, the same way we always thought Sky's kidnapping was. It's the mainstay of Denver's water supply, Con—the last stand before Denver's drinking water reaches the city's treatment plants."

"Dear God." Colleen's face was ashen. "I think she's got it, Burke. It has to be where DeMarco's planning to release the virus."

He was from New Orleans, Marilyn thought shakily. Of course he didn't know what they were talking about.

"The Cheesman Reservoir on the South Platte River, Con," she said urgently. "It's about an hour southwest of the city. If Colorado Confidential moves fast, they can still prevent DeMarco's thugs from carrying out his plan."

"If I'm under arrest, Burke, I want an attorney."

Even before she saw Con stiffen, Marilyn realized who the harsh tones belonged to. Her startled gaze went past the knot of Confidential agents to the open doorway where a handcuffed man with cold, dead eyes was standing between Lexy Kanin and an agent she didn't recognize.

"We stopped him as he was leaving the parking garage, C.W.," Lexy said, addressing her remark to Colleen. "He gave us a phony name, but I recognized him from the photos you distributed. Say hello to Mr. Helio DeMarco."

Chapter Sixteen

"How does it feel, being the sister of the governor?"

Marilyn, Con's arm around her, looked swiftly over her shoulder as Colleen Wellesley came up behind them. She managed a smile at the brunette.

"It hasn't been twenty-four hours yet. I'm not sure it's really sunk in, even though Josh won by such an overwhelming majority." Her smile dimmed. "When Con and I phoned to congratulate him last night, Celia and Father invited us to Thanksgiving dinner today with the rest of the family. We would have loved to have gone, but it doesn't look as though we're going to make it."

She turned her eyes once more to the silent tableau being enacted behind the tempered-glass window in front of them, and as if by unspoken agreement Colleen did the same. Con, Marilyn realized as his arm tightened around her, hadn't taken his gaze from the scene in the first place.

The Royal Flush looked like a ranch. It *was* a ranch, as Con had told her when they'd arrived here two nights ago after Helio's capture and the last-minute thwarting of his plans to release a killer virus into the Cheesman Reservoir. An ex-employee of Denver's water board had been caught just moments before he'd been able to carry out his assigned task of cracking open the vial he'd received from a man who fit the description of the late Simons and dumping its contents into the city's water reserves.

Buried in the back pages of yesterday's *Denver Post,* Marilyn recalled, had been three news stories, seemingly unrelated. One had concerned the apprehension in a downtown hotel of a Dr. Halid, who had been charged with practicing medicine without a license and entering the country illegally. Hotel security were praised for alerting the authorities when they'd arrived to the suspicious actions of Halid, and providing them with the number of the room he was in.

The second story was briefer, reporting only that a certain Captain Breen of the local police had died of a gunshot wound apparently suffered when his weapon had accidentally discharged while he was cleaning it.

The third snippet of news Con had drawn her attention to had been the sketchiest of all—a vague line or two about a disgruntled water board ex-employee being arrested on suspicion of attempting to destroy property near the Cheesman Reservoir. None of the three stories had appeared on the television newscasts later, mainly because the election and Josh Langworthy's thrilling landslide victory over former governor Todd Houghton had taken precedence over everything else.

Maybe one day the public could be informed of the disaster that had been so narrowly averted, Colleen had gently warned Marilyn upon her arrival at the ranch two nights ago. But Colorado Confidential's effectiveness depended upon it remaining a shadowy, behind-the-scenes force for justice.

Which was why its headquarters was disguised behind

the facade of a real working ranch, Marilyn thought now, feeling the tension in Con's arm around her. Even the Royal Flush's basement had appeared to be a perfectly ordinary storage area until Colleen had pressed some hidden release on a dusty wine rack, revealing an entrance to a spacious and well-lit meeting room. Even more clandestine was the entry from the meeting room through what seemed to be a broom closet to the surveillance room they were presently in.

This was the nerve center of the whole operation, Colleen had informed her. All ranch access points were visible on the bank of videos that took up one wall, as was the Denver office of ICU. The computer system rivaled those of the federal authorities—and necessarily so, Marilyn had gleaned from the ex-cop's veiled references, since it could link to federal and state files.

But the video and computer systems, as state-of-the-art as they were, weren't what was holding the attention of the scattering of grim-faced agents, including Con and Colleen, at this moment—in fact, at almost any given moment during the past two days, Marilyn thought worriedly. Colorado Confidential's agents were watching through a room-length, one-way glass window as Helio DeMarco skillfully volleyed his latest interviewer's questions.

''What's her background?'' Con's question was abrupt, as was his nod toward the woman seated across the interview table from DeMarco in the glassed-off room.

Colleen exhaled tightly. ''Apart from being our new governor's fiancée, she was FBI. She was one of their best and we're lucky to have her. Don't let those brown-eyed blond good looks fool you, Burke—Fiona's a skilled interrogator.''

"And she's tired. How long has she been in there with him now? Four hours?" Con turned decisively from the window, his arm leaving Marilyn's shoulders. "Take her out. Send someone fresh in."

A gleam of silver flashed between the fingers of his left hand, and then somehow the coin was in his right. Marilyn realized from his preoccupied frown that the sleight-of-hand had been entirely unconscious. If Colleen hadn't spied the worn coin on the Royal Flush driveway this morning and returned it to Con, she thought wryly, she herself would have turned over every piece of gravel to find it. Restlessly passing it back and forth between his fingers had seemed to be the only way he'd been able to take the volatile edge off his tension during these past two days.

Well, not the only way, she admitted to herself as he and Colleen, the latter with a quick smile of apology to her, walked a few feet away from the other groups of agents and herself to carry on a low-voiced discussion. Although she suspected that Colorado Confidential wasn't restrained by the strictures of other law enforcement agencies, at Colleen's insistence DeMarco was given several breaks from his interrogation during the day and all questioning ceased at eleven o'clock in the evening, not to be resumed again until early morning. Any break for DeMarco was a break for Con—and for herself, from worrying about the man she loved.

Familiar heat touched her cheeks as the memories of their previous two nights of lovemaking replayed in her mind. Ensconced in the Royal Flush's grand guest room, and with the glow of an antique oil lamp on a nearby dresser casting softly mysterious shadows on their massive four-poster bed, Con had taken his sweet time about showing her just what those skillful gambler's hands of his could do.

And even if she would never be able to shuffle a deck of cards as well as he could, Marilyn thought happily, she'd returned the favor, teasing him with her mouth and her fingertips until his eyes had been clouded with passion and his drawled entreaties had been edged with desperate need. When they'd finally set all teasing aside and come together, it had seemed to her that for a time they'd left the shadowy bedroom behind, and had soared through the crystalline Colorado night like two shooting stars blazing a sparkling trail across the sky.

After they'd made love for the first time on their initial night at the Royal Flush, she'd fallen asleep in Con's arms. Coming drowsily half-awake just before dawn she'd felt an unfamiliar weight on her left ring finger and known without looking that Con was also awake and watching her. She'd slanted her sleepy gaze at him and seen his smile flash white in the semidarkness.

A heartbeat later her eyes had flown fully open. Even as she stretched her arm out toward the bedside table and the silk-shaded lamp sitting there, Con lazily reached across her and snapped it on.

"I've been carrying it around in my pocket for about a week, *cher',*" he'd said huskily. "There's a catch, though. A no-good New Awlins gambler comes with it, if you'll take him."

Well over four and a half carats, the pink diamond in its pink-gold and platinum setting seemed to glow like a rose-colored flame on her finger. Unable to speak for joy, she'd only been able to throw her arms around Con and drench his bare shoulder with tears of happiness.

"If you want us to be married in Boston or Denver, that's okay with me," he'd said into her hair. "But if you'd like, I know Tante Jasmine and *Maman* would adore shopping for a wedding dress with you."

"A New Orleans wedding," she'd said promptly, lifting her head from his shoulder. "Oh, Con, I want to be married in your city. That's where we're going to make our home together, so it seems only right. The Langworthys and the Van Burens will just have to fly down for the ceremony. But it better be soon or I'll have to settle for walking down the aisle in a white pup tent."

His palm had gently stroked her stomach, and he'd smiled. "F'true, you're gettin' pretty big there, mama," he'd murmured. "Can you guess how it makes me feel, knowing I gave you that child growing inside you?"

She'd looked up through her lashes at him. "Children, Con," she'd said with quiet happiness. "The doctor who checked me over when I was taken from the hotel to the hospital this afternoon was mainly concerned that I'd suffered no ill effects from Halid's injection. But when he'd given me a clean bill of health in that regard he advised I take Dr. Roblyn up on her suggestion of an ultrasound as soon as possible. He seemed to think I might be carrying twins."

"A whole houseful of children, and a mama to go with them." His tone had been uneven. In the subdued lamplight she'd seen pure joy light up those emerald eyes, before they'd just as suddenly darkened. "When I think of how close that bastard came to harming you—"

He hadn't finished his sentence. She'd known from the tense set of his jaw that he was trying to bring himself under control.

"But it was a ploy, Con," she'd ventured. "Evil as the man is, he had no intention of killing me—not with an injection of distilled water."

He'd flicked an uncomprehending glance at her. "Of

course he meant to kill you, *cher'*,'' he'd ground out. ''Not in that hotel room, no. But as a pregnant woman, your chances of surviving that virus once it entered your body through Denver's water supply would have been zero, and DeMarco knew that.''

A chill had run through her at his words, and she'd known instinctively that he was right. When Con had taken her tightly in his arms and they'd made love for the second time that first night, there'd been a quality of fierce desperation in their coupling, on her part as well as his.

It had been the same last night, she remembered now. Con had held her as if he was afraid to let her go, had kissed her as if she was in danger of being snatched from him, and when he'd cupped his palms gently on the curve of her belly, for just a second she'd seen a flash of bleak fear shadow the joy in his eyes.

With an effort she attempted to banish the vague uneasiness shadowing her mood, and focused her gaze on the slim, pant-suited blonde questioning DeMarco. Her future sister-in-law, a woman she hadn't exactly given a warm welcome to the family. Marilyn planned to rectify that as soon as this ordeal ended.

Colleen had mentioned that the process was being videotaped, but Marilyn was suddenly certain that the mobster's skillfully evasive answers would yield no inadvertent clues even if those seeking them replayed his performance a hundred times. In front of her was a small speaker with a volume control, and although Con had lowered it to inaudibility, preferring to concentrate on DeMarco's facial expressions and body language rather than his spoken words, on impulse she turned the volume up.

''...greatly in your favor if you cooperated with us in

finding little Sky,'' Fiona was saying evenly. ''You see that, don't you, Lio? We're of the belief that abducting a baby wasn't any part of your original plan anyway.''

''What original plan?'' DeMarco's cold eyes widened. ''As I've already told you, Agent Clark, I'm a simple businessman. It's ludicrous to think I could be connected in any way with the kidnapping of a child or any other crime. If you or your fellow agents have any proof to the contrary, I'd be interested in knowing what it is.''

''We have the statement of the woman your people were holding in that hotel room two days ago. She'll testify that you gave the order for Dr. Halid to inject her with what you implied was a deadly virus—the virus that you instead had arranged to be released into the city's water supply,'' the blonde riposted.

Not by the flicker of a muscle or a change in her tone was Fiona showing the frustration she must be feeling, Marilyn noted. But Con was right. Under her eyes were slight smudges of exhaustion, whereas DeMarco looked as if he were merely engaging in an unimportant conversation. His voice even held a hint of good-natured disbelief as he answered her.

''I wouldn't count too heavily on any possible future testimony that may never come to pass, Agent. Don't many witnesses recant their stories when they get on the stand, if indeed they're still available to give evidence when the time comes? And don't some pregnancies prove risky for both mother and child, especially when there's the added stress involved of testifying at trial?''

Even as Marilyn swayed in shock against the glass barrier, Con was beside her, his strong arms going immediately around her. She felt a tremor of violent emotion run through him, and knew he'd both heard De-

Marco's last words and had understood them for what they were.

"He just threatened the life of a witness, Wellesley," he said harshly. "He just threatened the life of the woman I *love,* dammit! Tell me again how you're going to justify releasing that bastard!"

"…a threat, Lio?" From the speaker came Fiona's voice, and this time Marilyn thought she heard a touch of shakiness in her tone.

"Please." DeMarco sounded aggrieved. "I asked you two questions about the trial process. And although I've willingly cooperated with the authorities up until now, even to the point of waiving my rights to have an attorney present during all this, I can't really afford to take any more time away from my businesses. Especially since I'm currently in the middle of negotiations for opening a New Orleans branch of my importing firm," he added carelessly.

"New Orleans?" At Helio's reference to the city, a white-faced Colleen swiftly turned the volume control off, but Marilyn barely noticed. "New Orleans, Con? He knows I'm listening, doesn't he? He's telling me I can't escape him!"

"He's said nothing we can use against him to hold him any longer, Burke." Colleen ran a trembling hand through her hair, her gaze anguished. "Colorado Confidential was given a pretty wide latitude in this interrogation by the powers that be, but we've reached the end of the line. We have to release him. We don't have a choice."

"He's going to try to kill my wife and unborn children. And you're telling me he gets to *walk?*" Con's voice was thick. "Send me in again, Wellesley. Give me one more chance to get something out of him."

"You were the first interrogator, dammit." Colleen shook her head. "You got less from him than anyone, since he refused to speak a word until we replaced you. This isn't my decision. We were given forty-eight hours to hold him, and DeMarco's well aware of that. Our time's—"

"He wants Burke to be the one who releases him."

Now that she was out of the interrogation room, the ordeal she'd just endured showed in every fatigued line of Fiona Clark's delicate figure. She passed a hand across her eyes. "It's part of his game-playing, I think. He wants to rub it in that we lost. I'm sorry, Colleen. I just couldn't crack the bastard."

"No one could, Fi." Colleen's lips thinned. "But I'm not about to allow him to gloat over one of my people. I'll take the release forms in and countersign them, Burke. Why don't you and Marilyn go upstairs and—"

"He was my collar. He's right, by the rules I should be the one who tells him he's free to go," Con said stonily. "If I send you in my place he'll know he got to me."

"I don't think that's such a wise—"

"Con knows DeMarco. If he says that monster will see his absence as a sign of weakness, then I believe him," Marilyn rasped. "And we can't let DeMarco think that, especially after the threats he's made against me. Let Con go in, Colleen. It—it's important that he does."

The brunette hesitated. Behind Colleen Con's eyes darkened as they met Marilyn's. For a long moment she held the gaze of the man she loved, her own steady and unwavering, and then she flicked her glance back to Colleen.

"Let Con go in," she said quietly. "It has to be this way."

"Fine." Wellesley exhaled tensely. "He's your collar like you say, so I can't stop you if you insist. But if it looks like you're about to lose it in there, Burke, I'm pulling you out and finishing up the paperwork myself. There's a hell of a lot of it," she muttered, thrusting a sheaf of forms at him.

He didn't immediately take them. "You're sure you're all right with this, heart?" His question was low. Marilyn's voice was just as low as she answered him.

"I'm sure. But be careful, Con. Gators—" She bit her lip. "Gators bite."

"I'm a Louisiana boy, *cher'*. I know they do," he said softly, pulling her quickly to him and pressing a kiss to her mouth.

The next moment he had taken the forms from Colleen, and was pushing open the door to the interrogation room.

"I wish this had turned out differently." Beside her, Colleen shook her head. "We all know Helio was making a threat, but he couched it carefully enough that we never could prove it. What we need to do now is to make sure he doesn't get a chance to carry out his threats. I intend to talk to Con about the two of you entering the Witness Protection Plan, at least until we get enough on DeMarco to put him safely behind bars."

"That's how Con and Roland Charpentier first ran across DeMarco," Marilyn said distantly, her gaze fixed on the two men in the room. DeMarco was reading over the papers Con had pushed across the table to him. "Helio's organization found and eliminated a mob accountant who was in the witness program."

"I didn't realize that." Colleen frowned. "Wasn't Charpentier the friend of Con's that DeMarco killed? Do you know the details of how that happened?"

"*…the thing was rigged to release a vapor the second time it was used…*

"No." DeMarco had finished reading the forms, Marilyn saw. He nodded briskly, and frowned at the plastic ballpoint Con tossed his way. "Con never spoke of it to me," she added softly.

"We'll work out something." Colleen was watching too, now. "You've got yourself a good man, Marilyn. I suppose he told you he's been asked to head up the Confidential operation in New Orleans sometime in the future?"

From the inner pocket of his suit jacket DeMarco produced an expensive-looking pen. He clicked the small silver release at the top of it, signed his name with a flourish on the last page of the document, and passed it and the pen across to Con, clicking the release closed as he did.

"Yes." Marilyn's hand slid over the curve of her stomach. She stared with burning eyes at the scene. "Yes, he told me. He thinks he'll accept."

His gaze cold and dead, Helio seemed to be holding his breath as Con clicked the borrowed pen's release, signed his own name, and then hesitated. Out of the corner of her eye Marilyn saw Colleen frown at the delay and turn the speaker's volume control up to hear what was being said.

Con initialled something on a previous page. He returned both the document and the pen to Helio.

"…not actually arrested, only held for questioning. Just counter-initial that change and we're done, De-Marco."

With an oddly tense impatience, swiftly the mobster took back the papers, snapped the pen's release one final time, scrawled his initials. He sat back and folded his arms, his hooded gaze on the man across the table from him. Con stood. Without another word he began walking toward the door.

"That must have galled Burke, having to let Helio go." Ryan Benton, an agent who'd questioned DeMarco earlier in the day, grimaced. "I hated having to breathe the same air as that bastard while I was in there with him."

…a vapor that brings death within ninety seconds of being inhaled…

"Looks like Burke feels the same way." Shawn Jameson joined them. Marilyn vaguely remembered being introduced to him the night she'd arrived at the Royal Flush. "Or maybe that's what they call a poker face," he added wryly. "I hear he's a gambler."

"I knew he was a gambler when I fell in love with him," Marilyn said through numb lips. "I—"

Con came through the door, his expression unreadable. In the interrogation room behind him Helio DeMarco suddenly clutched at his chest.

"What the—" Colleen sounded confused. Her confusion turned to urgency. "The man's having a heart attack, for God's sake. Shawn, Ryan—give me a hand with him."

The two agents at her heels, she crashed into the interrogation room. Marilyn saw Benton loosen DeMarco's jacket as the other two got the mobster to the floor, saw Jameson grimly place his palms on Helio's chest and start CPR. She turned away from the window and met Con's gaze.

"He intended to kill you the same way he killed Roland, didn't he?

He nodded tightly. "The pen I used—"

"The pen you used was Roland's," she finished for

him. "But since the hand is faster than the eye you switched it back again when you asked him to initial the change. He was the one who used his own pen the second time...and he was the one who inhaled the vapor."

"It wasn't revenge, *cher'*," Con said hoarsely. "You taught me to leave that part of myself in the past. But I knew that while he was in the world you and our babies would never be safe, so I—"

It was over, Marilyn thought. The horror that had been Helio DeMarco was finally gone. And she and Con and their children had a future she wanted to begin right now.

She put her fingers lightly on his lips. "I love you, Con. When's the next flight out of Denver to New Orleans?"

Slowly the tenseness in him faded. A corner of his mouth quirked up and he kissed the tips of her fingers. "Tonight too soon, heart?" he whispered, bending to her.

"Tonight sounds just fine," she breathed happily as Con's mouth came down on hers. "I can't wait to get home to New Awlins, *cher'*."

Epilogue

"F'true, Cap—a boy and a girl. My little dawlin', she just sailed through the whole thing like a pretty mama Persian cat giving birth to one kitten after another."

Propped up against a sea of lace and satin pillows, Marilyn raised incredulous eyebrows at her husband sitting beside her on the edge of the bed. Unabashed, Con grinned and squeezed her hand before continuing his phone conversation with his old friend Wiley.

"She and the babies came home yesterday. Yeah, Cap, all here in the room with us. You want to say hi?"

"You wake these little ones up after they both finally dropped off to sleep, Mr. Burke, and you'll have to answer to Ingrid and me. Not to mention you're going to have to buy your wife another diamond necklace like the one she's wearing, just to get out of the doghouse."

The plump, coffee-colored woman folding tiny blankets by the two bassinets set against one sun-dappled wall of the spacious bedroom of Con and Marilyn's Garden District mansion exchanged smiles with her companion, a Nordic blond version of herself who was gathering up a rainbow of pastel-hued tissue paper and ribbons from a nearby dresser.

"Yah, that's right, Mr. Burke," Ingrid grinned, her

apple cheeks creasing good naturedly. "And I t'ink dose pink diamonds, they are getting pretty expensive if the husband goes in the doghouse too many times."

"You tell him, ladies." Marilyn dimpled up at the two women. "Or maybe let him get in dutch with me one more time," she laughed softly. "I'm holding out for the matching earrings."

It hadn't been quite as effortless as her handsome husband told it, she admitted to herself as Con brought her hand to his lips and pressed a kiss to her fingers while continuing to talk to Wiley. But he'd been beside her in the delivery room for the whole thing, and the love in those emerald eyes watching her as she gave birth to their newborn son and daughter had given her all the strength she'd needed.

She'd fallen in love with a gambler. Who would have bet at the time that she would have ended up with two babies and an adoring husband who just happened to be the head of the recently formed New Orleans Confidential?

Across the room Ingrid was setting out more of the dozens of baby gifts that had arrived over the past few days. The motherly Minnesota Swede turned to her, her blue eyes puzzled.

"These two, Mrs. Burke—they came together. It seems a strange present for the little ones, yes? The toy rabbits I think are good, but this heavy silver rattle—why would someone give that to babies?"

"Those are from my sister, Holly." Marilyn smiled, her gaze misting. Beside her she was aware of Con hanging up the phone, and he snugged his arm around her as she held out her hands for the odd pairing of gifts.

"But why these two things?" Ingrid asked. Her brow

cleared as she looked at Marilyn. "I think there is a story behind this, yes?"

"A very long story," Marilyn said softly, meeting the tender gaze of the man she loved as her babies gave contented gurgles in their bassinets a few feet away.

"And I'll tell you all about it one of these days," she promised happily as Con's mouth came down on hers in a kiss.

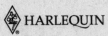

HARLEQUIN
INTRIGUE

COMING NEXT MONTH

Visit us at www.eHarlequin.com

HICNM1103

HARLEQUIN®
INTRIGUE®

Our unique brand of high-caliber romantic suspense just cannot be contained. And to meet our readers' demands, Harlequin Intrigue is expanding its publishing lineup to include **SIX** breathtaking titles every month!

Here's what we have in store for you:

❏ A trilogy of **Heartskeep** stories by Dani Sinclair

❏ More great **Bachelors at Large** books featuring sexy, single cops

❏ Plus outstanding contributions from your favorite Harlequin Intrigue authors, such as Amanda Stevens, B.J. Daniels and Gayle Wilson

MORE variety.
MORE pulse-pounding excitement.
MORE of your favorite authors and series.
Every month.

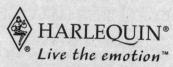

HARLEQUIN®
Live the emotion™

Visit us at www.tryIntrigue.com

HI4T06B

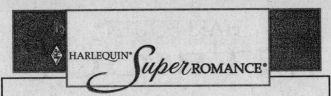
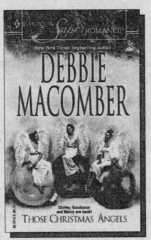

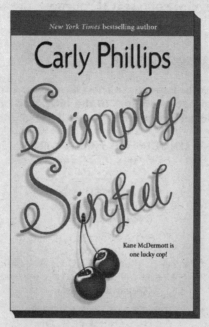
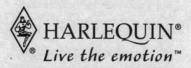

HARLEQUIN®
INTRIGUE®

has a new lineup of books to keep you on
the edge of your seat throughout the winter.
So be on the alert for…

BACHELORS AT LARGE

**Bold and brash—these men have sworn to serve
and protect as officers of the law…and only the
most special women can "catch" these good guys!**

UNDER HIS PROTECTION
BY AMY J. FETZER
(October 2003)

UNMARKED MAN
BY DARLENE SCALERA
(November 2003)

BOYS IN BLUE
A special 3-in-1 volume with
REBECCA YORK (Ruth Glick writing as Rebecca York),
ANN VOSS PETERSON AND PATRICIA ROSEMOOR
(December 2003)

CONCEALED WEAPON
BY SUSAN PETERSON
(January 2004)

GUARDIAN OF HER HEART
BY LINDA O. JOHNSTON
(February 2004)

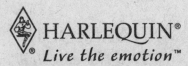
HARLEQUIN®
Live the emotion™

**Visit us at www.eHarlequin.com
and www.tryintrigue.com**

HIBBONTS

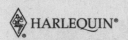

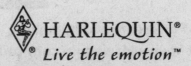